HELL'S DOLLHOUSE

JENNIFER R. LYONS

Hell's Dollhouse
Copyright © 2025 by Jennifer R. Lyons

Library of Congress Control Number: 2024927091

ISBN
978-1-964488-43-1 (Paperback)
978-1-964488-44-8 (eBook)
978-1-964488-42-4 (Hardcover)

You want savin', take yourself to the church up yonder, I hear they're open Sunday mornins, Survivin' is different though. Look around, no water, no cities, just dry, dry land. You want to survive, you're gonna have to pay the Devil himself. Might not cost your soul, but he'll take your life.

Advice for the newcomers

Death. The Tower. The Devil.

The three cards that lay before me on the small, dirty bed were all upright. I told myself they were just innocent cards but I couldn't quite shake an ominous feeling as I looked them over either. I had never seen tarot cards in all my life, but I instinctively knew this draw to be auspicious. I looked into the fortune teller's eyes hoping for some indication I was wrong. My heart skipped a beat as her black eyes widened and darkened as they slowly met mine after only a quick glance at the cards between us.

The woman before me was short and dressed all in black. Before she even began speaking, we'd known her homeland was as far away as one could get. She was a stranger in this land and she didn't try to hide it. She had a strange way of starin' through people rather than at 'em and as she spoke our guesses were confirmed. Her voice was low and her speech pointed. Her g's were too sharp, and all her w's sounded like v's, unlike the drawl familiar to our ears. The most striking thing about her wasn't her dress, her eyes or even her speech. It was the fact she seemed to be travelin' all on her own. We didn't see that too often. Us girls could tellshe definitely had money but it was all too obvious she'd earned every last red cent.

We saw it in the way she stood, fierce and defiant. We who lived with so little could see nothin' easy ever came her way. There'd never been no inheritance and no rich man ever saved her either.Her set mouth and jaw line betrayed how the small woman clawed her way up from pure hunger. I'd watched her walk inside, all the way from the stagecoach. Even at that distance I could see she was brave, cynical and completely in control of her own life.

I couldn't take my eyes off her.

She'd checked into a room upstairs but then come right back down makin' herself comfortable right at the middle table. She paid no mind to the incomin' men nor Dan's watchful gaze. At first, us girls were unsure what to do but after a few minutes of us gawpin her way, Jo sauntered over. We heard her ask what she wanted but couldn't hear her reply but we watched Jo brought her drink and food. Next, Jo leaned too close and asked her some question I couldn't quite hear. I found myself leanin' towards that middle table, strainin' to hear. A thick, Eastern accent growled out only two words.

"I see."

The two words prompted uproarious laughter to spew from Jo's ugly mouth.

The woman gazed at Jo with obvious distaste and when Jo laid one hand on the woman's shoulder, her and whispered, "Well ain't that somethin', that ya see," and she walked away. I watched them closely but was baffled by their conversation. "Who doesn't 'see'?" I wondered mostly because the woman clearly possessed sight.

The short woman chose to imperiously ignore Jo's ugly laughter. She turned, ever so slightly, away from Jo. Then, she proceeded to eat her meal remarkably unperturbed even though she was alone in such a place. There was no way for such a woman to be inconspicuous; no one came here to eat alone. People desired the companionship such a place offered. They drank with friends and of course, embraced us girls. Still, she ignored the pleasures others sought and kept her composure even as the fellas began fillin' the place up.Most of 'em looked her way but steered clear of her. That was another surprise in a place where every woman was longingly and openly desired. Jo mimicked the men ignorin' her entirely after servin' her. I kept my distance but kept a careful watch on the stranger still wonderin' what she meant by "seein'". Betty come over to tell me how her own grandma had "seen".

I listened in awe as Betty described her grandma's ability to see accidents or illnesses before they happened often savin' her kinfolk before certain death. As she spoke, my hazy memory pulled a memory from deep in a place I was sure I'd forgotten; Lord knows how hard I'd tried but failed to forget. Silently, I observed the scene playing out for its one-member audience remembering the smell of sweat and dirt and the sounds of the drum. It showed a ceremony I still couldn't quite understand. I turned to Betty, carefully keepin' my voice low.

"The Indians believe somethin' like that too. They do a sweat and claim to see visions. Is it like that?" I asked her. I was intrigued at such a gift. The dust was so thick and high in this high-desert place. I thought, "It sure would be somethin' to see through them clouds."

Betty whispered back, never takin' her eyes off the tiny stranger, "I guess, maybe. I can't say for sure but I thought those sweats are visions of the past, and they always seem to be teachin' somethin'." She pointed with her chin, "That woman there, she tells the future."

I forced myself to stop starin' and guiltily looked around. I was supposed to be workin' and needed to be careful. The place was near full with payin' men waitin' on drinks and filled desires. The simple gift of conversin' with a stranger did not belong to me.

I worked the room but kept a careful eye on her, I was afraid of losin' her before I could speak privately. Thankfully, it was a slow Tuesday evenin' and all our guests left early to rise early to work the mines. By dark, our place was all but emptied when I noticed she no longer sat at that middle table. Makin' sure no one was payin' me no never mind, I climbed the stairs as silently as I could and stood before her door. My skin bumped into goose flesh despite the hallway bein' the normal hot as hell temperature it always seemed to hold.

I hesitated there, I didn't want to knock and be heard by anyone but her. I also never barged in those doors. If men were in there, they was payin' for that time and never liked the interruption less I was fixin' on joinin' in for free. I stood, frozen on the spot wonderin' what I might do next when the door slowly and silently opened and a small hand beckoned me into the dark.

I looked around a room almost identical to one I myself occupied. A bed, a chair and a small dressin' table was in here with a small rug. It was cleaner than the others, this room was meant to be rented out by the night, not the hour.As I stepped in, I noticed she had the light burnin' real low. Still no words had escaped her small mouth and she pointed me towards the bed. I didn't hesitate. God hisself only knew how many times I'd been beckoned to a bed, this would be an easy evenin'; I was here on my own consciences. I sat on one edge while she took out a deck of cards that were nothin' like them cards downstairs. Fact was,I'd never seen such a strange deck.

"I guess this is what you are lookink for?" Her voice was quiet and harsh contradicting her petite figure. When she spoke, it sounded like ice falling on a cold, hard ground.

I only nodded too nervous to speak. I was surprised at my own cowardice. After all, I spoke readily to strangers, befriended and bedded 'em. There was something more to her that frightened the words right out of me though.

"Are you sure you want such a think? I can see so much about you, without these cards. Your clothes tell me what you are. You live here, and most people, they see that and they see your whole life. They call you a whore. They even tell you how your life, it will not go anywhere but here. You are stuck between being a whore and woman. You are not free." She shrugged and continued without waiting for my answer or even seeing my reaction to her all-to-true words, "Well, what others see, that is no matter to me. Any fool can see these thinks about you. I know you are seeking something more than judgement to your current, ahh, shall we say employment? Ya, yes. "She shook her head up and down at her own words, "You are asking for more and of course, to see that, it takes the gift only a few possess. I am one of those people, just like your friend informed you downstairs." If she took a small moment to raise her eyes, she would have seen my surprise that she'd overheard our quiet discussion. She didn't though. Either she was uninterested or perhaps she simply wanted to begin. She was already shuffling the cards around.

I was most astonished when she stared right into my eyes, I'd gotten comfortable bein' ignored by her. That icy voice cut the room right through to my soul opening old wounds and awakening worries I'd tried to forget. I desperately wanted to know my future but I wasn't expectin' feelin' this much, and this was before she even began. Her next words shook me to the core. She knew things but I hadn't even told her so much as my name.

"I can see somethinks about you. You want out of this dusty town, but this is no surprise who wouldn't? That is not a special wish." Her voice softened into a mere whisper. I had to lean in to hear her next words though being so near made my skin crawl.

"Alright, I am curious. I will do this think for you, because now I am curious what you believe could be told. You want more from your life. I can tell you what the cards will show." Though I was the only one in the room she spoke around me, not to me but around me. It was bizarre, I knew she was speaking to me but it was so indirect I actually looked around to see if she was addressing someone else.

She went on, finally addressing me by thrusting the cards into my hands and commanding, "So here, you take them now, you hold them and mix them. Sort them, move them all around," she waved her own tiny hands demonstrating how I should mix the cards, "All this while you think," she tapped her head, "you ask, not out loud, but from your soul!" Her tiny hands were placed on her heart and she closed her eyes commanding me, "You ask the cards what your future holds." Then, she was silent sitting there with her hands clasped in front of her and her eyes closed.

I glanced down at the cards. My hands were tremblin' so hard, they shook a little as I swirled them around. The strange pictures caught my attention. Faces, birds, signs all mixed together, then apart until finally, I held a neat pile in my sweaty hands. She opened her eyes and looked at the pile.

One hand waved to indicate her next directions while she spoke, "You, you take three, ask them, ask the cards which ones you should take. Silent." She held a hand up as if to stop any words that might escape even my throat. I'd never asked cards for nothin' but I did my best.

"Show me what I need to see, show me the way out of this hell hole," I desperately thought as I carefully chose three random cards from throughout the deck.

She was nodding yes at my actions, "You choose the three, yes now you take them. One. Two. Three. Lay them in front of you, I take these." She took the rest of the cards from me. I looked down at the short row of oft-used cards. All were facedown their shabby backs blank.

"Yes." She was nodding again. "Yes. Good, that is what you do. Now, turn them. One. Two. Three."

Death. The Tower. The Devil.

Her eyes widened in apparent surprise while she rubbed her eager little hands over the cards.

"You see, they are all there, all turned ovfer by your own hand, your own fortune is right here. One only needs to read these cards to see it." She quieted and looked over the cards carefully.

The candle flickered throwing shadows against the walls.

"You want the answers about the future so you come here. And now this." She rubbed her small hands again and went on, "I have never seen such a draw, you should know that." She nodded again, "I also want you to know, I never to a reading for free. Never. And yours will cost you."

I nodded neither surprised nor perturbed. Nothin' in life was free. Ever. I thought I was prepared to pay her demands so I nodded one time in her direction.

She shrugged at my acknowledgement, "Ok, well. Let me start then. This draw, the way the cards come together is what tells the future. The cards, they never lie but you must accept that they can mean many things in your life, or for the people around you. Look around. It is not difficult to see the harshness of this place, of your life. The cards reflect this. This place, this desert of land, it is a terrible lonely place. The cards show this." She studied them more, quiet for a time.

Finally, "The thing is we do not need these cards to tell us this or show us how harsh this place is, one can simply look around, try to breathe in air and only choke on the dust. This is no mystery. So maybe, these cards show that because they show you to trust them. You know this truth and now these cards show you this to begin. Yes. That is one important thinkg. You have doubts, yet you want the belief. So belief. Next, you can see this calamity that surrounds these cards. These images, they can be scary for some, I see efven for you, that you fear these images. This is in spite of the bonded life you live. Daily you ignore your own fears and dislikes. Yet, you fear these images. The first is someting all people fear, even you who hates her life. Death. Then, there is this falling Tower. Yes, change can be chaotic and scary because we cannot always see through the dust." She looked at me again, "and I see how much you hate dust. This, though. This is interesting. You do not even flinch at the Devil. I think, I see this means you made your pact with him long ago. "I was careful not agree nor disagree at those words. She looked into my eyes and I she knew enough. She went on, nodding her head again.

"Yes. You made your pact. Well that is no big surprise, is it? Again. Look around. This place is no Eden. So, we understand you know you made your deal with the Devil, you know what that means so instead look at the other cards. Yes, you live in harsh circumstances. But you want somethinkg from this place. You feel this place even owes you. You want and even desperately seek a change. No matter what this place takes from you, demands of your soul, you seek a change." She set her mouth and looked toward the window, "Yes. I see it now. You will get this change. Death shows us that. You are on the very edge of all you desire, but of course it will come at a price. Will you pay?" she shook her head a little, "You have paid so much already, yes, you will pay again. Next. The Tower assures us it is not far off. Days. You will not be required to wait much longer, certainly not weeks or months. Your desire will turn to reality and all that you lifve now, that will be change. This place, this dust," she gestured to my clothes, "those clothes. All change. You will only be a memory for this place and this place a memory for you. The Devil shows this life, this life you lifve right now, it is very hard, you make many sacrifice. Above all it shows you are not in control of any part of your life. Ha. That is not so hard to see. No one would choose this life. Well, you sacrifice and you pay the Devil for your life, no matter the hardships." She leaned towards me once more, "Mark my words, the sacrifice is not yet paid in full. And to change, you will make more." At those words, her eyes rolled up, and her voice dropped to a hoarse whisper.

"You. You have made a deal with a higher power. Maybe to survive, maybe to change. Maybe both. The price you paid and continue to pay is high. But then so is your reward. It is comingk but this is a terrible thingk; danger is all around. People, they run, they are hurt. You cannot stop this. But you must not freeze in the moment from fear or disbelief at what is happening. This will be your chance. There is fire. There are many gunshots. And when you see these thinkgs. Then you will know it is time for you to flee. You will try to run from this place and some will follow. You will not have much time. You will not have much time to choose to stay or go so take what you want; take what you will need to survive hell. You will see taking a new life will require the end of another. You will choose to sacrifice that life because returning to hell is no option. Be on guard. Be the lookout. Watch. Change is coming."

And then, she slumped forward, and her deep breathing told me she was asleep. I didn't know what to do, I hadn't paid her yet. I had questions too. What danger was coming? What worst danger could possibly visit this place? She was asleep so I could not ask.

I wondered how she knew so much about me too. It was all true. I'd made my deals with the Devil to preserve what little life and dignity I still possessed. There was nothin worse in life knowin' I owed him but she made it sound like it was time for a return on my investments. I wondered how the Devil repaid his mistresses.

I looked around the small, dingy room then I straightened up. No more answers would come tonight so I left her in the same position in which she'd fallen. I didn't bother to cover her or even move her cards. I was no maid. I did put out the lamp, though. Fire was comin' but flames frightened me and we didn't need the place burnin' down around us this night. And with that, I left her room and quietly went into my own.

I tried not to think too much about that strange woman or her cards but my dreams were full of fire and screams. I couldn't know if I was now seein' or if I was over thinkin' those cards. I woke, many times that night and finally only fell asleep early the next mornin', though my habits woke me not long after. I made my way downstairs and was surrpirsed to find her already there. occupien' the same table as the night before. Her cards was stacked neatly before her and she was surveyin' the room.

She gave no notice my direction or our conversation the night before in her own rented room. I ignored her, too and got my own breakfast, talkin' with the girls keepin' our eyes out for early mornin' customers. Unusually, not one man visited that mornin'.

"What a slow day, we should be enjoyin' the break, but I can't recall a time when the place was so filled with the softer sex." Betty nodded towards our one customer.

"Mmmhm. I can't remember a mornin' like this neither. Ya know what? I'm gonna get my bath in, right now." Jo loved her a hot bath.

Fact was, most liked a hot bath. We offered 'em real regular. Our customers worked the coal mines and we got the few cowboys in who ran cattle through the high deserts. Every man wanted bath, at least once in awhile and ours were highly sought after, I figured that was mostly down to the scrubbin' us girls did but it was a little different from our normal tasks so we didn't mind much. Us girls got to bathe once a week, if we chose and we could more often if we paid the two cents. Jo was the only one who could afford it and often paid for more.

We all liked the idea of havin' the baths to ourselves, though, without havin' to help men with their washin'. Bathin' on our own meant there was no actin' no placatin'; it was a time for relaxin'. We helped each other with washin' our hair and backs. It was an easy and unfair system, first come first served.

That day we all headed to the four tubs that were filled with clean water being's it was mornin'. What a treat that clean, hot water awaited us! 'Course, Jo was first in and Becky wasn't far behind. That left the other two tubs for the last three of us. Betsy and Sue, each stepped in one leavin' me behind to serve the winners. I sighed.

Even though I was terribly disappointed at both having to await my turn and the fact the water wouldn't be as hot or clean, I walked around the girls, pourin' water over their hair and helpin' to scrub their backs clean. I was used to keepin' my chin down and doin' what everyone else needed. Jo's was filled with both old and new bruises so I took extra care to stroke gently. I didn't ask where they come from, I knew. After all, we all carried bruises.

Sue finished first, and I got into that bath. It was still nice. Sue was cleanest of all the other girls and not selfish in the least. She even ensured the water was a little warm.

Sue washed my hair and back after she was dry. Then she left. The other girls finished and dried leavin' me to a few minutes on my own. I leaned back and closed my eyes, even with the water coolin' down, this was a fine treat. I closed my eyes and breathed in the clean lavender smell of our soap. "Life wasn't half bad sometimes, even here," I thought sleepily.

Maybe five minutes later, I felt as if I was no longer alone and opened my eyes to the strange small woman standing over the tub.

"Ahh, good morning," She said in her strange accent. I didn't say anything back, just smiled a little but deep down I was wonderin' what it was she wanted. I hadn't paid my debt yet.

"I see the other girls and you come out here. I heard about the bath house and I decide I want a bath. I waited for the others to finish. I wanted to get the clean water, and so they left and I come in here." My skin prickled, I felt a little uneasy with her watchin' me like that, though I couldn't say just why. She wasn't threatenin' in any way and I finally put it down to the fact she could see much more than my futures. She saw and used situations to her advantage.

Like now, she saw I would be here alone and that's why she'd waited. She was gettin' closer to demandin' payment.

"Yeah, well, they went back now, so take whatever tub ya want. Matt, he's the boy that fills these, he already filled that one over there, so go ahead. " I pointed to a tub at the end of the line. She didn't move.

"Yes. Well. I will wait here while you finish. I require help with this dress." She hardly moved as she spoke though her eyes traveled over my body. I closed my eyes again and ignored her. I wasn't ready to get out.

After a few more minutes, I felt her breath near my face, "You see, I told you I never do the readingks for free. I need help with this dress." I didn't open my eyes right away, wonderin' exactly what she was after. If she wanted me to get out, she'd have to ask. I wasn't in the business of guessin' her desires. If all she wanted was help with that dress for a payment, well, I figured she could wait a minute more.

"Now."

I couldn't explain the feeling that one word imposed, but that one word sent shiver down my spine and I opened my eyes giving her my full attention. "I want my payment now." She turned away from me, took a good four steps away from the edge of the tub and turned back around. Her eyes demanded me to leave my reprieve immediately. She knew I would comply, though that didn't take cards nor a gift to see.

Most expected it from me; girls like me always did as told, hopin' it was our deal with the Devil. It was how we survived. I stood up and smiled at her, just like I did at any other customer.

"You want a bath, then? I can help you with that dress. Let me towel off, and I'll be right over. Why don't you remove your shoes while ya wait?" I smiled again, showin' how courteous and compliant I was and began toweling off. She waited and watched.

"Ya want help with the shoes too? Alright, nearly done, here, I'll be right there." I finished and walked towards her, still undressed but ready to pay such an easy debt.

"The trance, you witnessed, it is not so easy to live with that. Always makes me so tired." She explained as if she were finally ready to make small talk.

"Mmmhmm. Well, I sure couldn't wake you after." I advanced towards her, and reached for the back of her dress.

"Yes, well, thankful it does not happen with every readingk." She shrugged a little, "Some have no effect whatsoever on me." She waved her arm and I nodded even though her back to me I nodded. I undid the many tiny buttons and slipped the dress from her bony shoulders. "Of course, such the experience it is, those customers I require more payment." Her voice had hardened again. Again, I nodded, even though her back was towards me.

She turned around, gazing into my eyes while I slipped the ugly dress off her body. As I reached down to remove her small shoes, she readily obliged lifting her foot just a little. I undid them and put them to the side.

"Your dress is awful dusty, want me to have it washed for ya?" I helped her turn around once more so I could undo the tiny corset. "Cook normally does the guests washin', or I can do it if ya want. For the trance." I slipped the corset off her middle. "I can wash your unders too. I don't mind." I pushed down the petty coat and then the slip beneath that. "Here, turn back 'round, lets get those stockins off." Once again, she obliged, silently but kept her eyes locked on mine while I undressed her. I tried not to touch her skin as I worked. I couldn't tell how old she was. Her skin was beautiful, no wrinkles no blemishes. When she spoke, she did so with the authority of an aged person. She was beautiful, in her way, I just didn't want to make that skin contact. Most times, I just clamped my jaw tight together to get through the necessities while I pleasured men but I found her repulsive.

I couldn't think why, she smelled like sweat and dirt but wasn't near as filthy as most our customers. I doubted she could even physically harm me much given her size. I shuddered beneath her gaze though and the bile rose in my stomach at the merest thought of pleasurin' her. I forced it back down. I would only do that if she asked out right.

"There, there ya go. Let's get ya in that water while its still warm," I offered my hand so she could step over the edge, but she didn't take it. I tried ignorin' her gaze and went on, "I have questions, ya know, about them cards. But I wanted to thank ya for the readin'. I will watch for the time you told me about." I was at the edge of the tub but she hadn't followed. I looked back at her, "Why, what are ya waitin' for? The water is nice and warm!"

"You can help me wash and yes, please launder the clothes. For the trance, I want the payment, though." She stood before me and again I wondered a her age. She didn't look a day older than myself . Tryin' to distract her a little or maybe to just delay the inevitable I complimented her youthfulness, which made her smile. I wondered if she was a witch who kept herself young through spells.

I'd never met any witch before but I never met any seers neither. "She might be both," I thought.

"Ah, yes, well. Time is the funny thinkg. It is kinder to some than the others. And. Your draw tells of what you pay the devil. You must remember, we all owe him somethinkg. And, in return we all get somethinkg. Never be fooled by the appearance you see, time is a funny thinkg." I noticed her eyes again. They was so black, like the coal brought from the earth just a few miles from that establishment.

I had no idea what she was talkin' about, either. Could she mean she didn't age? And what payment more was she wantin?

"So, this payment. I want you to come to me. I am a woman with needs. I don't want a man today. Sometimes I do but you are here, in your youth, your beauty. I want that today. I want you to take care of the aches a woman gets. Now."

I couldn't smile but I forced myself to answer, "Well, all ya had to do was ask, I ain't no seer." She smiled at that. I told myself more than her, "I do this for Jo sometimes, ya know." I didn't really like helpin' Jo neither. Her face was horrible to see even in ecstasy but I went on, convincin' myself further to just start and finish what she was demandin'", "She has a hunger that most men can't get at, so I help out. Here, come get in the bath. You can lie back, and I can stroke right where you need." I reached out my arm. She didn't take it and my heart sank. I wasn't no seer but I knew her next words before she spoke.

"Your tongue. That is what I want. I want you to kneel right here, and use your tongue." She was almost pantin' with her desire.

I normally only sucked on men's cocks. It was part of my livin' and sure, a few women had come through who liked other women. And some of the men really liked us girls to lick each other but that was pricey so it didn't happen often. This was different somehow.

She wasn't payin' me. She was holdin' me to my debt. I looked at the clothes I was already promised to launder and then at the soap I would use to wash her and finally, the jug I would rinse her long black with. I swallowed. I didn't' want to perform. I wanted her to be clean but she wasn't askin' to wait.

"Once you do this, you help me with the bath and clothes, you will be paid in full. No more debt." And she opened her legs a little.

I dropped to my knees and made my way to her, not the first time I had done that and not expectin' it to be my last but recoilin' all the same. In the end, this was my profession, nothin' more. It would be over in a few moments and I would move onto the next one, probably within the few moments after my return to the saloon bar. She took hold of the back of my head and guided my face towards her. I licked and licked tryin' not to think about what I was doin'. I just listened to her small groans and tasted the growin' wet from between her legs. Finally, she released my head and walked towards the tub.

I took my hand and rinsed out my mouth, best I could and turned towards her. She was lyin' back, relaxin' in that water. And Dan was standin' in the doorway.

CHAPTER 1

Dan was what Mr. Evans called essential. Mr. Evans owned and operated the business. Dan was our trainer and overseer. I know he did other work for Evans too but I was so tied to the establishment I wasn't all too sure what he got up to outside those four walls. I tried not show my fear as he spoke.

"I see you is real busy in here, Ms. Ruth. Real busy. Ya finish up, I'll be waitin'." And he walked out.

I knew what that meant. She wasn't payin' for me to be lickin' her like that and I was on the clock. I was always on the clock and anythin' I did demanded payment. Dan made sure no was ever pleasured for free.

I walked over to the tub and looked down. She was completely relaxed, her eyes was closed. She was completely unperturbed by the intrusion she continued to lie there. She didn't care I'd paid off the debt owed her, but in doin' so I now owed Dan. I wasn't quite finished yet though so I pushed Dan out my mind and washed her lovely hair.

It was long and course and near as black as her eyes. No signs of grey streaked it and when she stood, it nearly reached the floor. It took a long time to wash and rinse all that hair. Finally, when it was finished, she held up her arms for scrubbin', then her legs, her feet, and arms and hands. She never spoke and I didn't neither. I washed her back and she leaned back and indicated me to finish washin' the rest of her body too.

I gritted my teeth and finished up while noticin' Dan watchin' through the small window.

I helped her out of the water and dried her hair. Wrappin' her in a towel, I then put my own clothes on quick-like. They was nothin' more than the small shirt and pantaloons typical costume for my trade. I wrapped her hair in another towel and gathered up her things, followin' her inside.

Dan allowed us to pass but at the last second took my arm, hard.

"What are ya doin' Ruth. Ya followin' her, did she pay ya for all that?"

I didn't know how to answer him, I didn't want to tell him about the cards. I tried shakin' his arm loose.

"Did ya like it then? Is that what this is about?" He smiled knowin'ly, "I seen ya girls, when ya alone. Maybe that's it but she ain't one of us, and she gotta pay. Or you will." He bit off those last words with a hard squeeze that reddened arm and he walked off.

I knew I would be payin', he didn't even stop to ask her about it. And I knew how I would pay. Dan wouldn't forget neither.

Still, I followed her to her room and helped her dress, and brushed her long hair. May as well take my time knowin' what was waitin' on me, I figured.

"You will not ask me to pay. I can see this and yes, I heard that man talk to you." She nodded curtly. For just a moment, I hoped she might do right by me but then she went on in that icy voice of hers, "This is not my problem, of course. I never read for free. Plus, I did like you washinkg me and of course, your beautiful mouth and the way you moved your tongue. I am still wet." She stopped and considered for a fast moment then, "Still, I do not like the idea of you hurtinkg over such a payment. If you ask, I will pay and we settle your debt some other way." I didn't want to owe her again, though. I feared her more than I did Dan, so I lied.

"Dan ain't that bad." I shrugged through my lies, "I'll probably just have to suck him off later."

She locked eyes with me and I knew then, she knew I was lyin'. I looked away from her harsh gaze and gathered her laundry.

I did her laundry quickly and hung it in her room to dry. She watched me the entire time but never spoke another word though I could hear her pantin' a little as I worked. I felt cursed as I left her room and that was the last time, I saw her though I have thought of her every day since.

Dan was waitin' for his pay. Without a word, he pushed me into my room and demanded to know why I was "playin' her like that." He told me to show him just what I did to her. I was shocked when he didn't hit me, instead he put my hands on the back of his head and told me to show him. I let him. When he finished, he told me to stay in my room the rest of the night, no dinner. He made to leave but at the door paused and came back; at least it was only a few hits.

CHAPTER 2

I woke early the next mornin', happy to be on my own. A small porch stood outside my room's window, and I woke early to climb out into fresh air to feel sunlight during a time others slept.

Breathing deeply, I allowed the new day to seep into my soul through my skin. I wouldn't get to enjoy the outside long and even though I wasn't too sure the porch wouldn't soon collapse I relished this morning. It was early summer, the perfect weather out here. Winters were too long and late summers were so hot and dry, one could hardly stand it. I looked over the main street, really the only street, leaning a little on the wooden rail. I was careful not to slide my arms; those dry splinters hurt.

Even though I was outside, I kept an eye out for business, licking my teeth, feeling the new gap that still tasted bloody.

I ignored the soreness on my face and mouth and breathed fresh Rocky Mountain air deep into my lungs. It was invigorating, though I winced a little as I opened my mouth a little too wide to yawn. Dan really had left his mark there on my left cheek Still, I tried to ignore that and doubted any other air could ever be as fresh as those high mountains provided their few inhabitants.

The smell of the town was not quite as fresh, and I gagged a little on the dust that settled in the back of my throat after my too-wide yawn. This place was always dusty. Dust covered everything and everyone all the time agin' the relatively young buildings and folks alike. Everyone called it a town, but that was far-too generous a word, I thought to myself.

Firstly, there was just the one street; the main street. It was short and broad. There was one general store and and two saloons. The board-walk was not yet started but promised in the near future. For now, a generous number of narrow boards precariously placed offered a slightly protected walkway through the mud and horse shit that covered the street. How a place so dry always had such a muddy street was beyond me. I shook my head a little and looked down the other direction.

A few other new-but-worn buildings shared the street. Most were small and full of a few optimistic newcomers that changed hands every few weeks. Right now, one sold minin' equipment such as pick axes. Another sold clothin' that promised not to wear even with hard work. They wouldn't last long. It was just too harsh a place for most to earn the promise of abundance that drew so many westward.

A small church both welcomed and guarded the farthest end of the main street. It was a neat little building made of wood, like all the other buildings, but a couple of things set it apart from its neighbors. First, it was surrounded by a neat little yard that was surrounded by a neat little fence. Most peculiar though, was the fact that it somehow, it never seemed to attract quite as much dust as the other buildings lending it an odd, ethereal air in stark contrast to the others.

I shaded my eyes with one hand to better watch the few folks crossing the slow street. Sunday mornins were always quietly interestin'. Most of the men mined all week and spent pent up yearnings for something better on their precious Saturday nights. After those raucous nights most slept till noon. Most of them found their ways back to the shanty towns filled with tents or shacks they each called home.

The families that lived here occupied slightly better dwellings on smaller muddy trails that twisted and turned till they connected to the main street. While everyone was just tryin' to survive, those families had it the hardest. I doubted one was spared the harshness of life lost on the trail and it showed on their faces forever embedded in their eyes.

It was almost as if dust collected on them, just like the buildings was agin' them too. Sunday mornins' saw the families gather at the building safeguarded by its fence and yard. I watched 'em now, all holdin' hands in their Sunday bests, heads bowed to the sun or maybe already prayin' away their sins in the hopes they'd soon see the loved ones they'd lost to the dry desert or deep mines.

After watchin' the families disappear into the church, I turned my attentions to an arrivin' stage coach. It was early. Or maybe it was late, normally they never showed on Saturdays. I shaded my eyes for a better look while leanin' far over the rail. Look like mail was being delivered and one of the few new optimistics was crossin' the street with what appeared to be his young wife. I licked my lips takin' in the quaint little scene. It looked like she just came off that stage coach, though I hadn't seen her actual departure.

She was dressed well, if a bit worn. Her dress had a slightly faded look as if it had been hung in the glare of the sun one too many times. The hem gently rubbed over the earth with each quick step and from my vantage point I could see it had frayed and been repaired many times. Overall, though, it was a good dress. The material was not cheap nor frugally used; it was just a little old, maybe even an inherited piece. I concluded it was probably one of two or three she owned and like so many other unlucky women, she had left some luxurious city life by following the love of her life. She must have felt me watching her because she glanced up and made eye contact.

Grinning down at her I called, "Mornin'! What a fine day it is! You tired of him? I can give you a break!" And I winked.

She didn't like that. And even though I could tell she didn't like herself for doin' it, I saw her watch her husband's eyes to see where they were lookin'. To his credit, he kept his eyes forward. That was fine by me, we all knew his eyes well. He'd lived here quite alone for a few months before she could join him. I hadn't even known he was married! Made no matter if we lost one customer, there was always plenty new ones each week.

She threw a disgusted look my way and turned sharply. I laughed down at her.

It was too nice a day to be out alone on that porch. Four other girls now joined me in surveying the quiet Sunday morning.

"Thank God, the boss is still asleep!" I heard Bess mutter. I agreed it was better to have his sleep as long as possible though I didn't think Evans would mind, after all, its not like was headed into the church all dressed and no skin showin'. We wore same clothes as always advertisin' our skill.

I thought, "Actually, thank the whiskey." May as well put the credit where it was due.

It had taken me a few years, but I'd learned dulling my life with whiskey also meant missing out on these few quiet moments I could sneak in the mornings when no one else was awake. A few of the other girls and I always kept this unspoken rule embracing each short-lived gift of reprieve each chance we got not knowing when or if we'd get it again.

The young couple finally finished their crossing; she never glanced back but I waved again anways when I saw him glance regretfully back. Jo even squeezed her chest a little. His neck reddened as he let her through the little gate at the church yard. I could still see his red neck even as he crossed the threshold. I shook my head. "Men," I muttered.

We stood out there as long as we could, right up until we heard footsteps and voices find there way outside. I was the last to go inside.

Ducking through the low frame, I carefully stepped over a small bed meant for one that normally held two. I stopped to tidy the room I called home.

It didn't belong to me, but I preferred it tidy. I'd always been that way, preferring tidiness over clutter or worse yet, dirt. "Maybe that's why I notice the dust on the buildings so often," I thought to myself. I threw the nightly contents of the chamber pot out the window and turned my attentions to the rest of the room.

Today, I even removed the linen from the bed and hung it in front of the window. Though I tidied daily, Sundays I took special care of the few items in the room. I shook out the blankets and fluffed my one pillow. Finally, I straightened the furniture and rug. I listened at the door. After not hearing any conversation, I decided it would be a slow day I left the linens hanging. I left my room.

I went down the stairs to the kitchen. Stepping down those stairs, I realized this was my home or as close as I was ever going to get to one, like it or not. The thought made me a little sad.

This was the place I slept. I took in company here. I ate here. This wasn't the home I'd ever wished or planned. Wishing wasn't gonna change one thing, though, so I forced myself to stop thinking of homes and kept going through the kitchen out the back door. I reminded myself to find joy in the small things.

I waved to Cook as I passed through. She was going about her day. She was a small colored woman; her skin was almost black as the darkest night and though she was tiny she was strong. She was muttering to herself. She often muttered to herself, I thought it might be because she was so often on her own. She didn't take in company like the rest of us girls.

"Girl. Where you been? You better hurry up. You 'bout missed any chance of eatin' this mornin'." Her low voice meant her words were never much more than audible but she spoke harsh enough I always paid attention. She was not a woman to overlook even though she was small in stature. She was strong as any man and her resolve was at least twice of anyone I ever met, includin' myself though I didn't like to admit that much. Unlike me or the rest of the girls, she was free to come and go and because she fed everyone. They needed to eat and far as I knew that is all they required from her. The kitchen was more hers than the boss's. Cook wasn't expendable or replaceable. And she knew it. Everyone knew it.

Cook fascinated me both with her skill and intellect that most overlooked due her gender and skin color. She kept her kitchen was near spotless. She didn't allow anyone but us girls through either doorway. No men, ever, stepped a foot over either threshold. It was hot inside, year-round but she never seemed to mind or at the very least, the heat never slowed her down. No meal was ever served late. The space was lined with a long counter, shelves and one entire wall was dedicated to the fireplace and chimney. Cook even slept here on a mattress that was now neatly rolled and tucked into a corner. Her few personal belongings were kept in that same corner on short shelf.

The two doorways almost flanked the space or maybe guarded it. One lead to the saloon and hotel. The other to the back where she kept a kitchen garden as the seasons allowed. I remembered when she had insisted on the fence to, "keep critters out". I always figured she wanted it was really to keep the men out. I'd asked her once and she only laughed her crazy laugh never really answering. That fenced in area also held an outdoor fire pit and she roasted all sorts out there, pig, sides of beef, chickens. She didn't take well to criticisms but her food was good enough and I'd only heard one complaint in all the years I'd been there.

That memory almost always made me laugh, no matter how tough a day I faced. We had some new girl, she'd died since, but she was something. I always thought she must have been from a rich family. I'd never learned how she came to be employed under this roof but I could tell rough living was not familiar to her. Hell, anyone could tell from her speech to the way she carried herself; nose up higher than anyone I ever saw.

She was picky about everything. No matter the warnings or even outright smacks, she still grimaced and wrinkled her nose at the food, the furniture, the company, anything and anyone. She was still popular enough with the men, though and that is probably how she lasted long as she did. I think the men must have felt like they were in for a real treat picking someone so "refined."

Anyways, one mornin' she dared complain about Cook's hot cakes and sausages. She hadn't been with us long enough to know most mornings there was no sausage and that Cook never took criticisms easy or well. And she never forgot, neither.

There that stupid, spoiled girl stood with her plate held out to arm's length, wrinkling her nose and told Cook, "This stinks. I can't eat food that stinks." Cook never said a word, took the plate and gave it to the next girl in line. "Excuse me, but what do I get now?" Cook ignored her and I was proud of Cook thinkin' this time might be different.

The rest of us ignored her and the stink on that sausage too; we were all hungry.

We got two meals a day guaranteed if we worked. If we didn't, we might get one. Christmas was the only day we got a good three. Everyone was hungry almost all the time and we sure weren't going to throw away a good breakfast. Why, we even had decent coffee that morning. I remembered wondering what that mad bitch was thinking, turning away a plate of food.

Cook must have wondered the same thing. She walked over to that woman and in her low voice asked just what it was the girl wanted. I knew then, I'd been wrong; Cook might have tried to ignore her but that nicety was over.

"I want something I can actually eat. I was busy last night. I'm tired and hungry and tired of smells. I want something good." Her hands were on her slim hips and she glared down at Cook, who was at least four inches shorter. She never saw it coming.

Before anyone really could guess Cook's next move, that girl was on her skinny ass holding her face. Cook had knocked her clean off her feet. "Now what did you want?" Cook stood over her, glaring.

The girl then asked for her plate back but of course, it was all eaten. I think she ended up takin' a few scraps that were destined for the pigs. None of us ever heard her complain to Cook again.

Cook had made biscuits this mornin' complete with a thick gravy. I ate every last crumb and even wiped my plate clean as I finished. There was no more coffee so I offered to bring in the water. I often did that for Cook, and I always felt she appreciated it even if she hardly said so but I didn't need no thank you's. I was used to servicin' without 'em.

If I carried in the water, it also meant I could get fresh water. If not, our water went into two barrels and throughout the day, grime and a thin film of grease collected at the top. I was always careful to set the dipper down as far as I could, disturbing that layer of film but it never tasted so good as straight from the well.

Carrying the water also meant missing out on any early rising customers. Some men liked it in the morning. Most mornings, we had to wait around tending to those desires but if I was seen carrying water, no one bothered me. It was one more moment to of peace and freedom. I took as much time as I could gettin' the water that day. My sides were hurtin' meaning my time of the month was coming and I just didn't feel up to straddlin' any man.

As I walked, I recalled a life I'd lived a few years before.

Ma and Pa had decided to leave an overcrowded city, I didn't which one, but I remembered the dirty, crowded streets a little. He'd dreamed of a life ownin' his own land and a house clear from neighbors. She loved him and he was her dream. So, she followed him, no questions asked into a near road-less existence void of industry or civilization.

I remember the day they packed up a wagon and it seemed we just started walking west. I was oldest of three, and I was only five. I had two younger brothers. One was just a baby and Mama had to carry him, still nursing. I was excited and so was James. He was only a year and a bit my junior and we held hands walking alongside the wagon. It was slow going and Pa told us how we would soon meet up with other travelers.

"Soon" actually took over a full, lonely week of walkin'. We saw a few folks but it was mostly just us and the wide world. Both me and James developed blisters on blisters all over our feet. We tried not to complain but those blisters hurt. We took to takin' our shoes off walkin' barefoot and even the rocks were less painful than those blisters constant rubbin'.

The wagon constantly rocked and the baby John was just big enough to want to grab and lunge for everything. It was easier to walk than ride holding him, or so she said. I wondered who it was easier on, though and honestly, one look at her face we all knew it wasn't easier on her. Still, she never complained and Pa never offered an alternative or even extra rest. He was busy enough keepin' the horses to pullin' that wagon. I watched him, how it took all his strength to keep his arms up holdin' them reins, strainin' this way and that tryin' to keep to a road that weren't quite there.

We had a long way to go. Miles needed to be covered or we would find ourselves without provision and without shelter in a harsh winter. So, we walked and did not complain; there was simply no point to it. The move out west actually turned out fine. Eventually, we met up with others and it wasn't so lonely a journey. After a month or so, we'd reached a vast prairie. Mama and Pa got a little emotional and they decided that was our destination.

I'd raised my small hands to my eyes and looked every direction searching for mountains or water or trees or anything. All I could see was prairie and sky forever. We'd settled on a piece of land without so much a road leading to us. I heard Pa ask Mama that night how she liked breathin' in the fine, unsoiled air and they both laughed. That first while, we'd slept outside with only the wide starry sky shelterin' us. Only a few folks that were going further out west passed by our home. Sometimes they stopped and rested a day or two but most moved right on unmoved by the sea of grass that allured our Papa to stay.

I could run in any direction and only find silence and wind. Pa dug out a small home, framed the earth with the wood from our wagon and Ma did what she could to make it livable. And it was real nice. A few years passed real peaceful. It was just us and we all worked hard to get by and we all survived though Mama was skinnier than I ever recalled. She never had any other babies and as the years passed, a few neighbors moved nearby.

I always thought Mama was as relieved to see new folks as I was. Why, I hardly knew what to do with other kids my age but I made friends easy and fast. It was my daily chore to fetch the water. I bet I'd carried more water than almost anyone else on the earth and back then, I didn't really appreciate the chore as I did now. It took me away from other things I'd rather see or do and besides, full water buckets are heavy. If I ever complained Mama just smiled and thanked me for working so hard and reminded me how strong it was making me. She also reminded me to be grateful for the water. My complaints would stop there out of my love for her. I loved helping her and I actually was grateful for the water. My new friends also had the water chore; we often walked together chattin' the whole way despite the heavy burden.

Mama never failed in bathing us once a week. From the time we deemed that place our home right on through, she demanded cleanliness. Of course, that meant more water but every Saturday, she made sure I had help. All of us, even Papa would bring back buckets of water and fill that wash basin. Papa would heat it and hang a blanket to curtain off the front door, just in case any visitors stopped by. No matter what, he made sure Mama enjoyed the first bath. Her water was the cleanest and warmest. Papa helped wash her hair. I could hear them laughin' through the curtain through it all. Papa always went next and never took long.

Finally, I would get a turn. Mama took time scrubbing my back and hair. Then, the boys would get in together. Mama would scold them for splashing too much; after all, we still had laundry to do and needed that water. Papa would heat the water again and Mama and I washed everything. I loved the way our little dug-out home smelled after bath days.

I loved our life out on that prairie. It was simple but we was free. It was just us but it was nice enough and there was enough to keep us all busy. After only a few years, Papa announced it was time to move but I couldn't understand why. Even after he explained we were getting too many neighbors, I couldn't understand. I thought it was just gettin' nice. No one asked me, though, and no one asked anyone else so we all followed him west once again. I had a terrible feelin' leavin' our home that day. Even though it was bright as day, I felt like we was headed down a dark road and we couldn't see where to step next. I shut my eyes and forced myself stop reminisin' for a spell or I'd lose my footing right here present day.

I sighed, and put down the water buckets. There was time, this morning, to sit for a spell. I wiped tears from cheeks that I hadn't felt fall. Sometimes, especially right before my monthly, I noticed missing my mama and family more than I could bear. Oddly enough, it was also these days, that I could find some solace in my existence.

I sat and looked around. Conflicted. That is what I felt nearly every second of my waking moments. I was grateful to be alive. I was grateful for food and shelter. Yet, I always looked for the few peaceful minutes I could be alone away from prying eyes and hands. I was constantly looking and planning my escape. This morning I tried to content myself with the extra break and notice the beauty around me. It did not last. After a few moments, I became conflicted once more.

As much as I loved feeling the few minutes of precious freedom or fresh air, I also hated it.

It reminded me of everything that was no more and everything I wasn't and possibly never would be. The beauty only reminded me of the ugly existence I currently survived each day. Life existed beyond my boundaries where people lived in homes and owned their own time. Other folks owned shops and fell in love. They fell out of love. Women had babies and fed them. They raised children whom they tucked them into small beds each night, kissing precious cherub cheeks, fanning out their hair while they slept. That was true beauty and nothing I experienced.

My life was not my own. And these stolen moments were the only true happiness I might ever have. Normally, I could muster some sense of it and even accept it but today, the sun shining, the cool breeze, even the quiet of my journey to retrieve the water only served to remind me of all I'd lost and would never have.

CHAPTER 3

Iwiped my face again and took up my burdens and water careful not to spill either and made my way carefully back to the saloon. I was nearly complete with my short journey when Jeremiah stepped in my path. "Mornin' Ruth. That water heavy?" He smiled showing he was missing his four front teeth.

"Morning, Jeremiah," I smiled back, careful not to show my actual disdain I held for the young man. He was my age give or take a couple of years. He was also always filthy and a stench hung around him no matter the day nor time of day. Still, he was kind and when he bought my time, he was always gentle. I still found it difficult to be in his presence.

Trying to breathe in as little as possible I asked, "Why don't you take one bucket for me and walk me the rest of the way? You could come in and have a drink." I winked at him just a little. He grinned and took the bucket gladly. My first customer of the day.

We walked in together. I was careful to let the proud owner and proprietor of the establishment see I brought in a customer. Mr. Evans was pleased. "Why Jeremiah, nice to see you this day. Why don't you sit, put your feet up. I'll tell ya what, first drink on the house." Mr. Evans smiled leanin' over the bar to shake his hand. All of us girls knew what drinks on the house meant and I went to the barrel that held the "house" drinks. It was the one that held the beer that was watered down about half. First one was on the house but house drinks weren't our best. The trick worked though. Most of the guys only got thirstier after that first drink and ordered more. I filled a cup and brought it to Jeremiah.

He took the cup in one hand and grabbed my waist with the other. He sat me down on his lap and I forced a giggle. I gave him a little slap as I tried not to breath as I smiled and wrapped my arms around his neck.

Evans called out, "Found you a good one there, this fine day Jeremiah. I'm watching the time though, so don't you waste my drink."

I felt Jeremiah's shoulders slump, just a little at the reminder of who I was and where he was and who owned me and my time. Not wanting to miss out on a paying customer I whispered, "I sure am glad I ran into you. You carried that water like it was nothin'. Why, I could barely keep up!"

I felt him straighten up again and chuckle, "I was watchin' for you, Ms. Ruth. I figured you could use the help." I smiled but wondered why he hadn't taken both buckets, then.

Nodding my head, I asked, "And how can I ever thank you enough, or make sure you help me next Saturday mornin?" I reached my hands down his chest and rested one lightly on his growing crotch. He blushed a little.

Nearly every weekend we played this little game and I still never got him to ask for what he wanted. After all this time I knew what he could afford and what pleased him most. I got down on my knees and unbuttoned his pants with my teeth. I locked eyes with him and put his small firm dick in my mouth.

I had worked this job long enough; I got a certain satisfaction making someone come. I hadn't always been a whore, though. And, there were times, I allowed myself to hate the satisfaction, hate myself and all my customers. Jeremiah, even though he smelled, was not someone I could wholeheartedly hate, though.

He was too innocent and gentle. And it never took long to finish. He never pushed into my mouth further than I allowed and he had never hit me or struck my face. He just wanted someone to love on him and it was difficult not to oblige.

Once I'd finished with Jeremiah, I was free to go to my room. I was careful to kiss him on his cheek and whisper I hoped to see him soon. Thankfully, no one else was comin' in just yet; it was still early. I wanted to wash up best I could and get my bed clothes back on my bed before Mr. Evans took notice. Suckin' Jeremiah was an easy trade-off for some more free time and even was allowed a cat nap on my fresh bed all alone.

Becky opened my door without knockin' to call me back down to work. I jumped up and fixed myself up a little, slappin my cheeks to make me look more alert. I was surprised when I got to the top of the stairs. The place was filling up fast.

Becky was her typical excited self and from what I could make out from her chatter, there was some sort of commotion at out the mine. Men were filling in to discuss those goin' ons and to drink their opinions. It was going to be a busy night. We linked arms and went down together. The place really was crowded. Bawdy men leaned on everything there was to lean on; the girls, their friends, the bar, the tables. Every column had at least two guys leaning towards each other talking about whatever it was that happened at the mine that day. And everyone was bein' over loud. It was real comfortin' linkin' arms with Becky like that as we walked into a sea of strong emotion. Not one voice was calm. Evans caught my eye and then Becky's. His face was sober but Becky and I knew what he wanted. He didn't have to ask twice.

We needed to mingle and calm this growin' crisis with no explanation exactly what that crisis was. We walked towards other girls and I was careful to hold my mouth open in my widest grin. We leaned in together attractin' attention and I whispered, "Gals, they need us more than ever now, if anyone person is too heated, you know what to do." We all laughed and broke apart heading towards the loudest voices in the place. No one here was quiet like Jeremiah was that mornin'; this was a real workin' night. Evans watched us real close and finally called out, "You girls are in for a real treat tonight!" I was used to this work, used to the men and all they said but I still cringed, way down deep inside, every time Evans spoke. It didn't matter what he said, the mere sound of his voice was reminder enough he owned me.

Minin' towns were volatile, everyone knew. Some folks said desperation sparked such unlawfulness but I often wondered if the explosives that blew apart mountains somehow seeped into men's blood causing them to act so wild. One minute they would be just fine talkin' and playin' their cards. Next, they might be at each other's throats threatenin' death over nothin'. This evenin', though it was early, everyone was already inflamed. I couldn't even see any cards out yet. Nor was anyone drinkin' whiskey. Looked like everyone was sippin' ale..

I threw my shoulders back and walked to the loudest, dirtiest miner. Standin' real close and starin' right into his eyes, I lifted his arm around my shoulders. He took little notice keepin' up his tirade. I didn't interrupt. Instead, I allowed his arm to slip down, just a little, off my shoulder. Again, he responded without even looking. His hand grasped my slim hip and he pulled me in closer. I laughed loudly and put my arm right on his chest, and let it fall, slowly, right down the front his entire abdominal front. His talking quieted ever so slightly and he looked me in up and down. I grabbed hold of a hardenin' cock.

"Now, ain't that right, Ms. Ruth? Ain't ya agree?" His voice was directed outwards but I had his attention, for now. I squeezed a little and then let go and looked to the other men he was talkin' at.

"Ya know I do, Johnny, ya know I just do agree. After all, wasn't I just sayin' the other day, how you called it the last time it all went down." Course, I had no idea what they was really talkin' about since I'd been in the saloon all day but it sounded right and got the response I needed. Johnny quieted down, just a little. He liked my words but wanted my attention on him. His interest shifted from the other men to me and the little group broke up. The entire place was quietin' just a little and I chanced a quick glance around.

Just like I had done, each of the girls infiltrated little groups and got attention drawn towards themselves. More men were gettin' their drinks at the bar and I saw Evans emptyin' the first whisky bottle of the night. I kept Johnny's eyes on me as I brushed my chest against his ribcage. He liked that, I could tell. His mouth opened a little and his voice softened.

I walked my fingers back up his front and chucked him under the chin, "Now, then, what is really your talkin' about tonight?"

"Well, you know them Orientals takin' our jobs up there at that mine." He drew a long drink and wiped his mouth. I sure did know how most of the miners felt. Trouble began brewin' few months back, when the owners of the mine had introduced a group of the small men to work in the mines.

CHAPTER 4

I'd never seen an Oriental before comin' here and didn't have much to do with them. 'Course that was mostly due the fact they lived in their own quarters of the town. They even had their own women. Instead of a saloon, they had some sort of den where they smoked their opium and ate rice. Our men went there but we barely saw them on our side. I had never been to that part of town. I was fascinated by their dark hair and slender frames, though. Most weren't any larger than myself and many even shorter. I wondered how they could work such long, hard hours but they seemed to cope alright.

"Well, ya know they won't refuse work no matter how low the pay is. Why, when we decided we needed higher wages and they stepped up, takin' our jobs. Fact is, today, one of them even took on the spot Old Riley been diggin' yesterday. Went right in, took the load and took the pay." Johnny was shakin' his head sheer disgust on his face. I wondered at the sheer audacity of the Oriental wonderin' if he knew how things worked out here. And, I knew Johnny enough to know he exaggerated most things.

The fight was always the same. Coal miners got paid per load. This meant they could dig all day on a load and not get paid till they brought it out. Most dug a spot then had to leave it at least overnight and sometimes even days until they loaded it up. I'd heard the rumors the Chinamen didn't play by those rules but who knew. They might let a man work and dig, then get in early and take the payload. Or, they simply might be victims of some sort of prejudiced plot. No one outside those mines could prove this was actually happenin' either. It was their word against their word.

In the end it wasn't goin' to matter overmuch, who was right or who was lyin'. This could cause an all-out war. If one group was willin' to strike for better wages and another group willing to work, the strike would be unsuccessful fannin' already hot flames. Most men felt their very livelihoods were threatened by the Chinamen, Irish, and even Mormons who willingly took lesser pay. Whether there was any actual truth to men stealin' others' payloads was another problem all together. It could be very well exaggerated in an effort to remove those willing to work for smaller wages. Then again, it could be true and no one might ever know or agree on it because we sure didn't speak no Chinamen and they didn't speak English.

That much of the story was all fact. Everythin' else was heresay or opinion but my job was not to find those facts. My job was to calm the fears these men were feeling and keep them drinkin' in this establishment. That was all girls like me was good for.

CHAPTER 5

Except I was a person with a fine workin' brain in my head was figurin' on how best to use this situation to my advantage. I'd have to be careful though and wait for my moment. That woman, the seer, she saw calamity, this just might be my chance.

If it weren't, well I might have my own set of other problems. If the mines only employed Chinamen and Mormons, our own establishment could be forced closed. Chinamen had their own vices and Mormons couldn't be counted on as regular payin' customers. Oh sure, we had the odd one sneak in and out the back every few days but those quick visits weren't going to pay to keep us open. I couldn't change no one's minds, alls I could do was wait and watch and be ready. That wasn't today though.

I forced myself to listen to Johnny for a while longer, never taking my hands off him completely unless I was offerin' another drink. Lookin' around, all the girls were doing their jobs. Most of the men was quieted down. Becky was nowhere to be found and I guessed she was already upstairs with that loud-mouth brawler we all called Smiths. I was glad she got him. We tried takin' turns with the rough ones; my last turn ended with a black eye that angered Evans. He said I wasn't fit for servin' the men in that state and offered to give me another one if I didn't yell for Dan the next time. I hope Smiths was bein' nicer tonight. Johnny was ok except he finished fast. Smiths took a long time but he paid for it.

After another round, Johnny put my hands down his pants and came that way. An easy job allowin' me to move on quick. He took another drink and quieted down after that. Evans nodded my way glad for my quick work that evenin'. It was strange, I didn't much care for Evans but still liked his approval.

Mr. Evans watched from the bar, careful to see we were all busy, workin' the men. All but one man was drinkin' and conversatin'. Dan stood near the front door, thumbs looped into his belt loops, takin' in the entire scene.

Dan was Evans' go to man for runnin' this place. He was replaceable but loyal to Evans. No customer wanted quarrelin' with him and all the girls knew Dan was the real strength of the place. Rumor was Evans inherited his wealth and squandered most of it during his youth. He liked thinking he was influencing men far greater than himself and prided himself on cunning. In reality, he lacked the true traits that bred real leaders. Next to them, his true traits were displayed showing nothing more than a short, sneaky man who had just enough money to capitalize from the work of others. People always put up with men like Evans because of their money. And only because of their money. Men like Evans aren't attractive, friendly or loyal. He acted as if the town needed him but I knew, deep down, he knew the truth and simply accepted it long ago despite his distaste for it.

Dan was who people really wanted on their side. If Dan wasn't on their side, he was on the opposing side and no wants a man like Dan to oppose them. Dan had no money outside his earnings but held the quiet influence of cold strength. He feared no man, loved no woman and only survived that unforgiving landscape. His duties included but were never limited to breakin' in all the new girls, collectin' money due Evans and breakin' up fights. In all my time, I only ever saw him drink when the new girls came on. Other than those few occasoions, he was stone cold sober all the while watchin' everythin' so close we called him Hawk behind his back. It was really only thanks to Dan that swarmy

Evans had any sort of business at all. Even though I'd hated him more than anythin', my own survival demanded I trust him for many things.

It was hard to tell if Dan was even good or bad lookin'. He was average height, dark hair and skin darkened from his time spent out of doors. His eyes were dark and I had only seen him smile once or twice revealing straight yellowin' teeth. His body was hardened and lean from a life of hard work. Dan was always there when men like Smiths became too rough. Just last week when my tooth went flying from that hard slap, Smiths hadn't been far behind; Dan really laid into him and we hadn't seen Smiths for two days after. I could tell Dan was listenin' hard for any distress from upstairs even as he watched everything else.

I made some rounds while I'd been thinkin' and got pulled into a group of laughin' men who didn't seem to care too much about the mines. They definately sided with the strikers but they were like most men content to follow the current mood. Their loud speculations leaned towards the idea someone would "make it alright" and it would "all come out in the wash". My guess was they would happily drink to the winners whichever side that turned out to be.

"Oh come on, Rusty, you know you have a stronger opinion than that, I've seen it myself a time or two." My voice wasn't soft and the men all laughed appreciatively. Rusty smiled down at me and took another drink.

"You know Ms. Ruth, I knew you'd be missin' me today. Why, I woke up and thought of ya down here all alone. Make yer rounds, come back in a bit, an' ya won't sleep all alone tonight." He winked and slapped my ass as I walked on a little disappointed at his dismissal. Rusty was easy and quick to please. Not all men were like that.

Actually, I'd been hoping for a busy few hours and not have to share my actual bed if I'd stayed busy down here. I smiled and offered him another drink. If he drank till he passed out, I'd still sleep on my own. He accepted and I hurried off to retrieve it.

"Now, here's what I was hopin' for, there's the prettiest girl, with the prettiest feather. I was hopin' you weren't too busy just yet, Ms. Ruth." A low voice whispered to my left. Despite knowing better, despite me willing it different, my heart gave a small unwanted leap. Jed, or Jedidiah was there that night.

Tall, wide shouldered, long hair and the brownest eyes I do believe I'd ever seen belonged to that man. He wasn't young but he wasn't old and he knew his way with a woman. If my life had been any other way, I'd dared dream of spendin' it with a man like Jedidiah. Oh sure, it was nice when he visited. He paid well and when he stayed into the morning, he even brought breakfast to the room. He always paid and I always serviced his desires but after, he talked about hisself and about his old life.

He told me his ma and pa had several kids out in some city back East. It sounded like his dad did pretty well but then lost his small fortune in some scheme. After that, he lost his ma to the last sibling during child birth. His pa remarried and Jed left soon after. He was fourteen when he hitched onto some wagon train west, working his way out here. He kept in touch with his father and his brothers who managed to gain back their lost fortune and make even more. I often wondered if he now wished he'd stayed back.

He must have inherited his father's business mind though, because rumor had it, Jed did just fine. He visited the saloon every month and never kept a tab. He paid his visits, in full, every time. He detested Mr. Evans, we all knew. He was savvy enough to know how best to talk with him without being too friendly or makin' an enemy. He ignored Dan altogether, like one might do when stepping through the streets full of cow shit. He knew he was there, and purposefully stepped 'round him. I'd caught Dan glaring absolute hate at him several times but to my knowledge, neither man ever addressed the other.

Despite me telling my own heart to wise up, despite me tryin' to ignore those soul-full brown eyes, I couldn't. I was ecstatic to see Jed each time and tonight was no different. I didn't show it though. Each man here thought of themselves as the absolute favorite of each girl. We didn't need a fight.

I didn't answer his whisper with words, just gave him a nice, long side-ways glance and sauntered off towards more loud talking. Jed would wait for me, I knew. He always did.

I made my rounds and was sure to offer Johnny enough rounds to get him fast asleep before the night was too late. He'd sleep 'til mornin', I was sure. I kept Evans happy by takin' two more clients upstairs for short trysts; they couldn't afford more nor were they the lastin' type. One more followed me upstairs and caught me while I was seein' one out my door.

He pushed his way in and pushed me right back on the bed. I'd never seen him before and assumed he was hungry for a woman.

"Wastin' no time, I see. Well, let me just get comfortable enough and you can jump on any way you please." I patted the bed beside me, invitin' him over and I could tell he liked that. I was relieved to hear the heavy footsteps I knew belonged to Dan just outside my door.

I called out, a little louder, "Well, ya was so excited, what's keepin' ya over there?" I knew Dan was out there listenin' and though some of that was keepin' watch over me, he was also always workin' for Mr. Evans. He was makin' sure we was doin' what we did and our safety was just part of the pay. No girls, less pay. Simple as that and no real love lost on any of us.

Lucky for me, that night, I'd been right. The gentleman was simply hungry for a woman and came easily after only a few hard pushes. He slumped across me and I allowed him to save some face for comin' so quickly. I breathed in, deep as I could with his weight against me and told him how pleasant he was and after another minute or two, I told him I hoped to see him soon. He didn't say another word, just got up, left some coin on my dressing table and let himself out.

I closed my door, grateful for the chance to clean myself up and freshen all the areas that needed it. I looked in my mirror and even brushed my hair. Jed was waitin'.

CHAPTER 6

I put on the cleanest thing I had and threw a shawl over my shoulders; the night had grown cold. I pushed open my door and stepped towards the stairs, coin in my hand from the last stranger. Dan stepped in front of me, blockin' my way.

"So, Ms. Ruth, that last gentleman didn't stay long. What was that? You aren't waitin' on a favorite, are you? Rubbing the guys off early or somethin'? He didn't even stop for a drink." Dan's voice was low.

I *was* waiting on a favorite, but I'd done my job well that night. I was practiced enough to not show any emotion; especially not fear. Keeping my voice steady, I hissed back, "Dan, I didn't rush that man, and I sure offered him drinks. He never said a word but he left money." I took up Dan's hand and dropped the coins, folding his fingers over them. I shrugged, "Maybe his was Mormon and unused to a woman. He came fast. I never saw him before."

Dan was mollified and let me go. I didn't head straight for Jed. He was in his corner, head down, waitin'. Alls I could do was walk around a little more, see who was still there and blend in as much as possible before heading his way. It was so late, no one was truly interested in anything more so I slowly made my way 'round to Jed and sat opposite him.

"How are you, stranger?" Dan was back downstairs, so I spoke a little loudly, a little lively like I had nothin' to lose; like I hadn't been thinking about Jed since the moment he'd walked in a few hours earlier.

"Ms. Ruth, you finished with all the boys?" Jed mostly looked to the ground when he talked with me and today was no different. I moved in closer. If he wasn't looking at my face, I'd ensure he was lookin' at some part of me.

"Why? Ya think I need time with a man?" Funny thing was, I did need time with a man. Sure, I'd been servicing men for near twenty hours straight now, but things were different with Jed. Jed knew his way around a woman. I leaned over, letting my corset slip open just a little more. I tried not to think of what this might look to Dan or Mr. Evans but to quiet my own, very real fears, I asked what he wanted to pay for this night.

To my surprise, his face flushed just a little.

"Why, Jedidiah," I knew he liked me using his full Christian name, "what were you thinking of paying for this fine evening? Its dark out there, and cooling down. Were you lookin' for somewheres to warm up a little?" With every word, I traced my finger up the middle of his thigh until the end. I just rested my hand right there, close enough but making him want more. I could see how hard he'd grown. Locking eyes, I licked my lips a little and waited for an answer.

I didn't have to wait long. He all but jumped up, and all but pushed me towards the stairs. I stopped, abruptly, and pushed his hands away a little, playing like I was fightin' him off. As if I would actually try to stop his body coming onto mine. He liked that, I could tell. Next thing I knew, he was pickin' me up and actually haulin' me up those stairs. I couldn't help but laugh and call out to Becky, "Becky! Help me! I been taken by this brute!" Her laughter followed us up the stairs.

I saw Mr. Evans watchin' so I called, "Be sure you get the payin' for all the holes, Evans!" Raucous laughter and whoops followed us but Jed didn't put me down.

My room was fresh and ready. He carried me right over to the bed, falling onto me causing a small crash and more cheers from below. For the next little while, I allowed myself to dream. I was just a woman who loved a man who loved me back who showed it in all the right ways.

Jed must have tired me out because I slept right through till morning. As I woke, I let myself lean towards a man whom I knew would keep me safe and loved every night if I allowed it. As my arm stretched towards the other side of the bed, all I felt were the coins he left behind. The sheets were already cold.

Out of habit, I counted the coins from touch and was relieved, same way I felt after any customer. Same as any customer, my anxiety dropped as I felt exactly what I was owed. Evans would be happy and Dan wouldn't ask too many questions. For now, I was safe and for a few more minutes alone.

That day was same as most others. I ate the breakfast Cook supplied; biscuits and gravy. There was no time to clean my room as I'd done the day before though. Almost immediately the place filled with men talkin' about them Orients from the day before. I sauntered around, same as the other girls.

Energy was lower today, and my guess that was thanks to all the drinks from the night before. The guys were still angry but it was a subdued with many a heads bein' rubbed and lowered brows. Voices were low and gruff, not boisterous and loud. The whole atmosphere was foreboding but lacked the energy to ignite into anything more today.

As I walked around, smilin' at the boys, I smiled and acted coy but I was listenin'. Nothin' would happen today but I was sure something would happen soon. The more I listened the more convinced I became of something happening and soon.

Ever since I'd come here, nearly four years now, I'd watched for my chance. This life was not my destiny and I just had to keep tellin' myself that. The place quieted down and Evans motioned for us girls to back off the men. We each made our ways to our favorite spot on the stairs.

Becky always went to the top, Jo just down from her, then myself, Sue and finally Betsy. It was nice to have a moment, if not a whole lot of space to ourselves. None of us fell asleep and none of us paid to close attention to the same talk as yesterday. It was hard to sort the truth and I imagined it was like everything else and the truth was actually somewhere in the middle.

Thing was, and this was a big thing, the men had positioned to strike. Whorin' was a hard, hard lot in life but coal minin' that was something else altogether. Coal lay, deep in the earth. It was dangerous to get at, and it didn't come easy.

Miners would venture down narrow shafts, withstand explosions, tunnels and almost continual darkness just diggin' at their "payload". Once that "payload" was freed, brought to the surface and weighed, miners were paid its weight. This meant no miner, no matter how lucky or hard working they was, none got paid for workin' each day they worked. Diggin' just didn't pay. Only coal paid. The miners had rallied, wantin' payin' for each day, each dig. Betsy had said this was only fair, "After all, no matter what we do with their pricks, we get paid." Us girls, even a few men had laughed but Dan slapped her anyways. Most of us thought she had a point.

Not only did most of think the miners should get paid for each day's work, there was also the danger of a payload getting' stole. Miner leaves a payload; his team knows he'll be back for it and they leave it alone. If a new team comes in, don't know any better or don't care, they take the payload and collect on his prior day or even week's work. Owners didn't agree too much on those things though.

Owners said if miners worked a day, the weight would pay off next day. And they were right. If the man got to that payload, if the team didn't move on or if a new team didn't take it over. Both sides had their points. Today's words were low, carried less volatile energy than last night but it felt different. Some words carry meanin', they carry change. I'd learned to tell the difference between talk and talkin', it'd taken a few years but I prided myself on my listen' skills now and the ability to tell the difference. I let my mind wander back to the first time I'd even known the difference.

CHAPTER 7

Iwas nearly fifteen the year my family was lost to an Indian raid. Lookin' back, I should have known an attack was just a matter of time. After all, we'd moved into their territory, onto their land. For the first few years, our family had been one of a very few to live out there and no one took much notice of us; not even the natives. We did our thing and they did theirs. We might see each other once in awhile or we might hear them; sometimes I could still hear the sound of their drums and cries carry across the prairie. Other than know the other existed, though, there was nothin' more to the relationship. Then, as more and more people moved in, more and more land was takin' and the already-fragile relationship grew tense.

Then came the soldiers. And, at first, we only hear or briefly saw them same as the Indian groups livin' near us. As the months turned over, though, tensions escalated. Pa told us not to worry but I could hear him and mama talkin' in hushed tones when they thought we weren't listenin'. Just like anything else, nothin' lasts under such strains. There were a few attacks on our neighbors but nothing too violent. Food stores broken into. Then a house was set on fire. And another. A few families up and left. Pa decided with the soldiers so close, we were safe enough so we stayed.

The attack came at night and didn't take long. It was hard to piece together what happened that night. I know some men entered the house even though Pa had barred the door and held off a few with his shotgun. I think the roof was set to blaze and four or five men rushed the house. Pa was killed right off with a hit to his head by their war hammer. Mama was next. They killed my brother but for some reason left to live and remember. I always felt they didn't see me. There was no other explanation to leave me alive or behind. Next day, I ran as far as I could until I finally stumbled across some men movin' across the country.

I must have looked a mess; I was starving and terrified. They took me in and fed me and put me in their wagon to sleep while we went on to the next settlement. Thinkin' I was safe, I'd fallen right to sleep to the rockin' of that wagon. Then came another attack.

I couldn't tell if they were the same group that killed my family or not. I just didn't see anyone clear enough. They moved fast and it was dark. It all only lasted a few minutes. This time, they saw me.

That part lasted forever. It was the last man, and I must have moved just enough to catch his eye. He turned faster than I ever thought possible and was on me faster than I ever could have imagined. There was just no stoppin' him. My head was stretched far back, exposing my throat which I'd been sure he was fixin' to cut. Instead, and I never understood why, he just cut a large section of my hair off, then sliced my face from eyebrow to lip. He was gone as fast as he'd come and I was on my own, surrounded by my dead for the second time in as many days. This time I didn't run.

I walked, my face drippin' blood until another band of men picked me up. They shared their water but never offered food. I didn't ask for it either. I was sure my life was over and there just seemed no point to eatin'. They asked my name and a few other questions that I left unanswered. They left me with Evans the very next day. Turns out, I'd been right, my life ended that day.

I don't recall what the men said, or what Mr. Evans' response was, but I do recall Sue takin' me right upstairs. There, she'd bathed me and washed my hair and I had a plate of food. She cleaned the cut to my face. I heard all she was sayin' but didn't really listen. I was too busy wondering about my parents and brother and if heaven was real. I was too busy fearing bare-skinned figures walking through the doors to really hear her explain what I had to do to survive. I barely heard or even seen Dan waltz in and ask how I was. Sue told him I needed time. He'd agree to come back later. I was given a full three days to rest and simply sit upstairs. I had no idea what was going on that first day. The second, I'd begun to collect my senses and could hear the raucous downstairs. The evening of the second, I could guess my fate, though I still had no idea how truly trapped I was. The morning of the third, Sue was ordered to take my clothes. Thankfully, by then heard some of what she was sayin'. She told me who she was and where we were. We were followin' a long line of men moving west to mine coal.

"Minin' is hard work. We is here to lighten that, lighten that and their pockets." She looked me in the eyes, then, "Listen up, there just ain't no way they gonna let you go. I done talked to Dan, hell, I even talked to Mr. Evans about it. I told 'em both you're too young. They asked if you had hair below and I had to tell them yes. They gonna look anyways. So, you listen. Dan, he breaks all the new girls in. You're next and they ain't gonna wait much longer. You heard of sex? How a man owns a woman? You see, women and men, we's different." I nodded, very afraid. I knew a little of what she was sayin'. Ma had lost a baby, and told us how she'd gotten pregnant and how we could help her clean up. I'd also experienced my own bleedin' for a year or so by then. I knew things but I also knew those things went on between man and wife. I was raised religious. People who didn't keep by those rules went right to hell and mama called them whores. I turned my head to the wall, numb with this new shock.

"Listen!" I'd turned my attention back to Sue then, "you don't get clothes till ya earn 'em. That's how it works here, Dan will tell ya when ya do. Ya do whatever he tells ya. But if you want this to go easy, you put his dick in your mouth, real gentle and just slide up and down a few times. Then, he'll finish real fast in your pussy. Let him . He may let you wear a shawl right after that. Got it?" I nodded even though even thinking about what she was saying brought tears to my eyes and made me shake.

"He's gonna come right back at ya again. This time, he's not gonna give ya time to do anything, so you just lie back and take it. Try not to cry. He's gonna turn ya over and come in from behind. Let him .

He likes it that ways best. He's gonna keep at ya most of today and tomorrow. He'll leave and come back. Just let him. He's gonna tell you to suck him and to sit on him and he's gonna use every hole you got. Let him. Here, use this, it will help." She slipped me a small vile of oil. "Don't let him know you have it."

Dan was much worse than she'd said. I was shakin' so much that first time, I'd forgotten to try and suck anything. He took me, fast, and slapped my ass asking if I'd liked it. I hadn't but I was too afraid to tell him anything and he left. Soon, he was back. He knocked my face, so hard, I fell back into the bed, making him laugh. Then, he was on top of me doing everything Sue warned me about. I tried not to cry and tried to keep up with his movements, but couldn't. He forced me on all fours in front of him and got in behind me, I wasn't expecting the pain that exploded as he eased into my anus and I cried out. He stopped, and still inside me slithered up my back and whispered, "You're our whore now. You don't own you. You don't own anything, not clothes, not even your ass. You got it? Now, you take it until I say." And he pulled my hair until my head was high and he took his time. He slumped against me, making it hard to catch my breath and stayed in me all deflated.

He put his hands all over me, telling me to like it and that if I wanted my clothes ever, I'd learn the tricks. Then, he stayed there all night, watched me use the chamber pot and laughed as I tried to clean myself without him seein'. He made me sit in front of him with my legs apart and mouth open. We stayed in that room for three days with the food brought up. Finally, he threw me into the hallway and told me to get downstairs. I still didn't have any clothes. I noticed the other girls glance my way with short but sympathetic looks.

I made my way down, terribly conscience of my nudity, dirty hair and bruised arms. I tried to cover myself a little but a big man drew me onto his knee before I could say or do anything. I saw Evans wave to him and call, "She's new, why don't you go with Becky or Sue, Tom? They know a good time! She doesn't know nothin' yet. Same cost, and not as fun." The big guy ignored him and put his hands between my legs right there. I was cold and tremblin' which he seemed to like. He'd paid Evans for just a touch when Dan pointed out the front of his pants were moist. Then, Dan moved me onto another guy and another.

I was hungry, cold and learned my life that day. I was given lunch later but it took a good week to earn my clothes. Dan relished in standin' over me tellin' me what I was doin' wrong offerin' to let the men have such a disapointin' ride for half the cost or even free.

Only two weeks later, I was earnin' my keep. Two weeks after that, I learned how to get the guys goin' shorter without them even knowin'. A few weeks later, I even enjoyed some of the men. That was when I knew I was a whore. There was no escape. My survival depended on it. I'd paid the devil his dues.

As the weeks grew into months, I'd grown ever more dependent on Mr. Evans. We'd followed those men until we reached this place and a permanent establishment had been raised. Inside, I was sheltered and fed and protected from most attacks. Dan kept most men in check and Evans kept the drink flowin', which kept the rest of 'em in check. Us girls formed a sort of family and did what we could to make our lives better. It wasn't much but it was something:.

We shared food. For those monthly times, we shared rags. On cold nights we shared blankets. We even snuck small celebrations in where we could. I loved them girls as if we were blood sisters.

Still.

Most of us planned our escapes every single day even though we never talked about it. We watched for signs that might give us the next step to get away from all that protection. In four years, nothin' had ever happened to promise escape but I still watched. And that set me apart from simple whores, or so I told myself.

In the early days, I had begged forgiveness from a God who never answered, who never showed me a sign He was even listenin'. I hadn't stopped believin' but I'd let a little of the Devil in me when I had the first man who showed me what loving really was. After that, I'd stopped askin' forgiveness and if I felt like pleasurin' myself, I did. The respite was brief but guaranteed. I was a whore, a good one and there was plenty of time I didn't think I minded so much. I just kept my options open. I never even heard of any old whores.

CHAPTER 8

This talk in the saloon that day, this promised somethin' and I was gonna keep keen on it to see how I might use it. I'd paid my dues in hell; I was ready to leave. But like most things in that desert, this would take time. The next few days even the talk dwindled to hoarse whispers and I found myself givin' hand jobs to guys strikin' just to keep their hopes up a little. Evans promised a free hand job to any guy with a drink. Becky was soon complainin' her wrists were tired and our food got cut. No one was minin' and no one was gettin' paid. Becky stopped complainin'

An entire week went by, and though none of us dared complain, all our wrists were sore. "Thank God their drinkin' money wore out," Becky whispered late that Friday. I wasn't so sure. There was only a few customers and no one else comin' in. They didn't pay, meant we might not eat. I didn't like those odds even if it meant a nice rest from it all.

For two days no one came into the place. The girls and I were booted out onto the porches by Evans and Dan. We waved, we flashed and hollered but it seemed most of the money had simply dried up. I hoped we could entice them back to their mines.

Evans ordered Dan to walk us through the camp, "Walk 'em through. Once you get down between the canvases, take their tops down. Remind the men what they're missin' not workin'. Tell the girls to take those dildos with 'em."

We walked through the town, tauntin' the church goers, "Hey, beautiful!" I yelled at one young woman walkin' with her husband. He looked my way before she did. "Yeah, you! Wanna come play? Your husband looks like he wants ya too." We laughed as the blush rose into her cheeks.

We all sauntered right up that main street, right into the shanty town most miners lived in and loosened each other's tops. I slid the narrow wooden dildo down my chest and back up. "Look all ya! Look at how lonely I got without any visitors!" I yelled. The other girls did the same. I do believe every man there turned watched. Even though it was too hot for it, we took our time but no one followed us.

Two more days went by, just the same. Finally, the third day, that shanty town was void of most men. We guessed they were back to the mines. By the end of the week, our walks outdoors were over and our hands and mouths full again. We stopped tellin' 'em how lonely we was.

Becky and Betsy were talkin' early the next mornin', "My, God, I just didn't think the men would get that hungry." Betsy was sayin' to Becky. "I mean no one can hold their load, but there sure are a lot of 'em and most come back for seconds."

I let them to their conversatin' and went to fetch the morning water knowin' I was more than likelyto see Jeremiah along the way. Lookin' around, I let the summer breathe new life into me. The night before demanded a reprieve. Summer was a good time for reprieve. Winters were such an arduous journey of survival, summers often turned into mere spaces of time to prepare with so little thought or time dedicated enjoyin' the fact we didn't have to spend energy just keepin' warm. Of course, those thoughts led to others makin' my short journey even shorter.

So little of my time belonged to my own design. I suppose life was like that for most women. Our childhoods, even the happiest ones, were spent at our expense. Our youths were spent caring for our families and siblings with almost no break between caring for them and beginning our own families and caring for husbands. My own parents taught both my brother and I to read and write but I'd done nothin' with that for years.

"Mornin', Ms. Ruth." Just as I'd predicted, there was Jeremiah. I smiled his way.

"Why, Jeremiah, I just *knew* I'd be seein' you this fine mornin'." I smiled at him actually happy to see him.

"You know, Ms. Ruth, this trouble up at the mines, its got me thinkin'. You know this is a hard life." Jeremiah sounded more serious than I'd ever heard him before and I nodded I understood minin' was hard work, especially when that miner was Jeremiah. I looked him over as we walked.

It wasn't that Jeremiah was weakly built. It was more like a weak disposition towards work. There were many days the mines were full but Jeremiah was found elsewhere. Truth was, I think he found more pleasure in fishin' payload holes than coal payloads. He wasn't going to get rich that way but he wasn't exactly starvin' either.

"Now, you know me, Ms. Ruth. I never liked violence," he was continuing as though I was paying heed to every last syllable from his mouth. I looked him over again. Jeremiah truly was not a violent man. I certainly never saw him brawl. He went on, "I am just not too sure this is the life I was destined for. I hate goin' into the ground. At least we were gettin' paid and could count on that but now, well, everythin' sure is changin' fast." He stopped walking and looked to the ground. I felt like he was wantin' somethin', most likely the little suck he so enjoyed but I waited to see. I brushed his arm with the back of my hand.

"Well, I look at you, Ms. Ruth and I doubt ya want to stay in your, uh, position forever," he blushed a little and grinned at me. I grinned back, focused on his face, waitin' to hear what he wanted from me. I began to think maybe he wanted to stay outside for it and though that wasn't Evans' favorite way to do business, I doubted he would complain much as long as he was paid. I waited further.

"I think, well, what I'm tryin' to say is that I'm gonna leave here, Ms. Ruth. I settled all I need to settle. Come tomorrow mornin', well, I'm outta here." He fixed his eyes on mine.

"Well, now, I am surprised, Jeremiah. I just thought you were gonna ask me to suck you out here." I smiled as a brief blush stole into his face. "But you know, I understand. You gotta go where you gotta go. I get it and I wish you luck." I was sincere, I was surprised and I did wish him all the best. I smiled at him and he returned it. He still wasn't goin' anywhere so I waited again. I set the water down at my feet. This was takin' too damn long to hold that up anymore.

"Ms. Ruth. I, uh. Well, do you want to go with me? I have a bit o' savings. I could settle what needs to be settled." He wasn't grinnin' anymore but his young face was full of hope.

I found I didn't know what to say. It was so much easier just offering him pleasure than to ponder goin' anywhere with him. Also, I knew better.

Just nearly a year ago, another girl left with some young miner she'd found interestin'. She was one of our best girls too. She never denied a customer, she didn't seek trouble with anyone and she was known to even help Cook. She was Mr. Evans favorite though I wasn't too sure why. She was not the prettiest girl and certainly didn't have a great body. I heard him say she was invitin' one time, invitin' to everything a man didn't have. He was livid when she'd gone. And we all heard they didn't make it far. Dan told us hisself, he'd shot her in the face at point blank range.

She'd been Dan's favorite too. She hadn't needed breakin' in when she came to us and Dan only went to her that first night. I wasn't Dan's favorite at all and he'd had no problem shootin' her right in the face.

"Awwe, Jeremiah, that's awful sweet of ya, but ya know. I like it here with Mr. Evans and the girls. I can only wish ya well." I reached for his cock, "I can give you a little somethin' to remember me on your travels though." I smiled as I felt how hard he was almost the instant I grabbed hold. He didn't smile back, though.

He pushed my hands away and grabbed me by the arms, "Now, you look here Ms. Ruth. You ain't like the others, ya just ain't. Ya ain't a whore, not in the true sense. I think ya need to rethink that and come with me."

I smiled even though I never did like being grabbed that way and I looked right into his eyes. "Now, Jeremiah, you know us girls, we *like* pleasin' you men. And you know me, I am real good at pleasin' you. Why, it's one reason I get the water." I tried putting my hands back on the front of his pants but he was back just far enough I couldn't reach. He gripped harder.

"I know I been nice to you, Ruth. But a man can't keep wantin' and waitin' like I been doin'." He was gripping me so hard, I knew my arms would show it. He was pullin' me, hard, to him and for the first time ever, I feared the look in his eyes. I'd seen it many times, in other men's eyes and what followed was never pleasant.

Even more troubling, I was out here on my own. If Jeremiah was goin' to force himself on me, so be it, but there'd be no coin to show for it and Evans wouldn't like that. I tried not to panic and steady my voice.

"Look, Jeremiah, I like holdin' your dick in my mouth, or you pick where you want to put it. I can put you nice and deep in me but you're holdin' me too tight. And I can't move to make you happy." I tried smiling at him but I didn't like this. Last time a man didn't pay, Dan left more bruises than I could count.

Jeremiah didn't let go, he pushed me right down, spillin' the water beneath me. It was so cold rushin' into all my clothing. The ground was covered in hard rubble and I doubted I'd ever been more uncomfortable. Each small stone dug into my skin and my hair and clothes weighed down with cold water.

"Jeremiah," I whispered into his ear, determined to gain control of this situation, "What do you want from me." He slapped me hard, across my face.

"Shut up, Ruth, just shut up." And with those words, he reached up into my dress and pushed into me, his hands cold and rough. I jumped a little trying to keep him from hurtin' me too much. He put the other hand on my face, squeezing. "Do you like that, you stupid whore." And he pushed into my front, then back, rough. I couldn't help but jump a little, it hurt bad.

"Oh, that's right, jump and squeal." I see you like it.

I could hardly breathe, Jeremiah was heavy and really leanin' into me. I tried moanin' into his ear to soften him a little but he moved his arm to my throat. It didn't take any pressure to shut me up for good. I felt him nearly come but then he stopped movin', I hoped he was finished but then he started in again. Each time I pushed further into the rubble beneath me. Each time, he pushed in harder and harder. His arm stayed on my throat making it impossible to catch my breath. I hated it when they choked me like that. All I could do was wait.

Finally, mercifully, I felt him come and relax on me. I waited for him to get up off me. He took his time and when he rolled off, I saw tears on his face.

I didn't care, I was gonna have trouble for this, I was sure. I got up and grabbed the waterin' bucket.

"Damn you, Jeremiah. If you care at all for me, go pay Evans." And I walked away without another word. I wanted to kick him but was afraid I'd only anger him further.

I collected the water and hurried back to the kitchen. The day was still sunny, the air still warm but I was cold. It seemed any man, even the sweet ones could turn.

And just like I feared, Dan was waitin' for me when I go back. I tried smilin' at him as I passed the water to Cook. He didn't say a word, just watched as I hustled on by tryin' to avoid eye contact. Just as I breathed the sigh of relief on gettin' by, he grabbed my already bruised arm and pointed to my clothes.

"What is this? Why are you all wet?" I'd forgotten about that. I closed my eyes and waited while he pushed his hand up under my dress. "And what's this?" He voice was low, cruel. He showed me a few glistening fingers.

I smiled at him and licked his finger, "Why, Mr. Dan. That tastes like day old come to me." His grip lessened. "And I am all wet because I fell out there. I was on my way to freshen' up, seein' as we got a full house out there." I forced myself to hold his gaze. He finally loosened his grip and I hurried on up to my room. I let the door hang open, just a little to prove I wasn't hidin' anythin' and hurried to get linens to dry myself.

As I undressed, I forced myself to wait to clean out the inside of my legs immediately. I could almost feel Dan watchin' from the hall even though I hadn't heard him come up behind me. Instead, I removed my outer dress, then slip and wrapped the linen around my torso to work on my hair. Thanks to lyin' in the dirt I had plenty of mud dryin' just about everywhere. And there was no time or water for the bath I truly needed. I settled for brushing my hair and decidin' the dress was beyond savin'. I would owe Evans for that too.

And though I didn't want to, my thoughts drifted towards Jeremiah as I slipped my stockings up my legs that were now clean from mud and him. Thing was, if Jeremiah was leavin' it meant somethin'. More men might be leavin'. The town had never been safe. No minin' camp or towns were ever safe. There was too much goin' on to guarantee somethin' as frivolous as safety.

Not that there had ever been any guarantees. It just didn't work that way. We were too far west. The treasures men sought were too deep in the earth. That sort of gamble left everyone on invisible tenterhooks, unhinged while they scraped daily survival dreamin' of riches nightly.

Men facin' such a tiresome living needed distractions which was why this establishment was so popular. Most of 'em were friendly enough, and just lonely. They had their needs but before this, a lot of those needs hadn't been much more than human touch. If men left, who would keep us in business though? I couldn't predict the future but it was worrisome.

CHAPTER 9

Right now, there were five girls and Cook. I wasn't sure how many men actually worked for Evans. That was a lot of people reliant on a transient community lookin' for distraction. Last week had showed us how precarious even our livelihoods were. No money had meant no normal past time drinkin' or whorin'. Even if the men made it rich took away stress. If they weren't survivin' they were livin', savin' for their own land, their own houses. They might cut back on spendin' or cut it out altogether.

And of course, the most worrisome of all was men leavin'. No men meant no spendin' at all. Jeremiah might be only one, but would more follow? The men discussed this all week. I could hear the place really fillin' up and chided myself for over thinkin'. After all, no one was promised tomorrow and I had work to do.

There was a change, I could feel it, as I let myself down the stairs. There was no shoutin', no laughin', and I couldn't hear any of the girls talkin'. I looked around from the third or fourth step, really takin' stock on where my services would be best used.

Becky was already downstairs, already at work. She was standin' with two men, her hands in one's pants. Sue was doin' the same for another man, and I could tell two were waitin' on her. One had one hand entwined in her hair. Becky was a professional, there was nothin' that she couldn't do. She was gettin' on in age, but no less desirable.

Becky had come here havin' been abandoned by her second husband. She only talked about it once, and I'd wished she hadn't. She married him after her first husband died and I believe the men had been brothers. She married the brother and followed his dream of findin' gold out west. They had several children, she never told me exactly how many that I could recall. I think they'd been happy. She did say she never liked laborin' to bring the children into this world though. She dutifully followed him and she did all a wife and mother could, then some sickness swept through. She said maybe some sort of a flu. All the children died. Every last one.

When Becky talked about it, she hadn't cried. She just sort of stared off into the distance, tellin' me how the older ones helped bury the younger ones. Then, each other and finally, it was just her buryin' the last one. After that, her husband never touched her again. In fact, he hardly spoke another word to her and dropped her off one day, right at the edge of town. She never saw him again. He left her with nothin', not even a shawl. It took three days of winter weather out on the edge of town when she somehow made her way inside. Dan took her right upstairs; no food was even given until he was done. At least it hadn't taken long.

Now, Becky was a favorite. She had a nothin' to lose attitude and seemed to like the hours filled with pleasin' everyone around her. She never complained and as long as Evans let her drink, she never asked for anything else either. She was a true professional and good at her business. Men lined up, not seemin' to mind the wait. She'd be busy all night.

I thought today would be good to team up with another girl and I started lookin' for Sue. Sue was easy to lean on and I liked to think, she could do the same with me if she needed. Truth was, Jeremiah hurt me worse than I dare admit. If I could work alongside her, there was the good chance I could keep my hands full instead of getting' on my back. I found Sue, already actin' a little drunk and tuggin' some guy. I grinned and joined in, it would be an easy night.

While we worked, I listened for more men plannin' on runnin' like Jeremiah. We were busy, there was a full house and it was easy to piece what was really goin' on down at the mines.

Minin' towns needed two things to survive and the more abundant those two things were in number, the more the town thrived. Minin' towns needed mines and men. Mines were the reason, they lured treasure seekin' men in by the dozens. Towns sprang up quickly scattering the wilderness with stores, boardwalks, and churches. But the mines couldn't survive without men. Once the men came, they had their own needs. Towns just sprang into existence to meet the demand. Towns that differed from just about anything else ever imagined.

I doubted the wild west could ever be tamed. Towns fed the needs and desires of mostly young men tied to nothin' and no one. That kind of a man has precious few needs. Survival is their game and no big, rich houses marked permanent success. Shanty towns barely kept men sheltered. Chow lines fed them and saloons entertained 'em. Most didn't care for religion just yet; they were too young to know their own demise could and would overtake them. Many didn't come with families, so schools for children were nearly non-existent. Lawless men with no rules fueled capitalism that didn't yet enjoy too many fruits of their labor. The few that tried law and order were beyond all the youthful lusts of life and were just as apt to look the other way in most circumstances. Others simply took bribes. The few religious leaders and law dogs who did act integrous were only in danger of standing quite alone. Integrity wasn't exactly lucrative.

Everyone came in search of wealth. They were escapin' the hard life of factory work desperately wantin' more from life. Minin' towns only kept them alive. They didn't feed them in anyway. Such loose men were dangerous and in desperate need of anything good in life. Which is why the saloons did all the business.

Drink numbed 'em and for lonely men, a turn with a girl, hell even a touch from a girl was all the love any of 'em felt for years on end. We fed each desire, each need. The wild west was one place men could seek debased goods of life with nary twice a look their way.

Trouble was, the west was big enough for all and attracted more and more men from all corners of the earth. It seemed the farther the men traveled from, the less they expected from life. They accepted harder work and less wage but still, their lives improved from their old countries.

Their counterparts, however, demanded more from life and soon all those groups were at odds with their own desirin' needs and in the end, somehow even the wide west wasn't big enough for everyone. And it started deep in the earth, down in the mines.

I guess it shouldn't be too surprisin' that's where such evil might begin. Darkenss reigns for twenty-four hours a day and those narrow tunnels afforded space enough for work. Light nor beauty nor love could penetrate such a space manifesting in threats of violence eventually erupting in the physical. We girls all felt it, men were rougher and Becky reminded us of how it was when we first started before the town was much more than a pile of rocks.

We'd followed the wagons out all filled with men hungrier for more than food.

"You remember how quick they were them days? But, even that didn't mean easy nights. They was rough. My arms was bruised for weeks. They held on so tight."

"I remember." Ruth stared at us. I'd forgotten those were her first days servicin' the men. "After them days with Dan, I figured I could handle anything. That was different though. They was like animals. I tried to have fun, just like Dan showed me. Mostly, I just leaned back and tried to forget they was there. I think I had me ten a night. You remember, we just slept all mornin' tryin' to keep up for the next night. That's when I made my deal with the Devil."

"I don't what you girls are talkin' bout. I like them busy nights. They was the best." Jo was the best of us all at servin' the men, she was the hardest too. She said she liked it. No amount of whiskey or beatins slowed her down. The last time Dan taught her a lesson left her with a broken rib and she was back to work that night. I think she did like all the men.

Betsy laughed and grabbed Jo's arm, "We know how much ya like all them boys on ya, how much ya like holdin' them in your mouth." We all laughed. Jo did like suckin' on the men.

"Well, what about you, did you like them busy nights?" Jo was askin' me.

I didn't answer her. She didn't need an answer, she knew it because it was the same with her.

None of us planned this life, all of us were raised to be pure, wait for our husbands. Only sleep with that one man our whole lives through. And the early days of whorin' had been rough. We were taught a different life, a different way to think. We had no choice and as our bodies grew used to men, we found enjoyment, and that wasn't our choice either. At least not in the beginning. We were betrayed by everyone and anything good, even our bodies betrayed us and at some point, we yearned for men.

It was an odd love between us and them, certainly an affection existed between us that was difficult to explain. Though each of us experienced the odd rough night, most the men worked to keep us safe. We didn't mind keepin' warm once in awhile. It seemed a good trade.

Chapter 10

The wide west was a lonely place, maybe it was the loneliness, or maybe just the lack of choice but at some point we all embraced whorin. We liked it. We might have hated ourselves for it but death was worse.

It was a delicate balance, survivin' such a time and place. And, the tension between the owners and workers didn't lessen. I wasn't sure who to believe.

The owners would come in and complain they was bein' cheated by their workers. They hired a man, for an agreed-upon wage. That man worked and in return, was paid that wage. If a man decided to strike, he wasn't workin' and he wasn't earnin'. It was a compelling argument but us girls noticed how well-dressed those owners were. They didn't live in the shanty towns neither.

They continued to argue, they were growin' their business, makin' more jobs givin' even more work to more men. Us girls noticed those men only drank whiskey, never ale.

The miners held the view they was the ones bein' cheated. It was them doin' the work, it was them puttin' their lives on the line. And, it was them missin' out on better lives because those owners hired any worker needin' a job, regardless of their station.

What it all came down to was the fact most Chinese workers were willing to work for a lower wage. They were bargainin' white miners out of work who dared strike for more wages. It was hard to take sides. It was hard to know which side was right. Lookin' around, all those men needed work.

Us girls tried not takin' sides but when we was alone we talked.

"The way I see it," Bess started in one of those slow nights, "they all need the work. The coal deposit is said to be the biggest any of 'em have ever seen. I can't, for the life of me, see what they fightin' over." Jo nodded her agreement.

I shook my head, I couldn't understand it either, "Jo, you're right but you know how men are. Once they get the idea they might be getting' a short deal, they dig their heels in and not much changes their minds."

Becky looked around, her eyes wide showing how unsettled she felt, "You know, I can't imagine what they gonna do to them Chinese workers if they get the chance. They talkin' about runnin' em right out of town. Now, I don't any of those Chinamen and of course, I can't speak to the women, I can't talk that way, but I sure don't like the idea of any of 'em being run out like that."

Her voice was low, scared and it brought all our attention right to her.

"I was out there, you know, in the desert. It was before Evans found me. I can't be sure what happened to the people, my own family, I was with, but the desert is no place to be on your own." She wasn't lookin' at anyone, just far off into her own wild memories.

"You know, I can't even recall exactly how long I was even out there. Could have been days, weeks. It was long enough I thought I was dead for sure. I can't wish that on another human." She stopped talking and shuddered.

Jo put a blanket over her shoulders. "You know, you might be right but there's nothin' any of us can do about that. Not one thing we can do to stop any of 'em. Now get ready, doc's comin' up for one of our twice month visits."

In our business, there was a lot to do to keep a doctor busy. Evans paid the town doc with room and board to look us over twice a month and take care of anything that came up on the way. He was charged with keepin' us healthy, which meant keepin' diseases spread through sex to a minimum in the town. Evans was proud of the fact he doctored us, he used it in his advertising.

That doc never quite knew what to make of all us crowded in a room, legs open, ready to be treated. He went from girl to girl offerin' an ointment here and there, askin' how our cycles were. It was him who got us a few days off each much, "to tend to our womanly bodies, " is what he told Evans. He'd taken care of the odd pregnancy, but those didn't happen as often as one might think. Just the same, he told Evans he didn't like dealin' with 'em and besides, if we just didn't get pregnant. Evans never paid.

Each girl had lost at least one baby to this life. Dan kicked mine out of me. I never got pregnant again.

At the end of his visit, he asked us what we thought of the China workers. I was surprised, he normally kept his opinion to hisself, and was too overwhelmed by his duty to us to conversate much, especially on the current affairs of the town.

I put an arm around his thin shoulders, he was one of the smallest men I ever had seen, "You know doc, none of us is real sure what to think about all that. Most of the time, we just think how we can best survive out here."

For the first time, in the four years I had been seein' that man twice a month, he looked right into my eyes. "You ain't the only one, Ms. Ruth. Alls we can do out here is survive." And with those words, he left.

I looked around our little group. "Anyone else notice that? He's scared."

Jo nodded and even Becky was payin' attention now. "Yup, he's scared alright," Betsy looked thoughtful.

I think we were all surprised when Sue spoke up. Sure, she was oldest, and maybe even the wisest, but she was also the quietest, and normally, Sue didn't share much. "Look, girls. I know I can't ya what to do, but I gotta tell ya, this ain't good. This ain't good at all. Minin' is always dangerous, always will be. I mean look at what they do, goin' so deep in the earth that way, diggin' their keep in the dark riskin' life and limb. This is different though. This could mean war. Don't take sides. No matter what side ya take, its gonna be wrong. Men this tense, they act it out in bad ways. No one gonna look twice at a couple of us goin' missin' or beat up just because. It ain't worth an opinion. Now is the time to keep your head down, and your ears up. If it gets rough downstairs, ya gotta get outta there. I'll talk to Dan."

Between her and the doc tellin' us their take, we was a quiet bunch as we headed back downstairs. Evans noticed right away.

"Girls! Girls! What is goin' on? Where's your smiles? Why, it is one of the finest nights this summer, didn't any of ya notice?" He lowered his voice, just barely to finish his warning and advice, "Look out there, just look, and then why don't ya remind the men what nights like this are really for. You get out there, and you make 'em forget their troubles. Make them remember just what their money is for and why they stay in this god- forsaken place. You know it ain't their work, or them getting' rich or even savin' up like they tell us. No, you get out there, remind 'em how good whiskey and pussy are. Now git. It's just like any other night." He glared at us till we moved.

We were practiced actresses, each day and night for a long time, now, we entertained. It wasn't so hard, most nights. When it was time for a show, you just smiled until ya laughed. You stroked the shoulders and hands of the men all all while tellin' yourself, you loved 'em. And at some point, we saw the men believe so we did too. Actin' was nothin', really, ya just do somethin' till ya believe it and forget who you was before.

The night was a short one, men were tense and even though they spent, they spent money and their loads quick. Evans didn't care they never seemed to really forget about the mine troubles, he was content to pocket their money.

CHAPTER 11

Life went on, just like that night for a week or so, right up until an unusual visitor came in one night. He needed no introduction, though, to my knowledge, he'd never darkened our threshold before.

Sue greeted him like she'd somehow known of his impendin' visit. She nearly ran to his side and smiled real wide, "Well, ain't you just the most important visitor we had this day. Why, Dan, can we get this man a drink?" She beckoned to Betsy to join them, "Don't you just look like ya have a pile of troubles that need forgettin'. Why don't ya just sit down here," she stopped at a large table just to the side of the bar, "See? There's enough room for all your friends." By now, Betsy and Jo were all saunterin' over to the table.

To the surprise of everyone, the mine owner stuck his arm out in front of Sue, stoppin' her from following him. He shoo, his heads at the other girls and waved off drink from Dan.

"I don't need whiskey, and I sure don't need no whores, right now." His voice was gruff, commanding. But Jo laughed.

"So you say, but why don't ya try it? Then tell us if ya don't need it." She laughed, her crazy laugh and went on, "Course, I'm talkin' about that fine whiskey Dan poured, no whorin' for you, you're too fine for us." But she let her eyes rest on his crotch and opened her terrible mouth so many seemed to enjoy. All us girls laughed when his bulge appeared.

He didn't stop though. He pushed past the girls and approached Dan, right at the bar. "Where's Evans? Huh? I need to talk to him straight away. We got a plan to keep the calm." His voice wasn't so low, we couldn't hear.

Jo, always too loud, yelled, "Your pants don't look so calm." The other girls laughed but the owner ignored them. Dan glared at Jo till she backed down and headed to the quieter corner table where a few novices were tryin' their hand at poker. She settled on one young guy, strokin' his shoulders, careful not to look at his hand.

Dan looked the owner in the eye but continued his chore of wipin' off some of the finer glassware used for whiskey. I, so eager for information listened with my back to the bar, but tryin' to look busy wavin' at the young men playin' those cards. I opened my legs a little when one looked over and blushed. I noticed, then, just how young those boys were. Still, I stayed, content show off a little longer. Dan took his time answerin'.

"Look around, ya know where ya are. If a man ain't here, he's there." Dan pointed above his own head, then looked around the room. "Looks like he is enjoyin' the company of Becky, one of his favorite girls. Ya seen her? She's the one with the biggest tits. A man could suffocate in those tits." Dan continued with his chores, almost igorin' the richest guest we ever had. Any fool could sense he was not a man accustomed to bein' ignored.

He let out a deep breath, "Well, maybe it is time to check on him, make sure he's alive then."

Dan nodded, slow, and put his glass and rag right down. "You know, you're probably right. It's been, what, more than an hour, right Ruth?" I should have known Dan would see how interested I was in that conversation. "You go up and check on Becky and Mr. Evans, now. Be sure to knock before you go in." He winked at the owner, " No man wants to be interrupted. Why don't you ready yourself, just in case he's ready for another and Becky ain't up to ridin' right away." Disapointed I'd be hearin' no more, I obeyed. Dan might be actin' obligin' but he was almost good an actor as me, and I knew he was just makin' the mine owner believe he was not much more than a dog of Evans' 'Course, all the regulars knew better and I sure as hell knew better, so I hurried up the stairs. I felt Dan's eyes follow me the whole way and only faintly heard him ask, "Now, just what is yer business here. We got girls and whiskey, if ya ain't in to either, you might go find whatever it is yer lookin' for elsewhere." I couldn't hear the reply.

I stepped outside Evan's personal room. He was owner, so it was no surprise, to any of us, how big a space that one man occupied, though it made most of us jealous. That feeling only grew when we realized just how much he favored Becky, she practically lived in there with him, sleepin' late and some nights, hardly even visitin' downstairs. He expected her to keep earnin' her keep but he sure didn't expect her to keep as much company as the rest of us. His room was both office and bedroom, effectively two rooms together. He also had a small sitting room he took important guests. Becky told us she serviced a lot of his personal guests, more refined gentlemen than most of the ruffians downstairs and they paid more. I guessed that was why she was given certain accommodations denied the rest of us.

It was a bit odd, though. Becky wasn't known to be the prettiest whore. She was a little chubby, probably because Evans let her eat and her figure didn't suffer like some of ours did from hunger. Her tits were big, and most men noticed 'em as she walked through. It would be difficult not to notice, how they bounced before her almost announcing some grand arrival. Her face was homely, though, and she was a little whiny. What I expected the men like most about her, including Evans, was the way she rode 'em. She would climb on top of a guy, straddlin' him, hard, almost squeezin' the air out of him and bounce, those tits nearly hittin' her own chin. If they was sittin' up, they was hittin' his face. I knew part of her act was enjoyin' this. But I also knew, from straddlin' men myself, the faster and harder she moved, the faster they came allowin' her to climb off rather quickly. After, she always made a little show of, "cleanin' off all that load!" makin' em feel like they was the biggest, best thing she ever straddled. Evans liked her show.

I heard 'em in there. Evans was too practiced with her to come over-quick and from the sounds of it, they was enjoyin' the bouncin'. I listened for a few seconds before softly knockin;'.

Thing was, Dan was was only half right, whether he only talkin' to his distinguished guest, or serious, I couldn't tell. Then, Dan never was known for his wide variety of vocabulary. See, Evans, well most men, didn't mind bein' interrupted while screwin' if *it were done right.* What they sure didn't want was an intrusion. Dan was the same as the rest of 'em, I knew that from experience.

If I went bustin' in there, especially when Evans was about to come, he wouldn't like that intrusion; I doubt anyone would. Just like other tricks I'd learned so long ago, I learned the difference between intrudin' and interuptin'. My aim was to interrupt in a way that was not intrudin' while they so desperately sought their moment's pleasure. The best way to interrupt was to join.

I knocked softly and opened that outer door, barely hesitatin' before going to his bed. There they was, just as I knew they would be. Her on top, him holdin' on as if his life depended on it. I walked real soft to the side of the bed and, bein' sure not to talk but makin' eye contact with Evans the whole way. She kept bouncin' actin' like she didn't even know I was there. Another act of the night.

I leaned over, right into his turned face and put my mouth on his, all the while keepin' my eyes open, lookin' into his. I put my tongue in his mouth, and he sucked it, hard. All while watchin' my eyes. He put his in mine, but I just held it there. Breathin' a little on it, lettin' it slide further down my throat. Becky was really holdin' him to it, really makin' that little bed frame move.

He didn't say one word, just knocked Becky back a little, not hard, but commandin' and pulled me in, then, "You two kiss." Becky groaned a little.

"Mr. Evans! I was just about finished, I just wanna finish," she panted, tryin' to get up on him again. He put his hand right on her forehead.

"I know ya was, but I ain't. Kiss." There was nothin' for it, so I leaned over and kissed her. I put my mouth full on hers and pushed my self up on her, I reached down and held her tits in my hands. He'd pushed her right down to the bottom of the bed, so I straddled his chest, while I caressed hers. I could feel him harden beneath me while he began puttin' his fingers in me. Evans had many faults but he had big hands and fingers but he used 'em gently when he wanted. I could feel myself wet his hands.

I didn't mind kissin' the girls. It wasn't so uncommon any of us was uncomfortable anymore. I still preferred men as my bed mates, but a smaller payment to the devil meant admittin' there was some fun with the threesome. Guys normally got so excited, they came easy just watchin us kiss. Evans took his time, though.

He plunged fingers makin' me rub back and he pushed my mouth onto Becky's nipples. He commanded I suck on them, while she suck his cock and she rubbed her own pussy. He was breathin' hard and heavy, we all was when finally, he came in between her deep breaths. I felt my own muscles tighten over his hand and Becky convulsed beneath us. He leaned back, takin' up most the bed, makin' us move sooner than our bodies wanted, just to stay on the bed. Becky lay over me, pantin' away. She was too heavy for me to really catch my breath. Thankfully, he was finished and didn't take long askin' what I was doin'.

"Ruth. I doubt, very much, you came up just for that fun. What did you want?" Evans voice, no matter the situation carried a certain cruelty with it. His questions were commands, and his shrewd intellect spotted liars faster than anyone I'd ever seen. Evans knew we was little more than actin' our pleasures but he often said if we kept rubbin' eventually we'd like it. We never hesitated long in answerin' his questions but kept up the games he liked. I panted a few breaths, showin' how much I enjoyed the previous few minutes. He gave me a few more seconds than would be normally granted, showin' his pleasure at the little game.

"Well, Mr. Evans. Dan sent me up here, someone real nice dressed is waitin' on ya. Course, I came in and saw you two like that and couldn't help join in the fun." Evans like when I lied. I knew he didn't believe a word of it, he would never fully trust me but he untangled himself from the bed and I saw him smilin' as he stood.

"That's just right, Ruth, I'll bet it is. Well, who is dressed real nice?"

This time I couldn't lie, " I only know he's one of the mine owners. Dan was keepin' it sly down there, and I know you didn't want no intrusion." He grabbed my leg, hard.

"That's right, girl. You can stay here with Becky awhile, keep your clothes off. I'm goin' down to see what they need." And he left the room.

Becky moved to the side of the bed, he took up and stretched her arms above her head.

"Ruth, you know how I dislike doin' all that with any girl. Why did you have to come in? I was almost finished, he was right there, then you come in and we had to keep goin'. I was gonna take a bath today. Now, he might be back for more thanks to ya." She arched her back a little. "I can't think why, but he's wantin' this at least twice a day. Yesterday, he kept me up here all day, he made Cook bring up a tray twice. He just wants me waitin' on him or whomever he's doin' his deals with. I wouldn't be surprised if your well-dressed man appears soon."

I didn't have anything to say. I rolled onto my side and closed my eyes, takin' my well-earned nap. It didn't matter. Becky's prediction turned false; the gentleman never climbed the stairs to that room and even Evans didn't show up till long after dark.

CHAPTER 12

Over the next day or two, I allowed myself to learn as much about our far-eastern locals as I could. We all knew the basics. They came for work, they accepted low wages. They lived their own way, apart from the rest of the town in something we called Chinatown. Few conversed in anything but their own tongue and somehow, they managed to keep to a diet brought with them from across the ocean. I wanted to learn more about them, though.

Their town numbered around a thousand folks. Most were men, content to work and save their wages. It was far cheaper to live in China than the wild territories we was accustomed. They could live cheap, work hard and send money to their families who was awaitin' their safe return. I'd learned a man from China could work for about ten years and retire in China on those earnin's. It made for an almost unfathomable dream.

Men, willing to work hard, journeyed across the vast ocean to an unwelcoming, hostile land. They kept themselves to themselves not least because of a language barrier. They accepted a fate of living eight or nine to a single room, barely enough room to simply sleep so they would save money on rent. Hardly any women followed them, so they lived a lonely, work-filled life. After hard days, they returned to crowded but lonely rooms sleeping on thin mats that were rolled and stowed away each new morning. Almost all the money they earned was hidden away or sent home to wives they trusted immensely. Wives lived nearly as frugally as their hard-working husbands; all agreeing to and upholding their ends of their bargains so they might one day, live together again frugally retiring on those earnings.

Chinese were not Christian like many of their white counterparts, so they made no deals with the devil who so plagued so many others. They didn't bother with Sunday morning services and though we knew they prayed we weren't quite sure to whom they was prayin' to. Each year, they celebrated a new year that didn't quite fall on the Christian calendar. They held a parade and danced and sang down the short main street celebrating on their own. They always drew a small crowd with their snake- like dragon weaving in and out of people, showing off their small feet beneath.

I couldn't understand their words. I never ventured into Chinatown, but knew it was almost a mirror of ours. There was a shop that sold goods. Homes stood in varying states of disrepair that held mostly men but also a few families. In place of a saloon, an opium den stood open, always busy. There were a few women who kept the men company for a price. Nothing too unlike our own town, except their town was not meant to last.

Most Chinese workers were not planning on making such a place their home. They stuck to their retirement plans and this meant Chinatown was little more than a shanty-town and no building was substantially built. I'd often wondered how they kept warm during the harsh winters. All my curiosities, though, didn't invite me to their town, and for the most part, they kept to their town. An uneasy peace was kept between them and white workers after the railroads were finished. Men were turned out of good work, forced to dig deep in the earth for the same pay.

I never understood how such a dusty, grimy rock could be so coveted. I never heard of coal just lyin' waitin' for someone to pick it up off in some creek the way some gold hunters found their gold rocks. Coal, lay buried, deep in the earth daring others to free it despite threats of bad air or tunnel collapse. Men died, almost daily, of such work but it still drew more. It seemed the more they dug, the hunger for it grew. The owners, from what I witnessed, cared little for the men nor the filthy work they so arduously performed so many hours each day. During their visits, they talked only to supervisors choosin' to ignore blackened faces with bright eyes.

The owners kept themselves to themselves keeping their own ends of the uneasy bargain between the workers.

The summer progressed, hot and exhausting like most any summer provokin' tempers amongst the inhabitants. When the mines first opened, white miners outnumbered other workers by about two thirds. Unions gathered strength out east spurrin' on vast changes eventually tricklin' far out west. Common workers were leanin' on 'em demandin' pay for work. Course, not all trades were backed by unions and not all workers respected by unions. But. White men demandin' better wages, workin' hours and such were takin' a foothold in many of the industries. Minin' was not yet backed by such unions.

Men collaborated and united demandin' better wages and eventually chose to strike. Mines were left unattended invitin' others willing to work angerin' and endangerin' the strikers. Deals were done to keep new workers in their place further challengin' the original workers. See, mine owners didn't just own their minin' claims.

They owned the homes miners lived, the shops where they bought their goods. Miners was charged rent, and their goods bought all went against their wages. When the men chose to strike, they still owed rent and still had buy general goods to survive, so strikes didn't tend to last or make much, if any impression on those owners. Still, no owner wanted to lose two weeks of earnin's here, and four weeks there. So, an alternative work-force was brought in settlin' for original pay agreements the strikers were protestin'.

They didn't end there, though. Many Chinese were offered cut rents due the fac they chose to live so frugally and even charged less for clothing purchased because they were smaller in stature. Even when the strikers returned for the same wages as before, they demanded better rent rates and lower prices in the stores. The owners held out, though. After all, we was surrounded by nothin', where was they gonna go to find any better or anything at all? The miners couldn't win against the owners, so their anger turned towards the new workers and as summer churned towards fall daily threats turned to brawls. The brawls turned to several gang-like beatin's and Chinatown began to stand guard against an increasing hostile neighbor.

The territory, like most states, had a governor and law upheld by various sheriffs and deputies. And, like most states, money talked. Mine owners held the claims and the money, just like Evans owned our own establishment. Evans, nor those mine owners, ever took any oaths to uphold any law or order, but they paid to keep their own order. Most men was armed, and most wanted the fairness of more civilized places. And they was willin' to use force when they deemed it necessary.

The saloon was full up the next few days. Men congregatin' talkin' of strikin' again. Those were union men, and reitoratin' over and again, the importance of a lastin' resolution.

"A lastin' resolution means somethin' for all hard-workers that doesn't go away with mines sold or bought!" One man, a loud fellow who I personally knew to like hand jobs better than pussy, was yellin' to the crowd.

"Oh yeah? We work on the hardest men around, is that for us too?" Jo hollered back. Even Dan and Evans laughed but the loud guy ignored her.

"We need a lastin' resolution, adopted by the territory to protect our wages. No one else is gonna fight for us! We are out here on our own. Who cares in Washington? They don't care, this is the west, too few of live here and too few tax dollars make their way to their door. No. We must unite and fight. The filthy Chinaman needs to go back to China and make his riches there. Its up to us to fight for this!" He was garnering more interest, the more he talked.

A normally quiet man answered, "That's right! We dig for days and those Chinese come in and take the pay-loads! No questions, nothin'. They have to know coal ain't that easy to get at. They ain't that lucky!"

"Right!" Another man, also normally quiet, spoke with fire in his eyes, " I think they must pay for the best rooms! Why, every day, they bring out coal, while we might dig, what two or three days with nothin?" The room grew quiet, tense at his accusation.

It was quite an accusation. He was accusing workers of taking unfair advantage against their own peers. There was no law tellin' anyone how to run their mines. But, just like our social class system, the mines held their laws. One week one group got a rich room, the next another group was given the advantage. In this way, peers were treated to payloads rather fairly and on little more than the honor system. It wasn't perfect but ruled comfortably with little challenge. Except. This group of Chinese workers were new, there was no way for them to know the system or keep to it without the mine owners advisin' them. Of course, the owners didn't speak Chinese nor did they converse with the miners, it was up to the supervisors to keep the peace and keep to the system. If they were bein' paid off, well, there was nothin' keepin' that peace no more. The owners cared little more than for the coal to come out of the earth preferably at a quick pace. Who cared how or who dug it out?

"Come now, come now. It is not the fault of the China man, stranger to this land, to know the ways of it. We must hold the owners responsible to better the wage of the worker. This is the only last resolution!" The first man was speakin' again. But no one paid him any mind. Too much was bein' spoke of the possibilities of the supervisors and or owners bein' paid off.

Snatches of conversation rose in and out of my ears. The gist was the same though. Not only did the Chinese workers have to pay the same rents due to their humble lifestyle, but they were smaller, and paid far less in the general store for goods such as shoes, or pants. And now, they get the payloads because they take those savings and pay off the supervisors. Men stopped drinkin' at the accusations. A few even pushed us girls away from them as we tried joinin' in their conversations.

Sue and I stood at the stairs tryin' our best to stay out of the way but engage those we thought showed signs of need to let off steam. Neither was over-effective. The growing sentiment blamed the Chinese workers for their troubles.

I whispered to Sue, "How? How can they blame other workers? How can the owners allow this?"

Sue looked at me and answered slow, "Sometimes, Ruth, you ask the most senseless questions. Those in power never get the blame."

I ran my tongue over my teeth at her words. My own missing teeth proved her words true.

Sue might have been the most interestin' one of all us. She was easy to forget, easy to overlook. She was stick thin and unlike Jo, preferred quiet. Dan even had to beat regular every two or three weeks just so she'd talk to the men. She kept herself to herself. Once, she told me she never liked any man touchin' her.

Sue wasn't old but she wasn't young and her life was empty. She told Jo one Christmas Eve, her life was full of emptiness. And, hearin' her story, it really was. Evans took her when she was young, before she even started bleedin'.

As they made their way out west, Evans put her to work cookin' and launderin' for him. Her days started early on that wagon train, as soon as the sun was up, she was expected to have the fire stoked and coffee on. Breakfast was served soon after, all while she packed up the camp-site. She never talked of Evans bein' cruel then. He simply allowed her to eat the food he said he bought in return for her cookin' and all. She told us it was just the two of 'em but there were lots of kids she spoke to and Evans was good at makin' friends. Days were hard but full and Sue told us how she walked much of the way thanks to the jostlin' of the wagon.

Evans, she told us, soon made friends with another single man. Evans and the man named Dan, soon became business partners. Evans was good with money and plans, Dan was a hard worker. Soon, Sue was doin' the cookin' for her, Evans and Dan. Then, she started doin' his wash. Sue told us how Dan never really talked to her. Evans made sure she was safe each day and night. We figured out, on our own, Evans was actually a cousin of Sue. When Sue's mother and father died, his parents took her in; his mother was her aunt. Sue was only four years old, when her parents died and she figured Evans was about sixteen when she went to live with them. She told how they were poor but happy. Her uncle had a good job helpin' out at a nearby farm. He didn't own any land but there was plenty of work in the area and they never went without house or home. Her aunt took care of the house and family. She taught Sue to read.

It sounded idyllic but it didn't last. Only four years later, both her aunt and uncle died. Only her and Evans lived with them by then, her other cousins had grown and gone. The two stayed together without much change in their day to day lives. Evans supported them on wages made the same way his father had and Sue kept up the house chores. Then, Evans decided to move west. Sue liked the sound of adventure and they joined another few people happy to head west.

Sue never complained about the hard journey, nor any treatment or mistreatments from Evans. Unlike a few unfortunate others in their train, the two alongside Dan made it all the way to Deadwood.

For nearly two years, Dan and Evans sold goods to others journeying westwards while Sue kept up the cooking and laundry. Sue told us it wasn't bad living that way. She had friends and after all, there were plenty of people comin' and goin'. A few months in, Dan came home real secret-like. Sue said he always kept himself to himself but it was different that night. The next mornin' Evans and him packed up their lean-to store and headed west. Sue went along.

A few hours into their trip, Sue overheard Dan and Evans talkin' about several large gold nuggets. Sue asked where they got 'em and Evans told her to keep quiet. Sue said she just went to sleep after that and rode in silence. No one ever told her how the two got that gold but she suspected Evans killed a man for it. She never asked though.

They'd continued west until they got to the minin' town and Dan actually left them then.

She thought life would continue on same as before; she'd wash and do the cookin'. Evans told her they was buyin' a proper buildin' and would have a business. Not long after, he did buy a property and built the saloon we worked in right there on the main throughway. He sold cheap liquor and she cooked for the two of 'em. Then, Dan came back.

He wasn't there long before he and Evans planned new business. Cook seemed to appear from nowwheres and took over the kitchen. Evans told Sue she was out a job and would have to earn her keep. Dan showed her how. A few months later, when Sue turned up pregnant,

Evans paid off the doctor to rid her of the child. Sue never knew any other life.

It was strange, knowin' her story. Sue was the brightest of us all, and I often wondered why she stayed on. Why didn't she just go? She would have had a chance, somewhere cookin' takin' in wash like before. I never asked, though, and she never offered. Evans hardly interacted with her at all.

The thing was, there was nowhere to go. Not really, at least. Sure, there was the railroad and stagecoach right here in town. But we didn't earn actual money and if we ran, the desert welcomed us like a bird might accept its prey. Between the six of us, we owned two entire suits that didn't quite fit any one of us givin' away our trade, even if we somehow survived. We was just an easy target for the next saloon owner. And there was little peace between us and the natives. Sue's best chance was whorin' right where she was whorin' just like the rest of us.

The men stayed late, though they went easy on the whiskey and us girls weren't kept busy. They was arguin' until one finally shouted that it was late and work was waitin' in the mornin'. He left and others followed soon after. We slept easy, knowin' there'd be no strikin' the next day, at least. For three days, we lived on in relative peace but by Friday night, men were back again, arguin' over who was keepin' them from gettin' their best pay. Things turned ugly quick, despite Evans buyin' a round for the room, or us girls wrappin' arms 'round some of the more boisterous talkers. I even heard Dan ask Evans if we needed to shutter the doors the rest of the night. Evans shook his head.

He lined us girls up, shoutin' above the others, how tired we was gettin' of all talk and no play. Becky, Betsy, Sue, Jo and I did a little dance number and Becky even sang. The men calmed down. The loud one, I think Billy was his name, grabbed Becky at the end, dancin' with her pretty rough. I could tell Evans didn't like that but Billy slapped some cash on the bar and Evans ignored him after. I saw Becky lead him right up the stairs; his hands never left her body.

It wasn't thirty minutes later, I saw Billy leave right through the front door. He didn't call out to his friends, he didn't even look sideways at no one else. Just walked, right quick, out those front doors. Dan saw too.

It normally takes us girls a few minutes between men. We like to clean up, catch our breath before actin' again. So, I waited for Becky to reappear. She didn't. I finished the hand job I was givin' and kissed the fellow on his cheek as a thanks for letting me tug his wiener. I ran right up the stairs, right to Becky's room an unsettled feeling filling my stomach spilling over into the back of my throat. I took two deep breaths, knowin' what I might find the other side of her door. Then, I forced myself to walk right in there.

CHAPTER 13

Becky was a sight. Her face was already so swollen, I couldn't know how she could even see. One ear was torn, and several chunks of hair and scalp littered the floor. She was shakin' hard, shiverin' in the middle of a growing pool of blood right in the middle of the room. He'd hurt, he hurt her bad. I ran over and put my arms around her tryin' to warm her up. She slumped against me and I just held her for a few minutes. I heard Dan come in behind me and swear.

"Jesus, look at ya, Becky. What the hell happened? I didn't hear ya yell or nothin'. I'll have Sue get the dr. Ruth, help her on the bed." Dan wasn't my favorite man but he did take care of business when it came down to it. I obeyed at once and helped Becky right onto her bed. Blood dripped down the backs of her legs and when she leaned over, I saw how torn she was. Her mouth was already turnin' black and blue and I thought some of her ribs might be broke. I swore at that bastard Billy under my breath.

"Ruth," her voice was hardly recognizable, and barely audible. "Ruth, how bad is it?"

"Becky, its bad. But they gettin' doc right now. He's gonna fix ya right up and I ain't leavin'," I whispered into her good ear. I felt tears on my face.

She had bite marks all over her beautiful chest. The knuckles on one hand were bruising and there was skin under some of her nails. Her ear was still bleedin' and I could only hope Doc could sew it back on. I looked at Dan.

"Doc's gonna need hot water and bandages. We should have Cook boil that and ready those bandages." Dan didn't answer, just left to get it started. I held Becky close to me, she was still shiverin'. I tried to keep her warm.

"What in the fuck did you let him do to you." Evans startled me, I hadn't heard him come in. "What did you let him do, you girls know to call out if someone starts beatin' you. Roll over, is all of you used up?" I stayed where I was, holdin' his favorite as he stepped closer and closer. "Ruth, move. I want to see her." I stayed. He shoved me out the way and slapped her, hard right across the side of her head. She slumped into the pillows.

"You take her outta here, this ain't no hospital. I don't want to see her again." I tried, standin' but my legs were shakin' at the cruelty he was displayin'. I couldn't believe he would do this to anyone, especially not her. He left the room, shovin' past the doctor in the doorway.

That man was nearly pale as Becky, he'd seen it all. He gently rolled her onto her stomach and wrapped a bandage around her head. Next, he wrapped her ribs and then, bundled cloth right into her crotch to stop her bleedin'. By then, Dan was back in the room.

"We gotta move her. Ruth, you can have Cook bring the water and bandages, but she can't stay here." I had never seen Dan cry, in fact, I never really saw him show any emotion at all, but I saw a tear slide down his face when he took in the sorry sight of the young woman knocked out before him. "Doc, I can carry her out the back. You lead." And he wrapped her in a blanket and followed the doctor right out. I stepped over the freshly spilled blood and followed.

None of the men really looked our way, but I know each girl saw. Cook and I brought the hot water to the doctor's and helped dress Becky's many wounds. It took a long while.

I finished up with gently washing her and laying her back in clean sheets and blankets. Doc allowed me to do so, I presumed so he could ready more bandages. I was startled, instead, to find him behind me watching over Becky. His hands were still bloodied. I tucked the blankets in, tight 'round her so she wouldn't move too much and stood up. He barely seemed to notice.

"Doc?" He didn't move. I tried again, a little louder, "Doc?"

He turned, and I saw how red his eyes were. "How is she? I mean how is she really?" I whispered. He beckoned I should follow him and we stepped away from her.

"Its bad, Ms. Ruth. She looks like she done some sort of battle instead of pleasurin' someone." As he said those words, more tears spilled out. He took a deep shaky breath. "You know, Ms. Ruth, I did what I can and she's not bleedin' no more. I can't see that she was torn inside at all, I think it was all external, so those wounds will heal. Ribs are terrible to heal up, though. Its hard to breathe deep and pneumonia can settle in lungs. You know her hair? Well, some of that can't grow back, too much scalp came with it. We just have to wait and see if her eyes was damaged and we can't really ask about that until that swellin' goes down some. I expect that is gonna take a week or so. She can't eat solids at least that long, and she's gonna need help to the latrine and what not." He let out a breath and more tears fell. He looked back her way.

I nodded. It wasn't really nothin' new helpin' us heal, we all got beat now and then, some worse than others. Becky was pretty bad, maybe the worst but it was a rough job.

Doc spoke again, "Thing is, I am takin' her away as soon as she can move. I'll not keep her here any longer with such a brute." That was a first. No girl ever left because of some beatin'. I doubted Evans would let her go for safety or hope Billy wouldn't come 'round again and I said as much.

"It's not Billy. You know, a few months ago, she was with child. Now, I took care of it but it wasn't easy. And Evans saves her for his own bidding and I'm done with that too. Evans can't know I am leavin' and takin' her with me." He looked right in my eyes.

I nodded, hopin' she would just live long enough to give the two of 'em some sorta chance. I could see he loved her. The baby had been theirs, not hers. I didn't say nothin' but he knew I was promisin' my help and silence. I left into a night that promised an early autumn.

The saloon was all but silent when I got back. I quietly let myself in the back and started my way up the stairs. Evans called out, stoppin' me 'bout halfway. He was drunker than I'd ever saw him.

"He's dead. Billy. Dead. Dan fed him to the hogs." He hiccupped a little and then, "Never say her name to me again. Doc done told us she died and I told him to take care of it. Don't tell me nothin' more about it." And he slumped forwards on the table, stone cold out. I went up to my room, and I never talked to no one in the saloon about Becky again. Two days later, the town was without a practicin' doctor.

After, Becky, the saloon seemed to roughen even more. Becky was the one who could sing. She was the refined sort that made all us look a little better. "Spoiled brat," Jo whispered between tears when Dan told the girls she was dead. No one really talked about her, even amongst us girls but I heard sobs late into the nights followin' the disaperance of Doc. Cook kept herself to herself but I caught her watchin' me a few times. She knew without sayin' Becky was alive and moved on.

Business didn't suffer. I heard Dan tellin' Evans that was good at least. Evans never answered. The girls and I walked downtown a few mornin's later, takin' in the late summer sun and noddin' to all. It was a fine day and we walked all the way down to the edge of the muddy river banks every shrivelin' in that hot sun. Betsy spread a blanket out and we sat and watched the river awhile.

I noticed birds playin' in the water. I'd seen their kind before but I'd forgotten. They were tall, graceful birds with long, pointed bills. Beady eyes looked out each side their heads and they fanned their feathers and trotted into the water. I watched the two of 'em a good long while until they finally took flight. The other girls said they was hot sittin' there, and wanted to go back. I promised I would follow soon.

I leaned back on the blanket, lettin' the hot sun warm my body over. It felt good not havin' to work to keep warm or cool. The hot sun beat into my skin but a slight breeze danced right over it coolin' me just enough to bask. A stirring caused me to open my eyes.

A woman, Chinese, stood near me, watching me. To my surprise, she spoke a broken but decent English. She smiled a little and pointed to the river, "You like the crane bird?" At first, I couldn't make out what she was askin' so I looked where she pointed. The birds were gone now, but she was definitely watchin' where they'd been bathing. I nodded at her, surprised someone else noticed such a trivial, common occurrence.

She smiled again. "Yes. Yes, I see the two, from over there," she pointed a little further down from my own spot on the banks, "You watch them, the others, they don't see, or maybe do not care. But I see. You see. Cranes bring luck." She smiled again and took quick, short steps away. I watched till I couldn't see her any longer and gathered up my belongings and left.

What had she meant, I wondered? Cranes bring luck. I knew those Chines held their own superstitions, their own beliefs. No one ever told me about some lucky sign, though. Luck wasn't how life worked out here. All there was, was hard work. Especially for whores. And I took up my post once more.

Talk around town seemed to grow more and more tense. Miners called for change, but no one dared strike again. The mines would close once it grew too cold, now wasn't the time to strike or over-spend. Now was the time to prepare for days without pay and cold windy nights, even though every morning was greeted with the sounds of birds chirping and even the nights stayed warm. Anyone who'd lived through a winter, knew better than a few nice days during later summer, though. And no one rested.

The hate grew for the crowded, little shanty town just outside our borders and us girls noticed Chinamen no longer dared walk the streets alone. They walked in small groups, careful to only do the business they needed and left as soon as they could. They didn't look right or left, and didn't answer the shouts thrown over them as they crossed the filthy street.

We heard they were bein' treated just as bad down at the mines. Twice, they'd been forced into other rooms. Each time, they'd gone without fightin' and continued to work just as if nothin' happened. Then, one day, right in the early mornin' one miner kicked one of them down. They wanted their room and were willin' to use a force that wasn't all too necessary. The kid went down, hard and took a kick to the side of his head. He stayed sleepin' all that day. When the supervisor broke up the ensuing fight, he'd dismissed the perpetrator for the rest of the week. The guy come lookin' for a way to let off some steam and complained about the Chinese overtakin' honest work to anyone who would listen. None of us could calm him down.

It wasn't till after dinner time, he finally quieted and left. The boy had woken up and would most likely, be alright after a few days rest.

By then, the saloon was filled up again and all us girls was busy tendin' to the needs of the men. We listened as they told us how they agreed or disagreed with the violence that mornin'. Some said they boy refused to move, others said he swore at the man who kicked him. No one bothered tellin' how the boy stood just a little over five feet and his attacker nearly six. They just talked on and on about how this was their mine and needing better pay. The girls and I distracted 'em best we could.

Sue and I talked how the men weren't stayin', they wasn't takin' their time.

"Plenty come in each night and they drink and fill up the rooms. But watch, they don't stay" Sue pointed out. I looked over the room, seein' what she saw.

Most everyone held a drink in hand, but they were finishin' and leavin' makin' room for more doin' the same. Even the ones that were upstairs, finished in less than thirty minutes. Evans was makin' a killin' that night and I said as much to Sue.

"You bet he is, that door hardly stops swingin'. I myself had six last night. What about you?" Sue asked..

I leaned my head back, thinkin' a second. "I think I had two blows, three hands and three upstairs." I looked at her. "You're right, we are busy for a middle of the week, its no holiday or nothin'." She nodded.

The men were restless and we knew the problems in the mines was doin' it, though it was hard to make out just why. There was always problems in mines. They were a god-forsaken place. And, when there is no god, strife ensues.

The men were used to sacrifice, long days, back breakin' work but they was reachin' a place no one was ready to reach, they had enough. We saw it as they came in, eyes dartin' left and right. It was as if they was lookin' for a fight but no one appeared for them to fight. It made 'em anxious, restless and though they slammed back drink and girl, they left un-satisfied. Some returned later to the same indulgences only to leave lookin' to feed their appetite some other way. Us girls kept up, and to be honest, most of us was relieved.

No one was lookin' for small talk or flatterin' words. They came for drink and pussy preferin' us to moan instead of speak.

"You know, I ain't rid no one all week. They all been ridin' me. Can't complain, easy money made on my back," Jo cackled out her ugly mouth. She watched the men congregatin' outside. "Hell, if whorin' was always this easy, I'd swear to keep at it till I'm old and my cunts full of gray hairs." Betsy laughed at her crassness.

Jo was right though. None of us were workin' too hard. And of course, none of us complained, neither.

It was nice break, that I hadn't really enjoyed since Jedidiah last been in town. Man after man crawled on top of me, slippin' in and out till he was done, requirin' me to hardly break any sort of sweat. Some even did it right, allowin' me a moment to enjoy sex the way some women got to. 'Course, we couldn't choose our men and most weren't who we would choose at all, missin' teeth, smellin' bad but they was quick and didn't require over long affections.

By the end of the month, we were wakin' to cool mornin's. Betsy and I was enjoyin' biscuits and gravy one mornin' when she voiced what I'd been thinkin'

"You know, Ruth, these past two weeks been some of the easiest livin' I done out here. There's a change, and I can feel it comin'. I don't feel good about it, the tensions about as thick as custard anywhere's you go. And, if I am real honest, I don't like that feelin'. Dread has settled into my very gut warnin' me. I don't like that and I don't like that we can't know when or where this is finally goin' to bust out. But I can't go back to before, eithers. I just can't do it. This changes things, even for us." Her voice was low, we never knew when Dan might be lurkin' and listenin'.

I nodded, "Yeah, I been thinkin' the same thing. For sure, something is gonna flare right up. Ya know, some weeks ago, you remember that strange woman, the one dressed in black on her own?" Betsy thought a moment, then slowly nodded. "Right, well, ya remember talkin' how she could see?" Again, a slow nod. "Well, I talked with her awhile one evenin'. She took out some seein' cards. I was told to draw three. Now, I can't recall the picutres on the cards or exactly what she said. But it was ominous for sure, she said. A warnin' of a terrible event comin' ours way. But then a promise of a different sorta life." I shuddered a little as the memory of the encounters with that small woman forced threir way through my mind.

Truth be told, I hadn't thought of her much at all since her departure. I continuously thought of the cards and the things she predicted. I hadn't spent much time thinkin' on her, though. Her odd beauty was a hard thing to forget, that was true. Even more difficult to forget was how she claimed to be older than her face and body showed. She was a cruel figure though, and I did my best to drive her memory from my thoughts with great success until now. I shook my head a little forcing myself to think of the draw, her strange predictions, instead of her.

"Anyway, she predicted some sort of calamity that would give way to an opportunity at a new life. I think it is time to plan for what ya might want next. I know I am." I stopped myself, there, I didn't want to share further. I trusted Betsy like a sister but us girls guarded our dreams jealously. They was all that was left all our own. We might share the most intimate details of the nights we work or what salves work to calm our aching pussies but the dreams hidden beneath the layers of our hearts stayed covered hidden to others fiercely protected.

Betsy nodded again. "Yeah, well, it don't take no seer to see what is happenin' right now, that's for sure. I mean, each day we see the poor souls at the mercy of them mines. Don't matter what anyone thinks, neither. They want their pockets lined is all." I noticed Betsy was careful with her words, too. She never blamed the owners in word but I felt what she was sayin' and not sayin'. She went on, "That's the way of this wide world. No matter where or when, money rules. Hell, even the promise of money rules." She paused a long moment, her eyes lookin' far away, thinkin'. She lowered her voice further for her next questions, "So, your seer, did she say anythin'more? Anythin' about anyone or maybe when to expect this calamity?"

I shook my head, "Naw, not real specific. Just sayin' soon and to be ready. I been makin' myself ready, though." I didn't say much further and Betsy didn't bother to ask. Besides me protectin' my fragile dream of freedom, truth was there wasn't much preparin' I could do other than watch and ready myself.

"That ain't all, Betsy. Just the other day, ya remember how we was down at the river? Well, I stayed whiles you girls came back, ya remember?" She nodded. "A Chinese woman was down that way, she didn't talk till you all left. I watched a couple of tall birds bathin' down near some reeds growin' right at the bank. She came right over, said she saw me watchin' 'em and that kind of bird brings luck." Betsy didn't answer. I jumped when I heard Sue's voice just behind me. I hadn't heard her enter that small hallway just outside the kitchen.

"I only heard part of your story, Ruth, but sounds interestin', real interestin'." She looked into my eyes, like we shared some secret. "I know I sure am ready for a change." And with that, she retrieved her own breakfast and went out of doors to enjoy it on her own. I wondered what dreams Sue's empty life could possibly even employ and Betsy and I finished in silence.

CHAPTER 14

Sue must have told Jo a little what she heard. Jo never asked, nor said nothin' specific but she grew quieter with the menfolk over the next few days. She was thinkin' more and even stopped drinkin' over much, much to our consternation. Her normal ruddy cheeks, lightened and her hand stopped shakin'. Like the rest of us, she daren't share even a second of her own dreams but I could tell she was growin' em. And, lookin' 'round at the other girls, I noticed other, almost imperceptible changes.

I doubted Evans saw or felt the strange phenomenon; he didn't take much time with none of us. Besides, the tensions in that town were just near unbearable, so anything that happened was merely blamed on that as some sort of side effect of the goings on at the mines. The atmosphere of the saloon changed, though and for those who chose to see, saw.

Sue's spirit changed. She took on more clients. She even chose to walk about more minglin' instead of seekin' the solitude she normally favored. She always mothered us girls just a little and now, she took on a greater role, watchin' over us. I heard Dan tellin' Evans he noticed but he chalked it right up to Becky's supposed death and Doc movin' on. I think he thought Sue simply saw a need and filled it. I interpreted her motive quite different but I didn't say nothin' to no one about that.

I know Betsy and I changed too, though I hoped less noticeable-like than Jo's tremblin' hands stillin' or Sue askin' if we got our dinners alright. I watwched Betsy careful that evenin' tryin' to spot anythin' that might tell the wide world what we so carefully kept hidden away. Truth be told, I was afraid if Betsy was actin' different, so was I.

Betsy weren't though. She walked around the room handin' out shots, laughin' at the jokes men like to tell. She was good at actin', so I mimicked her. I laughed at their jokes, and turned their heads with my words, darin' 'em to touch me, promisin' to feel love for a little while. And no one asked me or Betsy anythin' about nothin'.

Most the men were so caught up in the business of the mines, they wouldn't have seen nothin' anyways, but us girls couldn't be too careful. That was just life. I did start thinkin' with Jo sobered up, and Sue leadin' us girls stood a chance to reach for our dreams. The promised calamity exploded early one mornin' late summer, and though it started small, I knew right from the beginnin' that was just what I been waitin' on; no amount of warnin' could have prepared me though, for the violence that positively erupted from the mines that mornin'.

Miners gathered to work, same as any other mornin'. And, like most of the mornin's that entire summer, rough words were exchanged at whom was workin' where. And, per the new normal, the Chinamen were ordered away from the room thought most lucrative. Later on, we was told some refused to go or maybe they just took too long to go, either way, one was kicked to the ground.

We got a few accounts, difficult to sort through to find truth but what us girls ascertained was the Chinese workers arrived earlier to the mine than their white counterparts. Most of the white miners was unionized makin' their work day slightly shorter, they was expected at seven in the mornin'. The white miners would then be given the days' schedule, and who was workin' what rooms. Now, the Chinese arrivin' early posed a big problem, they started in that room claimed by all to have the most coal. Ten white miners headed down, takin' no mind the room was already bein' worked and they ordered the Chinese out. We never was sure if the two refused or just took too long or worst, were just easy targets. And it didn't really matter what caused the upset, they was the ones that paid.

By ten in the mornin' the mines were all but abandoned by both Chinese and white miners. The white miners seemed to form some sort of strike demandin' the Chinese leave. Predictably, the Chinese took their own injured men and retreated to the relative safety of Chinatown. They seemed to be waitin' on some sort of instruction from the mine supervisors as to what should happen next. After all, they couldn't very well work in such condition.

The white miners grew in number and converged on the main street, kickin' up dust and anger. They asserted their usual complaints; the Chinamen didn't belong, the pay unfair and how their very jobs were threatened. We heard 'em before we saw 'em and Evans ordered us down immediate. The crowd was growin' there was money to be made.

CHAPTER 15

All summer long, we dealt with the men and their troubles. We felt their muscles harden beneath their shirts, readyin' for a fight and that mornin' was no different. Dan poured the shots and ordered us girls to sing, talk, dance anythin' to put the men at ease. Cook was ordered to make up biscuits and gravy that Evans sold. The place was so crowded, us girls could hardly move among the men. Sue even got pushed right out the front door.

She walked up and down the front of the saloon, advertisin' what men might find inside. A few of the overly- excited men pulled her to 'em kissin' her while she pulled away. The chase seemed to excite 'em further until Dan finally ran out and got her. He pulled her inside and reminded the men she wasn't free. If they wanted more, they needed to, "Come on in. You can taste our whiskey and our women all ya want, all of ya all know we don't charge much." And he pushed Sue back out onto the floor.

The noise was unbelievable, even comparin' to our busy summer nights or the party that was held that July 4 celebratin' freedom. The floor absolutely groaned beneath the weight of so many men. Everyone was yellin' above the others, tellin' their version of events that mornin' and what they expected would happen later. By noon, Evans and Dan was kickin' good payin' customers right out the doors. There was just no way to contain those men in such a frenzied state.

Things was turnin' ugly and threats was made to anyone within earshot. Besides all that, there just weren't room, not even standin' room, for all the men that mornin'. Some took to standin' on the chairs and by the end of it, us girls had been forced right up on the bar. There just wasn't nowhere else to go. All of us danced on that bar-top, but this was different, somehow. Men were grabbin' and pullin' and we kept fallin', though we never hit the ground. We was just pushed right back up. If one of us had fallen right through to the floor, we'd been trampled by accident. There just wasn't no place for the men to even place their feet. Dan locked the front door. Most unusual, Evans poured us each a shot and advised us to catch our breath. Normally, us girls were given leftover dregs of beer.

I looked around and saw, Dan had a bloodied lip and each of girls was wounded in some fashion too. Even Evans was wipin' a small cut on his right hand.

"What the hell was that?" Evans poured himself and Dan another shot. "I never seen such a crowd. Not even in Deadwood that time the injuns took over that one establishment, ya remember that?" Dan nodded. "Why, they don't cut it out, or someone stop 'em, they gonna form a mob. God knows what they'll do next." He downed the shot in one and shook his head, "Till is full up and I hate to miss out on makin' more, what ya say? Should we take business outdoors, see what we can make?" He eyed us girls, all nursin' fresh scratches and bruises from the crush of bodies we just endured. "No one looks worse for wear, least not terrible worse for the wear."

"Ya know, normal I agree with just about everythin' ya say, Evans. We go way back, you and I. But ain't sure about this one. Look out there." Dan indicated out the window, and I saw his glass, still full, rested on the counter that was normally high-polished. Our feet scuffed it all up, though and I predicted it would be us to polish it right again. Dan saw me lookin' and pointed that out to Evans. "Look around, there's plenty need doin' right in here. The girls need to put that alright and later, them men will all calm down and we can open the doors again."

Evans looked around, takin' in the damage then turned his attentions to the window. None of us girls offered any such opinion. Not even Jo.

"You're wrong, Dan, now's the time to fill up the coiffeurs. Look at 'em out there, they might kill each other off in a few hours' time. Then who will we open our doors to then? Let's make some money while it's out there and worry about the rest later." Dan didn't agree, but he didn'td disagree neither, he just waited to hear the plan Evans obviously had. "Cook's been makin' those biscuits all mornin'. We give the girls some, each to carry 'round out there and sell. One girl sells biscuits the other offers a shot, who doesn't like two girls together? If they want anythin' else, we let 'em in one or two at a time, they can go upstairs and pay on their way out."

"Well, I can't argue with that plan, it ain't bad. If they ain't crowdin' us out in here, least we got room to move out there." Dan sent us out the door and locked it behind him.

That street was full of men. It certainly wasn't as crowded as indoors but it still took a bit to walk around the small groups formed, discussin' what they was gonna do next. Us girls stuck to the idea laid forth by Evans and sold all the biscuits and whiskey we had. More than a few men lined right up at the front door, waitin' on their turns upstairs. Soon, all us girls was ushered back inside, and upstairs to feed that line. Sue passed by me in the hallway and remarked real quiet how she was sure Evans was makin' a killin' that day. I pictured the safe in his room, full of coin and notes, then I went about my business.

A good two hours went by and there was just no way to keep track of how many clients visited that day. Just after two we heard the last of the men leave and Dan hollered at us to leave our rooms.

"Ya girls come on down here, no others are waitin' out the door. Get down here and start fixin' this place up." We lined up on the stairs, surveyin' down below.

Sue took charge once more, givin' each of us a chore and what- not. Dan stood ready at the window, guardin' the locked front door. No line formed but the crowd never dissipated neither. Evans cleaned out the drawer and rushed upstairs. We heard his own door lock behind him. We knew he was countin' the money made that day. Us girls set to work, listenin' to the crowds outside.

It didn't take long, what-with all us helpin' to get that place shaped up once more and we lined up right at the windows, to see what was happenin'. It looked like all other businesses were shuttered too leavin' the men with nothin' more to do. I noticed most of 'em were armed and I heard Sue softly whisper, "Would ya look at that, there must be two hundred miners out there, and most got guns."

We couldn't make out if there was any one leader from our vantage point, so we headed right up the stairs to the balcony outside my room. It was a sight, from up there. Men all shoutin' and wavin'. None of us saw any sort of law minglin' in that crowd. I doubted it was safe for them to intervene. Soon, the men headed away from that main street, right over to Chinatown.

Chinatown was off, on its own. There was a crude bridge, made up of a couple of boards, makin' it accessible over the narrow bit of river that separated it from the rest of the town. The bigger railroad bridge was easier to cross, but further down-river. We watched crowd separate, as if they was givin' order to do so, and head for both bridges. It looked like was gonna surround Chinatown.

Then, we saw Dan leave our own front door. He joined the crowd and disappeared. My heart leapt.

Sue was first to speak. "You girls listen up. Nothin' gonna be the same here no more. Not after this. Now, I can't tell ya what is gonna happen to all those Chinamen over yonder. But we got a chance here, and all of us can take it now. Dan just left."

I doubt any of us had ever been more scared than we were at that moment. All the trials, the forced labor, the forced sex, all of it wasn't as scary- in hindsight- as takin' the reigns of our own destinies. My heart pounded and my ears roared with the blood that sped through my veins. I looked around at the others. Each face was wide-eyed, cheeks flushed. We held our hands out to each other. Some might have thought we was gonna pray for some sort of guidance. It sure looked that way.

Us whores didn't dare pray, though. We stole strength where we could find it and carried on needin' little on which to survive.

Sue had a plan, so we leaned in to listen.

"I ain't workin' for no man the rest of my days. I can't take it no more. I know, I don't know nothin' more than whorin' so I'm openin' my own place. You girls can follow if ya like, that's up to ya. It ain't an easy life, but it can better. I plan on leavin' here, today. Look around, though, we can't leave and worry over Evans huntin' us down." She drew a deep breath and didn't go on, we knew what she meant. We had to take care of Evans. "Dan too. Evans is in there on his own, he don't know that I have the keys to his room and that safe. I think we got a real good chance. If we all work together, we can surprise him and take what's ours." She didn't sound afraid, just determined. I looked out at the street, if Dan stayed away, I think we did have a good chance.

"Now, you girls, you all follow me, we go right into his room, he'll be sittin' down, and that's where I'm gonna shoot him. I took a pistol from his room some days ago. Its loaded and ready." I was amazed at Sue's foresight. "Now, if I get him just right in the head or his chest, that first shot will kill him. If not, well, we gonna have to finish him off, anyways we can. After that, we split up, gettin' what we can. We don't tell Cook until its time to leave. The stable, ya know the one right up the street? We can get horses from there, if we are real quiet, no one should notice. Got it?" It was a simple plan; we all nodded our heads. "Betsy, you get all the clothes, blankets ya can, once Evans is out the way. Jo, you get food, whatever we can carry. I'll get the cash, and you, Ruth, you get the guns. Come on." She ducked back inside and we followed.

Up to this point, none of us had been over-violent people. We were rough, we was crass, and we talked big but none of us had killed anyone, ever before. Jo's hands was shakin' again but we followed Sue, right up to Evans' door. She pulled a gun out from her brazier and cocked it. The sound seemed to echo down the hallway, so we waited a few seconds, but no footsteps sounded from inside. I put my ear right up to the door. I could hear Evans humming faintly, but not much more. I nodded to Sue, it was time.

She opened the door. Luck was surely on our side, that door made no sound swingin' open. We hesitated, listenin' hard but the hummin' continued. Sue stepped right in front and led us right up to the office where Evans sat countin' his money. He didn't hear us before he saw us, and the look of shock that crossed his face was forever etched into our memories. He was lookin' straight down the barrel of a loaded gun. He dropped the coin he was countin' and made to stand up.

Sue was quick though, and the shot went off quick as any lightenin' strike. I don't think none of us even heard it. My eyes were shut tight, but I forced 'em open. Evans no longer sat before us, the shot, or maybe death forced him from his chair. I'd seen blood before, plenty of blood but the wall was covered in brains and hair, and the smell of spilled blood filled the small space. I gagged.

Sue waved us out, "Get outta here, hurry, that blast was heard by someone I assure ya. Hurry up. Stick to our plan." I nodded but couldn't quite remember what it was I was collectin'. I doubted more than ten minutes had passed since we gathered on that balcony but everythin' looked different somehow. I kept remindin' myself I didn't pull the trigger.

It was odd, I didn't feel loss at the extinguishment of Evans life. I couldn't love him or miss him. I sure was used to him, though. And we shared an intimacy that was fun though I wasn't fond of, I wandered towards the door, tryin' to slow my thoughts. Betsy took my arm, and forced me to look in her eyes.

"Ruth, get the guns. Go." Her words shocked me back into reality. I ran to get what guns and ammunition I could find. Dan could be on his way back, someone else could have heard the gun blast, we needed to get on our way. I handed out weapons to each girl and we ran out the back. Cook was right with us, she hadn't needed to be asked twice, and we headed down towards the stable, keepin' oto the back side of the buildin's. We didn't see no one.

The thing was, takin' that route, we was getting' awful close to Chinatown, somethin' we hadn't really planned or talked about during our few hurried conversations. Each step brought us closer, though and we could hear a few gunshots and screams. We pressed on, we needed horses. It was our only way out.

We reached the stables unmolested, to our surprise. Even more surprisin' was how quick we saddled up four horses. Before we mounted, Betsy asked where we was headed.

"The way I see it, if we take these horses, and have Cook hold 'em, right down there," she pointed to a small cluster of trees near the stables, "We can walk right up to that old plank bridge. Folks'll see us, see our guns and assume we are on their side. Once, we're seen, we can all meet back up by Cook and leave that way. If we all gallop outta here, right now, someone will see us and remember. This way, it confuses what we was actually up to." Sue was noddin' her agreement.

"That's about right, we don't need people payin' too much attention just yet. Once we run, we run and I got a place I'm fixin' on headin'. Its a couple days hard ridin' eastward. I don't want to go back to Deadwood, but there's a few towns in between here and there that could use some good whores. I'm goin' to one of them." Sue was leadin' again, but it no longer surprised us.

Cook took the horses down to the trees, and we followed Sue right to that dilapidated bridge.

Nothin', not even Evans' bein' shot, could have prepared me for the carnage that reigned down on Chinatown.

Screams filled my ears, and it looked like the hills were movin'. On closer inspection it was actually folks crawlin' towards a safety that didn't appear to exist. Small groups of men walked up and down the narrow lanes, yellin' at anyone they met, darin' folks to leave their homes. I saw two men shot right in the street.

"Girls, yell a little, make some noise. Let's make sure they see us." Betsy whispered. So, we waved and yelled, right as we crossed that bridge. I recognized most the men and a few even waved back. Then, I saw Dan.

He saw us and started rushin' right towards our little group. I doubted he saw we was each armed, if he did, he didn't stop. He just kept his stride up, and hollered, "What are you doin? Go back and wait, people are gonna need some relaxin' tonight. This ain't no place for ya."

We watched as grew closer and closer. But not one of us answered him. He stopped, a little ways away, confused as to why we wasn't obeyin' him. Sue held a pistol right on him and Betsy held her shotgun, he raised his arms. Sue shot the same time as Betsy. As we fled, I saw Dan fall but none of us went back to see if he lived or died. It was time to leave.

Terrified screams followed us back to our horses. We hustled right out of town, not botherin' to take any main road. We rode hard till we reached the top of a hill, some ways away. I couldn't hear any more screams but I knew the carnage wasn't over for Chinatown.

We never questioned if we could help anyone or if we should have gone back to see if we could find someone hidin' out there in the sage brush and prairie grass. We just urged the horses on into late afternoon. We didn't stop and no one turned back for a second glance.

We rode, real hard, for several hours, towards the east. It felt strange to be out there, on our own, free as the wind at our backs. It wasn't that we weren't thinkin' of the events that brought our freedom, we just grabbed hold of the opportunity and rode for it. I was happy we was ridin' so we couldn't talk about anything.

Darkness fell before we was really expectin' it. I think the world looked different somehow, now that we was free. We knew what to expect but there was a newness that made it all different. Once it was dark, we continued on, then earnestly looked for shelter. Finally, we decided to camp near the river we was loosely followin'. It made sense, the horses needed waterin', we needed water and there was loose branches for a small fire. We set to makin' camp and carin' for the horses. Cook was excellent and quick at buildin' any fires and she made quick work of some corn meal that fed us. Betsy saw the horses watered, while I worked to free them of their saddles. Sue kept watch while Jo made a couple crude beds right on the ground.

We crowded 'round the small fire and talked for the first time since our departure. No one talked about Evans or Dan.

"You know, those Chinese, they was sure scared," Betsy's voice sounded tired. "I know all they did was wrong, takin' the payloads but that was horrible. I wonder how long they wandered their town that way, lookin' for 'em."

Sue answered, "Thing is girls, we couldn't stop that mob. There was too many and gettin' away was all we could do. I don't know what's gonna happen to the men that started it or how those mine owners are gonna handle this but we got to make some good plans for us. Winter is comin'. I expect it's gonna get right cold in about two, maybe three weeks. We got to find a place before then, and dig in for winter. No one needs to know our story, no one needs to know where we come from. Ya hear? No one. If we hear about that Chinatown massacre, you be surprised. Let the folks tell you all about it. But don't ya tell a thing that we saw."

We all nodded. No matter, what no one could know where we come from or they might guess the rest. It was a wild west but they hanged murderers.

"I say we go as far as we can tomorrow, go right to find a town, ya was tellin' us about, Sue." My voice was quieter than normal, showin' how fatigued I was due the strong emotion of the day. The ground was harder than a rock and I wondered how we could even begin to rest out here.

Jo was next, "Yeah, I reckon that's a right good plan, we ride until we find somewhere's we can stay, then figure out the rest from there. I don't miss the saloon, and I sure don't miss no men. I think I miss the pillows though." With that, we let the fire die down a little and lay down.

To my surprise, I slept as well as, if not better, than any other night. No amount of horror could overtake my fatigue or keep me awake. I slept right through to a brisk dawn, and slowly opened my eyes.

I looked around before I sat up, tryin' to recall just where I was and why I was there. The blankets were damp with dew. The fire was gone, and the morning felt like the coolest one we had since spring. The horses were there. They was munchin' on the prairie grass, it looked like they was content, but my own stomach rumbled. No one else was around, we'd chosen well.

I got up and went about my mornin' particulars, and fetched the water we'd need for coffee and the cornmeal biscuits Cook was so adept at preparin'. When I got back, the others was wide awake, and Betsy was stokin' the few embers hopin' for new flames.

Jo was askin' Sue what the plan was again. Jo was always a little slow in the mornin's, and I ignored them. I busied myself, rollin' up our beds and repackin' the saddle bags. Cook finally announced breakfast was ready and we ate in haste. It wasn't a bad spot, but we all wanted further away. We saddled up, and rode easy, right into early mornin' sunrise.

The sky stretches farther than is almost imaginable, out west. No trees, no buildin's blocked nothin'. Not even smog or smoke impeded the view. It was easy, in the mornin's to see what drew men westwards. The land went on forever promisin' anythin' and everythin' a person could dream. It wasn't hot, nor cold and most early mornin's didn't even have the wind.

The air was filled with the sounds of birds and when we was close enough, the river. The heavens streaked blues and reds that could never be emulated by man. I looked at that beautiful sky, as a free woman, and thought how sad such a sight was missed by the very men it beckoned towards it.

We rode on, each of us takin' lead here and there, and after a few hours, we dismounted and walked the horses through a field of prairie grass. We took our time, the day was growin' hot, and the horses enjoyed the break. We rode on, then stopped for a lunch break and rode on through the wild prairie. Soon, we came to a small town.

It was strange to be by people seemingly going about their normal business. We was dressed so we didn't stand out, but while men traveled in small bands, I was not aware of the practice being held by women. We stabled the horses and Sue procured a couple of rooms and baths for us in the hotel. We didn't see no girls workin' those rooms, but we did see a saloon down the street, which we avoided.

All of us felt dirty after a night out beneath the stars. I hadn't bathed all week, and only god knew how much come was between my legs by how many men. The other girls said the same, so we bathed. Even Cook joined us, and we helped each other with our hair and clothes. We took turns doin' the wash while the others bathed.

"Honestly, I feel a hundred times better after that bath. The rooms ain't have bad either, I think, due our fragile gender," we all laughed; fragile our asses, "we best stay here. No one knows us, we can stay a day or two, get some good meals and rest. By then all our clothes will dry." Betsy must have been thinkin' that entire way. Her thoughts were right though.

"I think ya is right on, Betsy-girl," Jo was happier than I ever saw her before, "I mean, we can take it turns gettin' meals and no one gonna pay attention to a couple of girls on their own. If we stay careful, I think it's a good plan."

"Yes, but what happens after a day or two? We can't be far enough away no one won't recognize us. Then what? Ride on, sleep rough, and do this all over again until we find permanent quarters?" I was right, and they all knew it, we was just buyin' time to buy time. We needed a solid plan.

"Why not jus' buy some train tickets. We can go where ever we want then." Cook's voice was so different, I wouldn't have known she was the one to talk, if I hadn't seen her speak. Before I could voice that or answer her, Sue was talkin'.

"You sure is right, Cook. I'll sell the horses, you can come with me, Betsy, make sure I am dealin' ya all fair. We can take that money and buy the tickets. Once I get those tickets, I'll give each of us a share of the money from Evans. Now, you all heard my plan, who is comin' with me? Remember, the farther you go, the more cost the train ticket. It might dip into your earnin's."

I was noddin'. Her words seemed fair, though I wondered if Cook would get the same share as the rest of us. She never slept with men, as far as I knew. Her bed was always warm, always on her own. Not to say her days weren't good or bad, but it wasn't the same, either. I noticed all of us was lookin' at her, and we was all thinkin' the same thing. Jo was the one to ask though.

"So, before we go and sell horses and buy tickets, I think it's only right we know how much we gettin'. After all, how can we plan without numbers? And, Cook, we sure love your cookin' and all ya done for us, but if you get the same share as me, we gonna have some words." Cook didn't answer, just looked at Sue.

"Well, there's four of us and you, Cook. And, Jo's right. You are gonna get less. That's only fair." Sue's voice was low but full of authority and she looked Cook right in the eye, almost darin' her to challenge us. Cook looked around.

"I can't say its right but I can't say you all is wrong, neither. How about this, you buy my ticket, and then give me the share you thought fair?" Cook asked. Sue looked around for our assent. I nodded immediately, sounded right to me. The others followed.

"Right, well then, where do you want tickets to, Cook?" she asked before she answered Cook's question.

"I want to go back where I come from. I have a sister out in Philly, I'm goin' back to her." Cook answered readily, she must have been plannin' that a long time.

"Fine, Cook, we get your ticket to Philly and we give you half what our shares are, sound alright?" Sue asked, and Cook nodded. "What about you others, where ya goin?"

"I'm followin' you if the invitation is still there, Sue," Betsy answered. "I don't what else to do with myself, and I ain't workin' for a man again. But I'll work for you." Sue nodded and rubbed Betsy's knee. I saw the look pass between them and wondered how I never noticed before. They loved each other. Betsy would have followed Sue anywhere.

"That's real nice, Betsy, and yes, I am still extendin' the invitation. I think we can travel by stage, not train, so we can save some funding that way. It ain't far." Sue sounded almost excited.

"I want to go to Cheyenne, don't get me wrong, girls. I ain't real excited to go it alone but I don't want this life no more. I'm buyin' my own place and I'll live off my garden." I was surprised to hear my voice crack. I'd sure miss these girls but I was done with whorin'. "I figure I'd go by stage too." Sue took grasped my hand, but no one answered. Later, I would recall Jo never answered.

CHAPTER 16

We broke up our little conversation, and Cook and I left for a small lunch. When we returned, Betsy and Sue was all ready to go sell the horses and get their own lunch. Jo would get lunch on her own, she said. Cook and I watched them leave and I laid down for a nap. Our door was locked and nothin' could trouble my mind anymore that afternoon. Cook watched the three women from the window and contented herself with watchin' the street after.

I woke to the sounds of Betsy and Sue tellin' Cook of the sale and givin' her a ticket and her share of the money. Cook took both and hid them away on her person.

"Where's Jo, she ever come back?" Sue asked. I looked around, only Betsy, Cook and I were in the room.

"I ain't seen her. I don't know where she got off to. I was sleepin', Cook did you see her out the window?" We all looked to Cook who was shakin' her head, no.

"Well, I say we head downstairs, altogether for some dinner. No one's gonna notice that, and we can talk further, like normal people. Plus, there is some interestin' conversations about a massacre not far from here." Sue was talkin' like it was nothin' but local gossip but gave us a knowing look.

Sure enough, when we reached the tables below, there was plenty of talk about the prior days' events. It seemed the terror went on for several hours endin' in the burnin' of the shanty-town. No one spoke anythin' of any whores on the run, though. We finished our meal rather quick and returned to our rooms. No one talked about the fire that must have burned frighteningly quickly through such a place. Sue walked to the window and watched the street. Jo still wasn't back.

"Where would she go? Not the saloon?" Sue sounded confused.

"I was thinkin' the same thing, she wouldn't go there, she didn't have a dime on her, there was nothin' invitin' her anywhere. She just said she was gettin' some food." I looked out the window, too. No Jo.

"I saw her, she sort of followed you two up towards the stable. I figured you knew she was there." Cook explained. "I never saw her return, though." Jo didn't come back that night, and we all turned in early. Jo wasn't there when we woke.

Cook had her ticket and she was leavin' that mornin'. We all got one more breakfast, together, but without Jo. "I wonder where got off to," Betsy asked every few minutes.

As we finished our last bites, the doors opened up and a young man entered, lookin' 'round.

"He's the fella at the stable, he bought the horses yesterday," Sue whispered. He headed direct to our table.

"Well, good mornin', to ya." Sue greeted him first.

He tipped his hat at us, "Mornin', ma'am. Ma'ams. How many is in your group?"

Sue looked at him, calculatin' her answer, then gestured at our table, "Well, you can see, there's us four, right here. Why do you ask?"

"We cut down an unknown woman from our rafters this mornin'. No idea who she is or where she come from. We just wanted to alert the right folks, is all." He turned to go, but Betsy caught his arm.

"That's awful, tell us, what did she look like? How old was she?" Betsy's face was flush, maybe even threatenin' tears.

"How kind of you to inquire, she wasn't old, I say early twenties. I hate to speak ill of the dead, but she wasn't the handsomest woman around, more of a hole in her face than a mouth." He shook his head and left. He didn't notice how the news shook us. Cook was first to talk.

"I want a bigger share. It's only fair. Jo ain't usin' hers no more. We got to split her share."

And with those words we left the table. Cook was right. No matter how horrible it was, she was right. Sue split Jo's shares and we walked Cook to the train. She climbed aboard, turned once and waved farewell forever. I couldn't decide if I was sad to see her go or not.

The stage only came through that town twice a week. We had to wait a few days for its return. Durin' those days we learned the fate of the now burnt Chinatown, thanks to the talk at the diner.

"Smell is horrible down there, I don't think I can ever forget it. You know those Chinese, they always keep hogs or pigs and none of that mess was spared fire. You could smell burnt pig a mile away. When ya get closer, ya smell the rest." He paused, thinkin', "Sad to say, I don't know if there's a different in the smells. Well, anyways, those Chinese miners that did escape, some of 'em just stayed in the desert wanderin' round till they reached the next town over. Poor bastards, some of even had gunshot wounds." He stopped talkin' for a time.

His partner asked, "Then what, how they clean up that Chinatown? What they doin' 'bout that?"

"Well, now, that's the real problem. The town did nothin' to help those poor bastards. Fact is, nor the railroad. I heard tale, they asked for return trips to San Fransisco, wantin' to seek employment elsewhere. They was gathered on a few cars, thinkin' they was headed west only to stop at their burnt up town. The doors opened and there was their friends and families, dead in the streets. Some tried to hide, they're still find half burnt bastards dug into hidey holes beneath the shacks they lived in. There they stood, surveyin' all that damage and one of the owners told 'em they could clean it up and get back to work, or risk losin' their employment. They wouldn't give them passes to San Fransisco." The guy took a deep drink of the beer in front of him.

The two were quiet for a time, thinkin' on the scene he'd painted.

Sue, Betsy and I sat in a stunned silence. I couldn't think any man capable of such a crime as leavin' bodies out like that. There was dogs and coyotes throughout that entire country. I doubted they'd left them alone. I shuddered thinkin' of the little woman who promised me luck would soon visit promised by those cranes. I wondered what happened to her and to her loved ones.

Just last year, the Chinese did a parade for the town and let off their fireworks. Nothin' like I ever saw before. Their strange instruments and words echoed down the main street. All of them were so happy to celebrate, and happy to share with the town. A place they called home, however temporary. Nothin' could ever make up for this. Nothin'. I wondered who was responsible. The men continued their conversation, so I stopped thinkin' and just listened.

"Well, ya know what happened next. They actually decided to allow the Chinese to live in those train cars. Chargin' 'em only half the normal rent. They rounded up some of the ringleaders too. I guess even the women of the town was shootin' into Chinatown from some bridge." I looked 'round Betsy and Sue then. "I can't tell ya, how rough a place that is out that ways. Nothin' sacred. And, they got the ringleaders, so they say, in custody. But the others, they're threatenin' violence if the Chinese return. I think they're callin' military in to keep it safe out there at those mines. Can ya believe that? They gonna put soldiers out there to guard them mines!" The man took another swig, givin' his friend a chance to ask a couple questions.

"That is near unbelievable. So, who is gonna try the ringleaders? Will there even be a trial?"

The other man shook his head, "You know, so far, they're sayin' they need an eyewitness to testify sayin' they saw him call the men to arms and lead them into Chinatown. So far, no one come forewards. But I doubt they will, I really doubt they will. Look at the way their own women was behavin'? Naw, that town, they all are against those Chinese." He shook his head. "I never said I love all the Chinese, nor all the Mexicans, nothin' like that but all they got for bein' burnt alive, was a couple weeks to clean it up."

Betsy, Sue and I finished in silence and climbed the stairs in silence. Betsy was cryin' real quiet and Sue stroked her hair. None of spoke the rest of that night. There just wasn't much to say.

I lay, on my own, contemplatin' the last week's events. Evans was dead. Dan was dead. Jo was dead. It sounded like a lot of the Chinese was dead. Death. The Tower. The Devil. Those three cards surmised the whole of that place.

Run by the Devil himself, no one was safe. It was cruel and difficult, no place to call home.

I was free of it, though. Forever. And no one knew any different.

Next mornin', Betsy slept in later than normal. I wondered if she was gettin' sick but Sue thought it was her soul needin' rest.

"Ruth. I got somethin' I gotta tell ya." We were downstairs, just us two gettin' breakfast. It was our last day in that town, the next the stage would come, takin' Betsy and Sue one way, me another. I waited for her to go on. "You remember how crowded the saloon was that day, watchin' all the men comin' and goin'?" I nodded, and she went on, "Well, I know who started it, I could testify." I put down my drink.

"What do you mean, you could testify? What would you tell, what would you say? Someone has sure found Evans by now, and maybe even Dan if he wasn't eaten by dogs or coyotes. I'm sure they noticed the empty saloon and no girls. What would you say, Sue?" As sad as the stories of Chinatown were, as terrible as all that, we couldn't testify. I shook my head at her, "Just don't, Sue. Ya can't. Jo would've died for nothin' And if that don't count, then let me leave first. I see you and Betsy though. I see you love her. And I am fine with all that. I am glad for the pair of ya. But ask ya'self this, can you give that up?" I shook my head at her again and she didn't bother to answer.

Much to my relief and own sound logic, Sue didn't pursue her moral judgments. The next day, her and Betsy got into one stagecoach, and I into another. We leaned out the windows, wavin' till we departed. They was excited to start their new venture, and I was excited to find some peace.

We each had a little over a third Evans' life savin's that we earned him. Sue had her eye on gettin' a property that Betsy hoped to paint yellow. I never heard of a yellow whore house, but maybe it would draw business. Betsy said she wanted it yellow and white. Sue would never tell her no.

I didn't care too much bout the color of the place I was gonna call home. I figured I would know it when I saw it.

I watched them ridin' away, wonderin' how I would live without them in my daily life. We'd shared so much. Our trade gave us a deeper connection that most friends can experience, and it didn't matter if we was forced into that or not. Our days, and many of our nights were spent together. We ate together, bathed together, worked together, talked together and relied on each other. There was hardly a memory we didn't share from the past years. As often as I'd imagined a life away from that hell, I'd never considered saying farewell. I'd never been able to picture a day without those girls.

I waved. No tears fell, from my eyes, nor theirs. We simply waved good-bye.

CHAPTER 17

My solo adventure began not long after they left. It wasn't the first time I'd survived on my own, but I'd never before had the means to survive. Life looked so differently now. Nothing barred me from my simple hopes or dreams. I thought of all I wanted as I walked confidently towards freedom. Nothing was gonna stop me. I carefully stepped into the awaiting stagecoach and as left town, I kept my eyes forwards.

I had never ridden stage before. I was accompanied by two well-dressed men who I chose to ignore. The space filled with desert dust, the smell of horse and a non-stop sway. Soon enough, I was holdin' a hankie to my face, trying not to feel the sway or smell the smells surroundin' me. I could only think how thankful I was that I was not goin' to the ends of the earth. My journey was much shorter. Still, the minutes dragged by stealing my energy. By the end of the day, I was left without energy, hunger and even my hopes were waning. New horses were hitched up at a short break and we carried on.

Words can hardly tell how such a start to my new life actually felt. The experience was near surreal. There I was, once again trapped in a situation far outside my control or liking. Yet, as the miles increased, I no longer felt trapped. Rather, it was as if I was walking up a mountain; this was my final push to the top. I could see my destination and was determined to overcome this last obstacle. Looking back, I felt this part of my journey was easy. I had to accept it was not.

Nothing about my journey had been easy.

Still, the smallest glimmer of hope had somehow lightened my life before and it did now. I followed it without knowing too much about where it was leading me or what I would do once I arrived. It was that light I kept my eyes on through the desert that night.

And once again, the sun rose shining light into the darkest of corners, even out there in a god-forsaken desert.

The funny thing about freedom, true freedom, I found was how differently the world would *look*. Traveling through that first day and night was exhausting and bleak. The sun coming over the mountains was exhilarating. The night was cool, it was getting' late in the year, after all, and the morning sun took its time warmin' the earth. But that did not stop me seein' and hearin' birds or how dew sparkled atop stone and earth.

As the day wore on, I resolved my past to my past. In much the same manner as I had accepted the fate I had been forced into, I determined to put it behind me. No longer could or would people know my trade from a simple observation. I wanted a quiet life and began demonstrating such right away. I no longer needed to engage in every conversation or remark around me. I no longer would be made to praise those around me for sake of payin'. There was no need to look every man in the eye, darin' him to want me to soften around him. No. That was in the past and I was no longer whorin' to survive. I was no longer a whore.

Everything felt different. My clothing softer, more giving, the seat not so hard. I breathed deeper, easier and when I caught a glimpse of my reflection, I was surprised to see how little my appearance changed to how I felt. I felt taller, more powerful, confident. My features didn't reflect any of that. No matter.

I was free.

The territory of Wyoming was a funny place. It was hard. Took a lot of sand to get a person through the bitter cold of winter. And, it took a lot to get through the hot summer days, too. The desert ain't hospitable but it was beautiful. I doubt any place on the wide earth could compare.

After a full day in that stagecoach, I decided I didn't want to leave the territory. There was no need. I found myself a small town, nestled at the bottom of some mountains that I figured I'd make home. As happy as I was, as excited as I was, nothin' was easy.

Like the journey in the stagecoach, I found nothin' came easy. Not that I'd expected it but parts of it were that I didn't expect. I found a small dwellin' place easy enough but makin' a home was not.

I'd always imagined a little home with its own little vegetable garden, maybe a few flowers, off to one side. The inside was simple, a place to eat and a place to rest. I never figured I needed much. I thought I'd work the little garden, and turn money over from jams or such. It wasn't the money that made makin' a home difficult. It was lonely. Real lonely.

I moved into a small place just like I'd wanted. It was small but neatly finished. A small table and chair stood beside a fireplace fit for cookin'. A bed stood in one corner. It was a simple place, for a simple life. The town was nice, too. Folks comin' and goin'.

A few people, not many, paid me more mind than to my likin'. Each time I visited the general store, the wife asked me more than the polite, "How are you?" She wanted to know where I was comin' from. Who was I with, that sort of thing. I ignored, her for the most part, and each time her quieter husband would remind her to, "shhh."

I spent a lot of my days outside, knowin' the winter months was comin'. I stayed out patchin' holes, gettin' firewood, and just breathin' air that was coolin'. The inside of house was light and clean. No one but me kept my schedule.

For the first time in my life, I slept in late as I wanted. I ate when I was hungry. Some days I ate three squares, some not. I didn't talk to anyone I didn't feel like speaking to. The first few weeks, I rested and my soul rested. When I looked in the mirror again, my eyes were brighter, my hair fuller and back straighter.

Winter hit, same as every year. The wind howled over the town causing snow to drift right up to the roof of my little home, making it all the cozier. I whiled away the hours alone, sewing and fixin' up things readyin' for spring. No matter what I was doin' or where I was, another season was always comin', it was always on the horizon. Always somethin' to do.

A quiet time in life made for a reflective time. As the winter wore, on I experienced emotions I thought were long dead to me. I thought I was going crazy from bein' alone. I feared the day someone might find my dead cold corpse frozen because I'd wandered out alone seeking a refuge I never found. Instead and maybe surprisingly, I did not die nor lose my senses.

One of the first things I experienced was a deep sense of regret, then anger. I was angry at the death of my family, and the life I led. Mostly, I was angry at myself for the whorin' I done. The thing was, there were many gentlemen I enjoyed. They was the gentle ones and even the needy ones was fun. Especially facin' the loneliness of a long winter. As the days grew to weeks, I welcomed the anger though. I might be lonely but I knew I would never go back to whorin'. I liked havin' the choices before me now. Slowly, the anger abated into a sadness.

The sadness enveloped me like the snow enveloped our town and it refused to melt away fed by cold and wind. My sadness was fed by a yearning for my spent youth, my lost baby and something more difficult to understand. The years spent servin' all those men, Dan and Evans. The time I spent smilin' for 'em and dancin' for 'em and complimentin' was all lies. And I lied until I lost what made me happy, what made me smile. I lost myself. Lookin' around my own little home, I realized I no longer remembered colors might catch my eye or what women talk about, as if just friends and not workin' the men like that.

Then, one day, it rained. The smell filled the little house, it filled the air around the house and most of the snow melted with each drop. I breathed in the fresh, new spring air still cold from winter, but hinting at warmer days.

I remembered how I loved the rain. As a child, I never feared even the most terrible thunder storms. I simply looked for the rainbows, I knew was comin'. I'd step out the small one- roomed cabin we called home and search the sky over till I found it. I'd inhale the wet smell, fill up my lungs with it. Each blade of grass displayed tiny droplets reflecting the clear sky. And above it all a rainbow encircled a washed earth.

I stepped out my front door, I breathed in the rain. It was a spring rain, heavy and cold. The earth and my soul were one, thirstily drinking up all that was given. My clothes and hair became heavy with the rain, I was shivering with cold and wet but still I drank filling up all the dehydrated parts of my soul. I stood out there a long while until I could take no more water and no more cold.

I staggered inside and undressed. I stood, naked in front of the fire allowing my skin and hair to dry with the heat it put out, arms outstretched. My goose flesh smoothed as it warmed and soon enough even my shivering subsided. After I dried, I was no longer sad. I was no longer angry.

I stood, anew, with the promise of warm days near. I felt different. Younger. Happier. Lighter. Free. The rain washed away the years of fear and guilt. The fire dried up the anger and sadness leaving me a fresh-faced 24 year old looking forward to life.

CHAPTER 18

The spring was slow-coming. Winter always held on longer than most wished. After the day of rain, we had more snow and then another big snow before winter finally relented. I made my way up to the general store for the first time in months.

I spent time purchasing the few goods I needed, and talked with the owner.

"How was your winter?" I asked. She responded like we was old friends feeding my courage to inquire how I might sell some goods through her store. I enjoyed making jams and the like knew I would be in need of some income. I had some new ideas I thought the women-folk of the place might like too.

Women liked takin' care of themselves and the men liked clean, soft women. Us girls relied on a cream and scented it with flowers grown with the kitchen garden Cook kept. It was a gluttonous goop made with fat, honey and the scent. It cured most skin ailments and softened any skin. I offered to let her sell it from her shop. I was only minimally surprised when she agreed to take ten jars next time I was in.

"Why Ms, Ruth, how are ya?" the low voice of someone I had very nearly forgot greeted me one mornin' while I was out in my garden.

Jeremiah was leanin' on my own garden fence, watchin' me as I was workin'. I felt my heart quicken, I hadn't even heard him approach.

He wasn't smilin'. His hat was low and his eyes were hard. I looked up and I wasn't smilin' either.

"Jeremiah. Well. Its been a long while since I saw the likes of ya. What are you doin' here?" My voice was equally soft and I found myself lookin' for a weapon. My hands were completely wet with sweat. I desired not to see any one from the past life that I had so painstakingly escaped. I wasn't goin' back for no one. Ever.

"Nothin'. I don't need nothin'. Nice place ya got there." And he walked away, not botherin' to say farewell nor wait for mine. I watched him walk away, like he didn't have one care in the wide world.

I wondered where he came from, how he found me. I wondered how long he'd known where to find me. I'd escaped that life, I felt different, I was livin' different but here was a ghost from the past reminding me despite all my changin' the past still exists. I had a hard time sleepin' that night.

I wondered at my feelings. Jeremiah sure wasn't gentle the last time we was together. I'd said no, he didn't care. He didn't are enough to even pay for it neither. He didn't care one fig for me, that was the truth. I was done whorin'. Done with having men not care about me or what I wanted. I was done with that mess no matter the price and if I couldn't run from ghosts, I supposed I'd have to face 'em.

I lived in relative peace the next days. The jarred cream was even sellin'. I kept myself to myself, still not trustin' many and enjoyin' the peace in my solitude. I was too cynical to forget Jeremiah was close by but I refused to stop livin'. Then, I saw him again.

He was just standin' near my house, watchin' me while I worked the small vegetable patch. He didn't say nothin'. When I made eye contact with him, he looked me up and down. His mouth open a little. It sent shivers down my spine but I kept on workin' I didn't let him see. As soon as he left, I put my tools down and retreated indoors. I didn't fancy lookin' over my shoulder all afternoon. Then, it was a few days till I saw him again.

Since leavin' that life behind, I made a point to clean my little home each night. Afterwards, I sat and brushed my hair and washed the day's dirt away. I spent most evenin's undressed allowin' my skin to breathe. It was a real treat to care for my body this way after years of neglect and abuse. I felt cleaner than ever and looked forward to the evenin's this way. I'd eat my simple dinner and then begin my little ritual. I brushed my skirt clean and wash my undergarments. It was a nice way to put each day away and wake up to such tidiness each mornin'.

I loved how my home was all mine. The few possessions I owned were all mine, all neat and clean and just where I wanted 'em. I swept the floor each day and it was clean as the small tabletop. Each day was predictable and lovely in its own way. Lookin' backwards, I wondered if the other girls might laugh at me or think how borin' I was now. I was happy though. True, some night was lonely, no one to talk with and I wondered where Jedidiah might be. In this life, though, no one could take or demand a thing from me and at least for now, I was happy with this life.

Jeremiah shattered my peace the very next mornin'.

I woke up, same as always. I could tell it was a nice day, the sun was peakin' through the curtains. I breakfasted and stood a few minutes plannin' my day. I needed to harvest honey and dry some of the early blooms already showin' in my garden. I also needed to go up to the shop, speak about the creams sellin'.

I finally asked her name and was delighted she shared her given name, Mildred with me. She told me she just never got used to her married name or bein' called it so she gave up. Her husband, a Mr. James, had stood by her smilin' at her the whole time. He didn't seem to mind what folks called her. I told her she could call me Ruth. It felt friendly knowin' them this way.

I dressed and gathered the few tools and such I'd need for the mornins' chores and opened my door ready to step into what promised to be a beautiful day. I hadn't even stepped out and a hand went 'round my throat. I was forced back inside, hardly knowin' what happened.

"Ya think they don't know the whore ya are, huh?" A familiar stench filled the space that only moments ago was clean, peaceful. Jeremiah kept his voice low, harsh all the while pushin' me up against the wall. I could breathe, but barely. I'd forgotten just how strong men was, especially when they was wantin' somethin' or angry. And he was both.

"I'll tell 'em. I'll tell 'em all how they been takin' in by some whore, befriendin' 'em, sellin' that shit. What ya gonna do, then, huh Ruth? Dan ain't here to save ya, maybe ya shoulda thought about that before you guys shot him down. I can tell 'em that too." Then he spit on my floor.

I ain't sure what happened next. Maybe his words reached down, deep in my soul and inspired me to fight against 'em. Or maybe it was just the tobacca on my clean floor, either way, a strength I wasn't expectin' or plannin' filled my body, top to bottom.

I grabbed hold of the arm that held my neck and twisted with both my hands, until he moved. I kicked him first in the shin, then a knee and he went down, mad as hell and grabbin' for me. But I was ready. I took the garden hoe from it's place near the door and brought it down onto the back of his head.

He was hollerin' mad and lunged but I brought it down again. And again. He lay still on my floor blood spillin' out the back of his head. I ran out the door right up to get Mildred.

They wasn't open jus' yet so I banged on their front door. Mr. James stuck his head out the window upstairs, "Why, Ms. Ruth, whatever are you doin'? We don't open for a little while yet."

"I need your help. I really need your help. Jere.." I let my voice fade away. If I didn't tell 'em a name, acted like he was just some intruder, I'd have better luck gettin' outta this trouble. "A man, he surprised me at my own front door this mornin'. I got him off me alright. He's down, on the floor. But I need help. He can't stay there and I don't know if he's alright." My voice surprised me. I was shakin' with emotion.

For once, I was just another woman who was attacked against my will. I wasn't some whore or too young to fight him off. I was just another woman needin' help to get an unwanted man out of my own house. I couldn't be sure anyone would even help but I knew I needed to appear vulnerable.

"Ruth! Is that you? What is going on?" I could hear Mildred from inside. Soon, she opened up her door and beckoned me inside. "Here, sit, drink. Tell us what happened."

I sat and took the offered water glass. I took a couple deep breaths and forced myself to stop shakin'.

" I am so sorry to trouble, ya. I really am," I began. "I woke this mornin', didn't hear nothin' nor no one round my house. I just woke up and breakfasted, same as usual. Then, when I opened the door, this man, pushed his way right in and threatened me." I took another deep breath. "I was able to hit him, right in the head, with my garden hoe. I think he's still there."

Mildred nodded to her husband who then left.

"There now, can make us some tea and we can wait here while Joe figures it all out. He's a good man, Joe is." She looked more upset than I would have liked while she spoke.

"I am so sorry, truly Mildred. I don't mean to be a bother." I said while she fixed the tea.

"You know, it is quite alright, Ruth. Joe, he don't mind. I suppose you notice we don't have children of our own. Well. Around the time Joe and I was acquainted, a big fella, he knew my father through some business. Well, he come 'round the house lookin' for pa one summer evening. I was young." She stopped and stared out the window before startin' her own story again.

"Well, anyway, he came 'round, like I said, looking for pa. Pa was out and just me and my youngest siblings were home. I told him so and he forced his way right into the house. He hurt me that night. Joe, well he stuck by me and I guess him and pa took care of all that nonsense. I never saw the man again. Joe still married me too." She squared up her shoulders, real proud. "He knew I wasn't asking for it, he only has sisters, you see. Anyway, he'll know what to do."

She poured us each some tea and let me sit in silence awhile. She went about her normal mornin' preparin' their breakfast and all. I wondered how such a fine woman and man could be denied the happiness of children. The house felt emptier, knowin' their story. And though, I'd never tell her, she and I had certain things in common. I felt less alone than before.

It wasn't long before Joe came in with the deputy. Joe indicated me sittin' there, "That's her, that's Ms. Ruth. She owns the house right over there."

I hadn't met the law before. I guess I just never had a need. I had to close my eyes and blink a little to better focus on the man standin' before me.

The deputy was Jedediah.

CHAPTER 19

Nothin' could have prepared me for seein' him again. His hair was longer and he was a little slimmer than last summer. He was lookin' fine as a summer day is long. I fell back in my seat, speechless at the sight of him.

"Mornin', ma'am. I am Jedediah, law around here. What is Joe talkin' about, now?" He tipped his hat at me and looked into my eyes. It looked like he was as surprised to see me as I was him, but wasn't let our previous relations show.

I nodded, near speechless. I took another sip of water and Mildred took my hand. She was under the impression I was only embarrassed or nervous. I nodded again.

"Well, it was like I was tellin' Mildred, here. I woke up, alone, like normal. When I opened that front door he was just there waitin', I guess. Well, he pushed his way in and said a few awful words. He was chokin' me. I got out of it, though and I hit him with the garden hoe." My voice was low and shaky.

"I see, did you know him from before?" Jedidiah was watchin' me awful careful waitin' on my answer.

"Well. I don't know quite how to answer that. I seen him before, the weeks leadin' up to today. One day, he stood right at my garden watchin' me work, said hello and walked on. I seen him after that a few times." I finally let myself look into his eyes. He knew. He knew who I was, he knew where I came from, what I was and I'd bet money he even knowed Jeremiah.

He reached a gentle hand, turnin' my face a little, nearly stoppin' my heart. It was months since a man touched me and now, two this mornin'. His hand was gentle, unhurried unlike Jeremiah.

"Look here, Joe, Mildred. You see them marks? See how they make out a hand? She's tellin' the truth." And without another word, he left. Joe followed.

"Oh my, dear. I can tell you need some more tea. Here you go." Mildred poured the warm drink and laid out the fresh biscuits that I guessed had been intended for her and Joe's breakfast. "Eat up, you may need your strength. Worry not, though. Jedediah been here a little longer than you and he is fair. Town is a much better place with him around." She nodded at her own words and joined me with her own cup.

We waited in silence. I was still too stunned to speak and my mind worked overtime.

Leavin' caught me off-guard. Sure, I'd planned. I'd schemed. But I really hadn't known where I might end up or who I might meet once there. Jedediah was a little fantasy meant to fill some empty winter nights. Yet, here he was. Here I was. For the first time in my life, I even wondered that fate might be a real thing.

For now, though a heap of trouble was awaitin' my own destiny.

Bein' female brought its own set of troubles. Mine was layin', maybe dead, up in my home nearby. I couldn't own land. I didn't have family. I was unmarried and unknown in these parts. It was my word against a man whose own existence closely and ironically mirrored my own.

I doubted Jeremiah was married or owned land. Jedediah and Joe didn't seem to know him either. But, he was a man I might have killed. If my former life came to light, if I made too much a fuss about gettin' attacked, who would believe me?

For a few minutes I was nothin' but a whore again bent to do the devil's work at any man's biddin'. I couldn't help it. I sobbed till my shoulders shook, till my heart actually hurt filled with the pain my soul was feelin'. They say life ain't fair. But it sure ain't fair.

Here was all my dreams, right before me, just waitin'. I had my own home, my own legitimate income and to top all that off, here was Jedediah. Mildred did her best to offer comfort.

"Come on now, Ruth. You don't know Jedediah they ways we do. He is right and fair. He is a good deputy. You tell him just what you told us and he can help." She lifted my chin. "Things are a little different for women out here, why there's even women," she raised an eyebrow, "you know the type. Well, even they do alright for themselves. We just got news of two of 'em openin' their own, uh, establishment a few months back. They offer their services but they also started their own bank. Most the cowboys who ride through these parts, they tell how they keep their money with them because they got a more secure system. Times are a changing, they are! You wait and see, Jedediah can fix this right up." Her voice soothed me and I wondered at her story.

Were Sue and Betsy the women she was talkin' about? "Imagine that!," I couldn't help but think. "Those two girls bankin'!" I hoped Mildred was right, I hoped Jedediah might believe in me just like her Joe believed in her.

Mildred went out front to ready her shop for the day. She left me with a nice hot pot of tea in the prettiest tea set I ever drank from and assured me she was ready to listen when I was ready to talk.

I poured myself more tea and thought about Jedediah a bit more.

He looked much the same and had those same gentle eyes I so often dreamt about. He was polite and in control. When he'd leaned in, I smelled his smell, somethin' fresh and clean but mixed with the sweat of a workin' life. His hair was longer and I sure did appreciate that too.

I recalled the few private conversations we'd shared and once again found myself dreamin' about a life all my own spent with a man much like him. A good, strong man willin' to wake up each day by my side, happy to live beside. I was no cook, that was for sure and I weren't no saint. In the quietest parts of mind soul I believed I might make such a man happy, though.

It seemed to take forever before Jedediah and Joe come back. The men looked worn but resolved and didn't say too much. Joe kissed his wife and tied an apron on proclaimin', "Time for business and the day.

You have yourself a good day, Ms. Ruth. We will see you soon." He and Mildred went to the front of their shop leavin' me and Jedediah alone.

He looked down at me and said, "Well, come on now, I can walk ya home."

But I wasn't ready to go home. I wanted answers and besides. I had some business to take care of, so I asked him to wait for me and went to the shop to talk to Mildred about supplies and gettin' more jars on her shelf. When I walked in, Joe was whisperin' to her behind the counter, both looked up in alarm when I stepped in, then relieved.

"Oh, just you Ruth!" Mildred exclaimed. "Jedidiah done talking to you then? Already?" She looked confused. Apparently, Joe was telling her all about the events that transpired that mornin' and by the looks of it, hadn't quite finished the story. I guessed she was figuring Jedediah to be a man of far fewer words than even she'd suspected.

"No. I come here for supplies and to ask how those jars are sellin'?" My voice was quiet and as resolved as the men's. I was determined to get on with life as normal as possible.

Those two helped me out and we planned to get the shelf filled with the balm over the next few weeks. We wished each other well and I left to find Jedediah waitin' on me outside. He took the basked I was carryin' in one arm and ahold of me with the other.

CHAPTER 20

"I will walk you home now, Ms. Ruth. And you will tell me all that needs tellin' about this mornin'." He looked neither right nor left, just straight ahead and walked. I had to nearly run to keep up with his stride. Never before had I appreciated our height difference as I did durin' that short walk home. When we arrived, he opened the door and beckoned me inside.

I took a careful look around seein' most everything was just as I'd left it. Nothin' was broke nor missin'. Besides the pool of dryin' blood on the ground I might not even guess anything amiss happened there that day. I turned around as Jedediah came through the door, then took the only chair.

"What happened, Ruth? I seen that fellow before, when I was up your way," He was careful not to acknowledge my former profession, at least not yet. "I can't say I know his name but I ain't never seen around here before. How did he know where to find ya?"

I shook my head and looked down. "I don't know, I thought I left all that behind me. I ain't talked to no one, nothin' like that. I figure he was passin' through and seen me at the store or walkin' home and followed me. His name is Jeremiah, I don't know his last name."

"Well, his name *was* Jeremiah. He won't be botherin' ya ever again, that's for sure. When Joe and I got here, he was moanin' some moving around on the floor a little. Joe explained he surprised, ya. Ya know, Ruth, I knew ya was here in town before the winter set in. I been checkin' on ya here and there too." He looked me right in the eye. I couldn't' look away.

"What do ya mean, *was* his name?" My voice was quiet, skeptical. It was too much to believe I had nothin' to fear, no one watchin' me or waitin' for me in the shadows.

He reached for my hand. "I mean just that, Ruth. He ain't ever goin' to bother ya. He can't. Don't worry about him again. I'm guessin' he was threatenin' to tell folks where ya came from?" I was surprised to feel tears come to my eyes.

Out of everything Jeremiah was threatenin it was true, him telling folks my past employment was my worst fear. I'd paid the Devil his dues long ago. It was time for a little heaven on earth and I couldn't go back to whorin'. Whether I was a workin' whore or not. I was the way people looked at ya when they saw ya.

Women usually looked away, as if we was filth on their shoes. Most men looked at us like they might look at livestock. They inspected us and handled us like they owned us. Even though most was gentle, most wanted just to reach out to another human being; they paid for us and expected their payin' to get 'em somethin'. It had been a cruel life constant with reparations. It abhorred my soul to even consider. I wasn't goin' back, not even in name.

If word got out, others would wait, just like Jeremiah done. They'd watch me, demand entry to my own home. They'd demand mastery of body, my wants and desires and ultimately my soul. It filled me with such a dread I could barely speak. Jedediah gently rubbed my hand.

"Now, you know, Ruth. I ain't goin' tell anyone about nothin'. Ain't no reason to. Why don't ya come here." He gently pulled me closer.

I stepped closer. I'd missed this man more than I liked to admit. Here he was, arms wide open in my own home after he saved me from a very real possibility of hangin'. Maybe I owed him love. Maybe I wanted love. He stood as I came in closer and took me in close. He wrapped strong arms around me, warmin' my body. He put his mouth on mine and forced his tongue into my mouth. I pushed him away.

"Get out." My voice was hoarse. I wasn't sure I was right. I wasn't sure what I wanted just now. I needed to think. And I sure as hell couldn't do that with his arms around me and tongue down my throat.

For just a moment, he tightened his grip. Then he dropped his eyes to the ground and stepped away. It nearly broke my heart when I saw how sad he was. His face was drawn and his eyes lst all sparkle. Before he left, he turned and spoke briefly.

"Ruth. I never cared what ya done. I didn't like it because it meant we couldn't be together. But I never thought of you as just some whore. Ya moved to this town, why I could hardly believe it. The prettiest girl I ever saw was here, so close. I ain't sure what's wrong just now, but I'll leave. I just thought we had more between us than the money. That's all." And he left.

I did everything normal the next couple of days. I tried not think of Jeremiah or where he ended up. I cleaned up the blood best I could. I tried not to think too much of Jedidiah. I hadn't seen him once since he left that day either.

It didn't surprise me much, really. This was a quiet place, folks kept themselves to themselves. They was happy to live quiet lives, happy to go about their business makin' no troubles. I liked it that way, that's why I was stayin'. Just knowin' Jedidiah was so close destroyed some of the happiness and peace I'd been feelin'. How strange our feelin's for others make our lives.

Nothin' changed my life knowin' Jedediah was near or not. I was still on my own. I was still on my own. My nights were still alone. Each mealtime was on my own. No one was demandin' a thing from me. The very idea that brought so much peace just a week prior was now hauntin' me just a little.

I went through the events of that mornin' over and again. Jeremiah bargin' right in the door. Mildred and Joe helpin' and takin' me in like we was kin. Seein' Jedediah. I shook my head. "Seein' Jedidiah. You couldn't stand nor talk when you saw him. Then, you told him to leave." That horrible critical voice deep inside all of us chided me.

"Why did I make him leave?" I wondered over and over. The answer wasn't easy. I found I was restless so I walked up to the store to say hello to Mildred, perhaps take her some tea and see if she wanted to talk awhile. I needed to hear someone else besides that voice askin' what the hell I was thinkin'. After all, it was me who sought solitude. It was me who whacked Jeremiah over the head.

And it was me who demanded Jedidiah leave.

Some things can't be undone no matter how long it takes us to accept the consequences. Finally, that thought ended the voices of my makin' in my own head. I left the house.

It was a nice day I noticed. Perfect weather, not hot but not cold. The short was pleasant. Birds was singin' and bees a buzzin'. The sun shone warmin' my shoulders. I breathed in deeply feelin' both lucky and blessed. What a lovely reprieve!

I entered the shop and found myself surprised and relieved at Mildred's enthusiasm to see me.

"Ruth! I was fixing on coming on over today. I told myself when I woke up this morning I was going to and look at this! Here you come to see me!" She came around the counter and hugged me. I surprised myself when I hugged her back.

Genuine human contact did something to my soul. Images of my parents flashed through my mind. When I first went to work for Evans, Sue watched over me and held me through the toughest nights. The night I lost my baby and the girls held me as I cried through it. Jedediah warmin' me in his strong arms. I wiped a tear from my cheek and stepped back. Mildred pretended not to notice turning towards the door that led to her kitchen.

"Come on, Ruth. I'll put on the tea."

She readied the tea and thanked me for sharin' what I brought. I nodded and settled into the same chair I'd occupied those few days before.

"How have you been?" She asked placing her fine set on the table.

"Well I can't say I been over-good. But I ain't been over-bad neither."

She laughed a little.

I went on. "I guess I shouldn't talk bad because nothin' has been bad." I stopped to catch up with my thoughts, she was a patient listener and allowin' me the time to collect my thoughts. I wasn't sure how much I wanted to share after all years of quietly guardin' myself, I knew I didn't want to overshare but I needed to talk with someone.

"Nothin' been bad. I just got so used to bein' on my own. I been in that house for a few months now, really makin' it my home. Truth be told Mildred, it's been my only home in a long time so I worked real hard to find peace in that little space. Jere- that man, the one that surprised me the other day. I guess he broke that peace." It felt so good finally tell someone else some of the thoughts floatin' around inside. I hoped this released them.

Mildred nodded sympathetically, "I know. I know, Ruth. I told you my own story the other day. These things, they change the way we see the world a little. It takes away some of our light for a while." She reached for my hand and patted it a few times. She thought I was talkin' about the unwanted attentions from a man. Even though that was only a little part of what was troublin' my mind, it was wonderful to have her feminine empathy.

I nodded and continued, "I love my home still. I feel safe. At least, most times I feel safe. Joe and that sheriff-

She interrupted, "Jedediah? He's not the sheriff. Only the law 'round here. But he's not the sheriff."

"Well, whatever his proper title, I think him and Joe handled it all real fine. It was fair. I think it was fair."

"You know this isn't a state, not yet. Territories are different. Why, I just heard of a massacre some months back on some Chinese. No one even hanged for it. My point is things are done different here because they have to be done different. Sometimes they get it wrong. Those poor Chinese even had to clean up the damages to their little Chinatown. I can't say that is right. This time though, they got it right. Your safety was compromised." Mildred spoke firm.

We drank the rest of our tea in silence and I went on home. She hugged me again before I left, and I knew I had a true friend when I hugged her back. I walked home noticin' the day was gettin' warmer and decided to work in my little garden. I had a few early summer blooms and vegetables needed tendin'.

I let myself in the house and then out to the garden. The day had warmed. I was workin' pretty hard and it didn't take long before my back was wet. I stopped to catch my breath and leaned on the garden hoe a little.

My garden was growing beautifully. Each plant was gettin' larger by the day and the flowers surroundin' the space were fillin' in and bloomin'. It was a right peaceful spot to be despite the work callin' my attentions. I admired the space awhile until I heard someone behind me. Someone was clearin' their throat.

Jedediah was standin' at the gate. He tipped his hat.

"Afternoon, Ms. Ruth. I only stopped by to tell ya Jeremiah's body been found. Looks like he was eaten by some wild animal. They buried him in the church yard no marker since no one seems to know his name. I thought I'd ask ya what ya thought about that and if ya might want his name recorded. 'Course, then they might go askin' questions and I realize that might mean troubles come yer way." He straightened his back and finally looked into my eyes. His professional demeanor changed, just the slightest. His face became drawn and shoulders slumped until he took a deep breath and righted himself.

I shook my head. "I can't risk it. I suppose if you find a way to mark it without namin' me in any way, that'd be alright."

He nodded and turned to leave.

"Jedediah, wait. Please." My voice was soft. He stopped but didn't turn back 'round neither. I cleared my own throat, "Jedediah, I am sorry for askin' ya to go. It's just. Well. I can't right explain. I don't feel too sure your attentions. I been workin' hard to make this place my home. Then, Jeremiah came by and then, there you were. I didn't even know ya was in this town. I can't pretend it ain't nice but I just…" My voice faded away.

I just what? I didn't know. I wasn't sure what to say next. I wanted to ask him what he really thought of me, if he was lookin' to sleep with me then leave me. I wanted to know if he thought of me as Ruth the Whore or Ruth the Young Woman on her own. I just couldn't gussy up enough courage to ask all those questions. He refused to turn around.

He refused to answer. Just gave a nod and walked on leavin' me standin' in my garden in the sunshine.

I never experienced heartbreak for man before. As he walked away, though, I knew that's what was happenin'. My heart wanted to scream out beggin' him to stay. I wanted to throw my arms around him and hold on until he turned back 'round.

I just stood and watched him go. Then I turned back to my garden and day's work.

It only took a couple days that I left my little house in search of company. I was restless and in need of friend. I walked up to see Mildred that afternoon. Once again, the day was near perfect. Warm sun drenched the earth around me feeding the fragile summer plants and trees. I decided it was a right-pretty day and pushed all thoughts of heartbreak as far from my mind as possible. I'd ruined it with Jedediah and refused to dwell on it any longer.

I took my time walkin' up to her store almost absent mindedly makin' my way payin' no attentions to a gatherin' thunderstorm. When I finally looked up due the shortage of sunshine, I realized I was goin' to be caught in what promised to be a good but hopefully short rain.

I stopped and took a good look 'round. I'd actually walked far past my original destination in my desire to close off my own desire it seems I'd also shut off part of my brain. I sighed and looked around for a place I might shelter as the first fat drops of cold rain hit my head and face. A tall-standin' pine promised at least some protection from the wet. I ducked under some of the low-swingin' branches prayin' the lightenin' wouldn't strike too close. This land invited strong, violent storms that had an unpredictability that could be dangerous.

The storm let loose just as I made it into my chosen shelter. The rain drummed out with such a force it splashed against earth only to splatter up into my face. I heard a small squeak and looked to my right. A small blue bird shared my shelter, watchin' the rain beside me. If I had my choice, I doubt I would have chosen such shelter-mate but he was mostly quiet and not too inquisitive about me.

"Perhaps he wouldn't have chosen me either," I mused aloud.

The rain grew stronger and wind more violent shaking our tree. Thunder and lightening surrounded us with near-deafening crashes; what with the wind and the thunder the storm drowned out any and all other sounds. Soon, the branches of most trees bent heavy with their load of water causin' my little friend to hop frequently in search of a dry branch. I watched him for a moment trying to calm my heart hopin' the storm would soon end.

Odd for that land, the storm lasted. I watched and waited and even the small blue bird ceased his frequent hoppin'. A soft voice behind me caused me, and the bird, to jump. The rain drowned out all sound, I hadn't heard Jedediah step in behind me.

Without a word, he put his arms 'round me and pulled me in close. He kissed my forehead, then neck and finally, my mouth. His hands found my back and down my front. He reached for my breasts and groped until I doubted I'd ever stop feelin' his hands on me. "Ruth," he whispered.

Then kissed me not allowin' me to say anythin'. His hands did all the work and I was surprised to find how excited I was at feelin' his hard desire against me. In all the months since I'd entertained any man, I hardly missed the proddin' that came with what they paid. This was different though. I was out of breath, lettin' Jedediah explore as he wished. I can't say how long we was under the tree like that but the rain ended before we stepped out.

I smoothed my clothes and he straightened his hat and we kept a discreet distance between us.

"Where was ya headed in such a storm, Ms. Ruth?" He asked.

"I was goin' up to the store, it's such a nice day, I thought I might take a cold drink with Mildred before dinner-time." I pointed back towards the store.

"Well, looks like you missed the store just same as you missed all the signs of the comin' storm. I can walk ya there if you'd like." His offer was genuine. He was lookin' me straight in the eye and offered his arm. We walked the rest of the way in silence and he bade a short, "Good day, Ms. Ruth," at the door. I watched him leave; I watched him a long minute.

I stumbled in, shocked at all that just transpired and wet to the bone. The tree wasn't that great a shelter. I closed the door behind me and watched him retreat the way we came. Never before had a man kissed me like that, then left without finishin' what he started. I was breathless.

"Ruth! Why look at you! What are you doing walking out in this?" Mildred came rushing over and helped me into her kitchen. "Here, we got to get you dry, girl. You can't go around like that!" She helped me out of that heavy wet dress and wrapped me in a dry blanket. Then, she worked on dryin' my hair.

"Aw, Mildred. Ya just don't gotta do all that, I was just lookin' for a short visit and the rain snuck up on me."

"Call me Millie, Ruth. And this is the best time to "do all that". You look a fright! That dress muddy, wet and too heavy to walk home. You are just going to have to borrow something to get you home." She laughed. "Why when you opened up that door, I couldn't even make out it was you! I thought I'd seen two people, turns out it was just you caught up in the worse storm of the year!"

"Well, Jedediah walked me over here. Well, he walked me part way." I told her.

She stopped putting the tea together and turned around. "Really? You say Jedediah walked you over here? I guess you run into him out that rain? Well, what are the chances both of you would make such a mistake on going out in this!"

I'd been right in thinkin' I needed a friend that day. Mildred hung my dress near the unlit hearth and offered me one to get me home. Once I was dressed she sat me down and we talked proper about all the things that didn't really matter to either of us.

"So tragic, Ruth. You hear about that woman, oh, I guess a hundred miles or so from here? Well, she was a young thing moved out here with her new husband. He was wanting to live in the wild west and promised her a fine, quiet place they might raise their family. Tragic." She shook her head a little. "Well, I guess he built them a lean-to and they survived the winter. She had the baby about six or so weeks after Christmas, all on her own."

I shuddered. Even losin' my own baby had been painful. My womb cramped like nothin' and I suffered only a fraction what she must have.

"Well, I hate to say on her own, he was there and helped. Still." Millie shook her head again. "I guess they was happy enough together, though. That's what everyone's sayin' at least. He treated her real good and she smiled at him like so many young girls do. Well, just a few weeks ago, I guess they was attacked. It isn't a real surprise, they lived way out there on there own like that. They say four braves entered the house just before dawn. They murdered him and scalped him, raped her and killed the baby. Then, they took what food they could find and left her."

I was shocked. Even with the violence I'd grown up with, I was shocked. "They left her without food all on her own out there?" It was cruel to think of a woman alone in such a desperate place.

"Oh yes, they left her with the bodies. I guess she dragged them into her bed and for some reason a trapper decided to check on her. He found her inside, talking away to her dead husband and tryin' to feed the baby." Millie brushed a tear from her cheek. I didn't know what to say.

"He buried the bodies, the whole time she was screamin' at him. He had to drag her away. He brought her here, to see the doctor but she ran away. They think she made her way back to her cabin. That same trapper, well he came back through after and said he could hear her shouting and singing all hours of the day, all on her own out there." She paused. "God, I hope she left those bodies in the ground."

I left not long after our talk. Millie's story cut me to the core of my soul. The Devil always gets his pay out here. The young happy couple owed in the end. He with his life and her with her sanity. The devil of that desert cared little and demanded much. Even their baby paid with his life.

I made my way home, went inside ready to bathe and do my wash.

I didn't see Jedediah for several days and began wondering if our time under that tree was nothing more than a dream. I visited Millie often always hopin' to see him but was always disappointed. I worked on my garden, I worked on my salves that were sellin' so well in the shop and I spent my nights alone.

Summer was hot that year. I couldn't recall a summer so hot in recent years. I opened up my house windows each night, just waitin' for nightfall and temperatures to drop. It was too hot for blankets and one night I decided it was too hot for a night dress. Thankfully, the temperature dropped around nightfall and clouds gathered hintin' at rain.

I let the cool night air dance over my body, till my flesh was covered in the goose pimples and nipples were hardened. It was such a reprieve from the hot day, I dare not sleep afraid to waste such a treat. No rain appeared but a mighty wind kicked up that blew the curtains straight up over the rod, so I rose to fix 'em. I wouldn't want the mornin' sun to be shinin' in my eyes. I didn't bother to dress or even throw a shawl over myself, I was alone and the cool night air was too nice to hide behind a shawl or robe.

I made my way to the window and reached high above my head to draw the curtains down when a faint voice cut through the darkness.

"Ruth, I can't keep way. I miss ya."

Jedediah was out there.

I paused tryin' to see him but the dark proved to heavy to make him out. He could see me, though. I knew I was quite a sight, illuminated only faint by the one light I'd left burnin' on the bedside table. I paused, wonderin' how I wanted to answer.

Did I want a man, even Jedediah, invadin' this space? It was hard to say. I'd spent all these days thinkin' on him, missin' him; here he was in the flesh. It was time to decide. Did I allow him into the sacred space I'd created? I looked around. This was mine. All mine. Did I want to share it?

I stood at the window and looked into the darkness. It didn't take long.

I walked to the door and opened it, invitin' Jedediah inside.

"I am so lonely, so lonely," I whispered. He took me in his strong arms and held me tight against him. I felt myself falling more than I ever dared.

I sobbed against him and he held me up, taking all the weight from my past letting it spill against his chest. He never hurried me, never shushed me. When I finally finished, he undressed.

He removed one boot at a time never breaking eye contact. He unbuttoned his shirt, then his trousers. He took off his underwear, revealing his hardened penis. Then he walked to me and picked me up. He kissed me while carrying me to the bed.

He held me all night long. Hard or not, he did what I needed. He pulled me close to him. The cool night danced over our bodies, but he kept me warm the whole night through. He fell asleep before I. I listened to him breathin' a long time, no longer lonely finally noddin' off into a dreamless sleep. I guess there was no need for dreams, I was in the arms a good, strong man holdin' me, ignorin' his own desires demandin' nothin'.

We slept late the followin' mornin'. I woke in the same position I'd fallen asleep and so did he. The sun finally woke us, it was much higher than I normally woke to but we was in no hurry. Jedediah's grip tightened on my arm and he pulled me right on top of him. I grinned down at him from my perch.

"Did you ever go soft, Jedediah? Or were hard all night long, waitin'?" I took that hardness in both hands, leanin' back just a little and held it for just a minute.

"Don't wait too long, Ruth, I can't take it. I been waitin' a long time for ya." He murmured reachin' up to hold both breasts. Keepin' his right hand busy, he reached around my back, pullin' me down letting my left nipple land a little rough in his mouth. I arched my back, right over the top of him, teasin' the end a little. I rocked real slow, back and forth wettin' him.

When I was sure he couldn't take no more, I thrust my hips down, takin' all him at once, deep inside me. He laid back, lettin' me ride him hard, and groaned just a little. I reached down guidin' his hand to the front of me leanin' onto his hand. It was my turn to groan a little.

"Ruth. God damn." He took my shoulders in hands and rolled me to the right, turnin' me over onto my stomach. He pushed into me harder and harder till I couldn't hold myself up any longer. He held me tight onto him with one hand on my shoulder and the other my hip. I cried out when I thought I couldn't take anymore but he held on till he was spent, and laid back beside me, breathin' hard. I stayed on my belly, warm and relaxed, sleepin' next to this man I loved.

We stayed that way most of the day. No chores or folks called us from our love nest. We slept made love and slept some more. We spent the next day the exact same. And the next.

I felt as if I could spend the rest of my life like that, safe and warm and loved in a small space just big enough for us two. Jedediah gently told me he had responsibilities to attend the day after though. I watched him dress.

We'd shared a simple breakfast and I'd gone back to the bed we'd mostly occupied the last days. I would wash the lines after he left, I thought briefly before he leaned down to kiss me. I held on, makin' him laugh a little.

"Be honest, you need a break from all this as much as I need to go." He gently touched me between my legs, makin' me gasp just a little. "You rest awhile, I promise I'll come back. Don't expect me before dark, though. I ain't done much for the past few days, there's sure to be some trouble or somethin' folks will be needin'. I like this place, most folks just want to get on with their lives, not causin' trouble with no one. Still, there's bound to be somethin' between the sheep and cattle folks or the Jones' pickin' on the Smiths. I'll see ya later." He kissed my forehead and left.

I stayed on the bed awhile longer, just feelin' the memory of touch and love thinkin' of all I should be doin'. My mind kept re-livin' the last few days, though. It was absolutely lovely to share time and space with someone the way we was. It didn't involve money or schedules; just bein' together. We ate when was hungry, we slept when we was tired and talked if we wanted.

I was seein' Jedidiah was a quiet man to most but in here, he talked a lot about his work and his days. He said he liked workin' law and helpin' keep a peace that helped so many. He talked how his dad worked it when he was growin' up in Kansas. His ma never liked it and worried over his safety. His parents never saw him work the same, they both died when he was in his teens.

I looked around and decided all my thinkin' wasn't really gettin' anything done. I got up from the bed, collected the wash and began the day's work. I scrubbed and cleaned through most the day, happy with the results of my hard work. Before long, my small home looked just as it did before Jedediah's stay. As I worked, I wondered what his own home was like.

Tidying up I realized I did not want to leave this space. I wasn't sure what that might mean, did Jedidiah like it here? I laughed at loud at my own girlish planning. It was four days nothing more. Or it might be more but we hadn't mentioned the future at all during any of these hours spent so frivolously on love-making. The truth may well be, there was no future. There may just be him and I and the occasional night until he found someone else. And with those thoughts, I set my jaw and walked up to the store, the last four days may mean nothin'.

CHAPTER 21

I needed some goods and if I was honest with myself, I was right lonely after those days with Jedediah. I wasn't ready to be over-honest with myself, though so I sought the distractions of Millie.

"Ruth!," She greeted me enthusiastically, "I have news! I am so glad you stopped in today! I was going to walk right up to your place if you hadn't. I nearly did yesterday!" I briefly wondered what she would have thought if she *had* walked up yesterday only to find Jedediah and laced together on the bed. I decided to pick up some extra linen to cover the small windows at the back of my house; I could care about that now, even if Jedidiah and I were only together here and there.

"Ruth, I have news, come back here and have some tea." Millie was absolutely glowin' with happiness. It was somethin' about her. It felt warmer just bein' next to her, her happiness spille from her fillin' up the room. I watched her for a moment and knew before she even spoke, what she was goin' to say. I steeled myself for her next words but we was interrupted Joe.

He come in and kissed her forehead, eyes shinin', "How are you, Millie-girl?" he whispered, though I could hear him, I pretended otherwise. My heart dropped a little more as I watched them together. He took her by the hand and stroked her back a little, "Do you need to rest? Yesterday, you got real tired, if you need to rest, go on. I can take the shop." She grinned at him.

"Stop, Joe. I am good, you go on and get the shop anyways, Ruth come by for a visit." She waved him out promisin' "I am fine, I can rest and talk with her." She laughed a little and turned to me, "truth be told, I am still going to be tired. Ruth, I told you I have some news. I can't believe it, and I know we talked before. Some miracle happened." She put her hands on her belly and I set my jaw, just a little, steelin' my nerves for one more let-down but I smiled warmly at her. After all, how couldn't I be happy for this wonderful woman I called friend? Even though our lives would always be different, even though I could never experience all her happiness, she was generous to share this with me and I was grateful.

I stood and went to her, takin' her hands in mine, "Why it is wonderful, Millie, when do you think you will have her?" The words just tumbled from me. She hadn't shared her *exact* news, but only a fool would miss the signs. I was unsure why I called the baby her, other than it felt like a girl.

"Oh, Ruth. I'd given up hope long ago. I never thought Joe and I would share this. I will have the baby, of course, we can't know if we will have a boy or girl just yet, sometime before Christmas. Right before Christmas. The past weeks ain't been real easy, days I was sick in the morning. You probably never saw me, if you had, you would have guessed, you have such strong intuitions. That part is easin' up though. I just thought I was ill, blamed the food, blamed the water. One day, I blamed Joe. I had to sit down and think it through. We have a wonderful mid-wife right here, and she helped answer some of my questions. Can you believe it, Ruth? I'll be a mama before the year is out." She wiped a tear from her cheek and smiled again.

I didn't stay over-long. Truth was, she did look as if she needed a rest and I ran out of things to talk about. I bought the few things I was needin', even remembered to ask after the linen for my windows. There was some real nice, soft calico I admired for a few minutes. It was perfect for a baby blanket, and havin' the little dear right before Christmas, she was goin' to be needin' some warm things. I didn't buy it though, I just couldn't make myself pick it up, at least not today. I paid Joe for my few things and left.

Walkin' myself home, I was sure happy Jedediah said he'd be back again this evenin'. Even if it were after dark, even if I was a might sore, I could use the company. I kicked at a stone and ambled up the road, takin' my time. I was in no rush it was just me after all.

"Just me," echoed around my mind. I'd told myself it was no matter and I even liked livin' on my own these past months. Things change though. My God, how things change.

A few months ago, not even a year, I was whorin' to any payin' man. Now, I had my own place, my own life and even a friend. I was makin' money too. I was content.

Then came along Jedidiah. Things change. I could allow the change and I could give space for someone else. Hell, did it matter if things change? They always do. Maybe now was the time to allow the biggest change of all, let my guard for love down some and see what happens. I walked home thinkin' it was time for another change and I was fixin' on makin' sure I was ready for change.

I needed to feel excitement again. I needed to allow some love in without fearing it would be taken. As I approached my little home, I breathed in deep and went inside. It wasn't enough to want or even to build a new life. I wanted a life worth livin'.

I fixed a simple dinner and took down the now-dry wash. The space was warm perfect for invitin' any good man so I waited for the sun to set. Jedediah said he would be back then.

Except he wasn't.

The next few days were some of the loneliest I ever experienced. I didn't feel like sharin' Millie and Joe's unbridled joy for their bundle of joy. I didn't know how to find Jedidiah and was too used to stayin' away from law buildin's to go any where near there.

"Who knew what I might find?" I reminded myself over and again. I never really asked about his past, and he knew mine. I didn't know him, after all. I felt so stupid for lettin' my feelin's get the better of me knowin' life just don't work out for us all, all the time.

Four days of solitude and I was about to give up on ever holdin' much of a conversation with any human ever again. It seemed the devil still expected his dues though I'd paid so dearly all those years. It was near unbearable to think of my future. I'd dared hope, not even askin' for the things most folks wanted. I would never own this little house. I would never have children. I didn't even dare hope Jedediah would marry me in some happy ceremony. All I'd dared hope was to share this space with him and live out my days in relative quiet.

It hurt. I'd come so far, done so much and every day he didn't come by felt like an eternity. Knowin' Millie and Joe were expectin' only rubbed salt in those old open wounds. I wasn't proper jealous. It only served a reminder of who I was, even if I weren't her no more, I still *was* her. And sometimes, the past matters. I couldn't run from it, I'd tried hidin' it when Jeremiah found me. Then, Jedediah found me. And just like the past, I'd let him in with little thought of how long that might last. A true whore.

I forced myself out of the house that fourth day. I walked a long ways, down by the river. The water runnin' sounded good. I noticed it only ran one way never circlin' back. Strange, time was like that but time carried the banks it had visited and the river left those behind. I envied the river, that way. It was hard to leave banks of memory behind. I sat and watched a particular rough patch of water awhile. Soon, I was distracted by a tall, lean bird at the edge of the bank opposite me.

A crane was watchin' me real intent-like. He didn't move, his body nor his head, just blinked his eyes keepin' his gave right on me. He didn't make a sound but I felt he wanted me to see him. I ain't a true worshipper of much but watchin' him carry on his life without too much worry made me wonder. I wondered at the majesty of such a creature. He was well dressed in beautiful feathers that kept him warm and dry from the river in which he hunted his meals. They was plentiful, I could tell. He didn't hurry his day away with chores nor plannin'. He just walked about, lookin' for opportunity somehow knowin' it would come his way.

I thought of all those poor Chinese lost nearing one year ago. I wondered if the little Chinese woman who shared with me the crane wisdom made it out with her life. I recalled how she looked that day we spoke. She was small, with little features common to her people. Hair black as night. I vividly recalled her attempts at bein' friendly and I knew then, she hadn't made it. She was too good for this world. Perhaps this crane was part of her spirit, lookin' out for troubled souls on this river bank, guidin' 'em as best and simply just as she'd done.

I was surprised to feel my face wet with tears. I cried awhile, recallin' those terrible days leadin' up to that awful September mornin' and of course, the mornin' itself. I felt a bit selfish after awhile.

Here I was, sittin' cryin' over folks who were forever gone. Yet, none of us is promised tomorrow. I'd been wastin' days, precious days wonderin' what was wrong with me or a past that was long gone. I got up and brushed off.

The past was long gone. And I was done wastin' days I'd been given. I set off for the law building, sending a silent thanks to the crane bringin' me luck.

It was empty.

Jedediah stayed gone. I finally worked up the courage to as Joe and Millie after him, at which they gave each other knowin' looks and answered negative.

"Truth be told, Ruth, there are a few folks missin' from town these days. I ain't seen Jedediah nor the James' for, let's see, at least a week." Joe answered but seemed to noticc my displeasure. "I tell you what, as soon as I hear from him, I'll send him your way or notify you. Alright?" I nodded a thanks and bid them a good day.

Walkin' home, I worried more about the welfare of Jedediah than the mere girlish worries he might not like me anymore. Two days later Joe and Millie showed up at my front door. Their faces were grave but I forced myself to answer their knock all the while tellin' myself it was worse not knowin'. Though her face was serious, I couldn't help but takin' notice Millie was absolutely glowin'. Her cheeks flushed pink with their walk and her middle startin' to show, I complimented her as I invited 'em inside.

"Why, Millie, you look radiant!" I said warmly.

"Thank you, Ruth, I finally am over that awful sickness and sure feel better. The baby is moving around day and night, I can feel it all the time!" Her eyes shone with this news but Joe remained serious.

He offered the chair to his wife and took my hand in his, "Now, Ruth. I told you we would let you know as soon as we got word of the whereabouts of these townfolks. I hate to tell you but it ain't over good news." He took a handkerchief and wiped his brow. "The James', well they is dead. They was found, in their own home, lyin' dead for lord knows how many days but we expect about a week. Every one of 'em. Jedediah is alright," he answered my question before I even said it aloud. "They say the small pox is back. Jedediah got held up the next town over, tryin' to clean up the dead and keep the order over there. Ruth. A lot of folks are sick. Real sick. And they are dyin'."

My heart sank at this news. Small pox was bad. I recalled a few years back how it ravaged a nearby Indian village. Nearly every individual in that place died of fever. The few who lasted ended up gettin' it anyways and dyin' all alone at the end.

Millie was talkin' again, "We need a plan for our town, Ruth. Joe and I been talking about shutting it down for a little while. Turning folks away and keeping our shop closed. We talked to the saloon and though he wasn't excited about losing money, he didn't want to catch this either. Ruth, if we shut the town down, we are going to keep everyone out, no matter who they are to keep this from spreading. If they ain't here by sundown tomorrow, they are gonna have to wait to come home." She rubbed my hand tryin' to comfort me a little.

Her words, no matter how kindly said, reverberated throughout my brain. Sundown tomorrow was less than a day away and no real way to get a message through meant it highly unlikely Jedediah would make it home in time.

"You say the James family was found dead? Are you tellin' me this is already here and we just didn't know?" I tried to still a growing feeling of panic, this silent killer was amongst, us and we didn't even know. "So, we keep folks out who might be ill, might be showin' signs of their impending death but it if is here already…" my voice faded away. I didn't need to finish.

If the smallpox was here already, our little town was in true danger. No cure was known. Folks who got ill were often shunned left to fight off the illness on their own. Fever would overtake 'em leavin' most thirstin' for water and any food they could hold down. Some got lucky and survived only the scars left behind showed their sufferin'. Many died.

Once again, the unfairness and unjustness of life hit me hard. Here I was safe, on my own finally finding happiness that I'd hardly dare wish for just a year ago only to face an unseen killer. It might take my life. It might take Jedediah's, only time would tell.

Joe and Millie invited me to walk back with them to get what supplies I might need for the next weeks on my own. I accepted and we walked in silence. A few folks was waitin' on their return; it looked like news had spread and they were doin' just as I was. Upon our entrance one man nearly knocked Millie to the ground in his haste to retrieve his goods. Joe cautioned him to slow down.

"Easy, brother. We are all in want and need in these desperate times. There is time enough to gather what you are looking for and there is plenty to go around." His voice lowered, just noticeably and he leaned towards the man, "Now, you watch it, or you will leave with nothing." Then he turned to the rest of the small crowd. "Listen up! There are plenty of goods for us all. I implore you to shop in a Christian manner. Your neighbors are also in want." And he took his post behind his counter with his wife.

I paid for my own frugal share determined to make it last as long as possible. As I was leavin' I noticed the shelf which held my own salves that was so helpful in relievin' so many skin ailments and softenin' the hands and face. I wondered if it would sell at all now. Surely, most folks might see it as a nicety instead of a necessity. What little income I had enjoyed was surely in jeopardy. There was nothin' more to do and I couldn't change these circumstances so I left the store after waving farewell to Millie and Joe wonderin' when I might see them again.

The walk home felt empty. No one was waitin' on me. I faced a sure shortage of supplies and no income. I was already at risk as were the only folks I knew. I wondered how long it would last, how many days we was facin' on our own. No answers came.

I struggled to keep my mind at ease over the next lonely days. I was in constant awe at how well I'd navigated lvin' on my own so happily and contentedly in the months prior only to find myself at my wits end facin' this loneliness. Days were the same over and again makin' it real difficult to keep any sort of normalcy. I'd wake to a small breakfast and clean myself and place up. The place was so clean I felt one might eat off any surface as well as any dish. I kept up my small garden and continued makin' the salve though I had no customers. Every afternoon, I rested only to face a more restless night. Soon, I'd lost count of just how many days I'd lived in such isolation. No news, no messages, no encounters of any kind plagued my days.

I tried comfortin' myself with the fact I'd had no symptoms of the smallpox. I surely would not get it. When I felt relief at this, my mind only turned to those who might have got it and I'd have no way of knowin'. Most times I worried over Jedediah.

CHAPTER 22

Our last words were kind and those four days seemed unreal. I tried allowin' my mind to rest on those days wrapped in his arms, in the very bed I was so alone in now but my mind struggled against it. I missed Millie too and was keen aware how much of her pregnancy I was missin'. The next time I'd see her she would be bigger. I could almost see Joe holdin' her gently throughout the days and nights, rubbin' her back against her aching muscles with her growin' belly. Thinkin' on those two only made me lonelier so I'd force myself to stop. The summer grew into late summer and the days hotter and dryer. I wasn't lookin' forward to the winter we was assured was comin' so I tried to enjoy my little garden despite the heat.

Finally, after I don't know how many days, I could no longer take the isolation. I needed news. I needed to know how or if Jedidiah was farin'. I needed to talk with someone, so I gathered most the salve and made my way to the general store. I wasn't surprised to see the door closed so I went to the back of the building, to their kitchen and hammered on the door. No one came. I looked up towards their bedroom window and knocked again. Then I shouted.

"Millie! Joe! Its me, Ruth. I brought some salve for your shelves. What news do you have for me?" I waited a moment and tried again,

"Millie! Joe!" Finally, I heard a key turn from the inside unlockin' the door. Joe stood there.

"Joe! Why I am relieved to see you standin' in front of me. I couldn't take another moment on my own, so I brought this over and thought I would hear what news you have. Where's Millie?" I glanced behind him, expectin' to see her wavin' me inside. Joe didn't answer but moved aside a little allowin' my entrance. I entered and called for Millie again.

"Ain't no use, Ruth. She ain't here." I looked at him closely, Joe looked drawn, weak as if he'd lost weight. His eyes was tired and had great circles beneath him, even the lines on his face had deepened.

"Well, where is she? I could use a friend." I was more talkative than I'd ever been in my life, which surprised me but Joe took no notice.

"Ruth, she ain't here. She won't be back." And two tears ran down his face. I looked close at the man standin' before me and noticed fresh pock marks for the first time. I took an involuntary step back.

"She ain't here. Ruth, she died. Near seven days ago. We got sick about the same day. I was real bad from the start. The fever and chills had me shakin' day and night. At first, she didn't seem so bad. She got more marks but didn't seem to have the other symptoms so bad. She nursed me all the way through. As I came through the final day or so of fever, she took to our bed sayin' she just didn't feel well. Said she was just overtired from caring for me through that night. I believed her so I let her sleep." He drew in a sharp breath and his shoulders shook with sobs. I was backed up, far away as I could get in that small entrance, tryin' not to breath the air from that sick-house deep in my lungs. A dread filled my heart knowin' his next words.

"I came back after awhile. I was surprised she hadn't been up tellin' me what we was gonna have for dinner. She was just like I'd left her, turned on her side, she said her belly was more comfortable that way. I called and she took no notice so I called her name again. When I went to the bed and rolled her over, she was gone. I could tell. Her eyes was wide open, her face already grey. I didn't even know she was that sick. I left her, there in our bed all the rest of that day. And the next. I couldn't bear to take her anywhere." His shoulders was heavin' again but I made no move towards him, still afraid to touch him. My hand was over my mouth tryin' to not see what he'd seen, his dead pregnant wife alone in their bed for too many hours. He went on.

"I finally come to my senses and knew I had to move her. It was gettin' bad so I decided to keep the linens on her and try to carry her out that way." He got a far away look to his eyes, seein' the past and took a deep breath before he went on. "It was bad, Ruth," he said lookin' right in my eyes. "I never seen nor heard nothin' like it before. I tried cleanin' her up a bit, you know. I thought she should be buried in a clean dress at the least. So I rolled her over and removed her skirt." Again, he had to stop talkin' to compose himself. I knew he needed comfort but I couldn't make myself lay even a finger on his arm. I just watched, mortified at his next words.

"I took the skirt down and there was the baby comin' out of her. Just the head. I didn't even know. I'd just let her lay there, dead like that. There wasn't much blood, but the baby was dead too. I tried, but I couldn't pull it out the rest of the way. I just left her like that, the baby stuck that way and wrapped her in the linens. Then I picked her up and buried her over yonder near the church yard." He beckoned the general direction with a quick nod of his head. "I tried askin' the good Lord if I was to bury her inside the church yard, if that might matter on that last day. He didn't answer." He shook his head a little, eyes hardenin', "Can't say I was surprised at his silence, I'd asked him to release her from that awful death and no answer came then, neither. Out here, we all pay the devil his due and I guess God just figured I still was in that debt. Millie wasn't though. Neither was the baby. Anyways, they don't rest inside the yard but near enough it. I prayed over it as I dug the earth. There ain't no box. The old Swede, the man that normal builds all those, he's dead too. I just kept her wrapped up and assured her face was covered and filled in the hole."

He stopped cryin', maybe relieved at havin' told his awful nightmare but I took no comfort in these facts. His eyes were less wild but mine were widened in a sickened disbelief. Not only had I exposed myself to this house, I'd lost one of the only true friends I ever had. I'd envied her growin' belly and the life she held within only to find it dead too. I had to get out of there. Joe was still talkin', asking if I wanted to visit where she lay. I couldn't answer and pushed my way past him right out the door.

Gaspin' for fresh air, I sought to cleanse myself of the virus has soon as possible. I nearly began undressin' myself before I even reached my own front door. I wondered if I should burn my own clothes, if I should seek medicine of some kind but all I really could do was bathe myself as best I could; I threw my outer clothes out the window and wrapped myself in a robe. I tried to still my beatin' heart and finally turned my fear towards grief.

"Millie is dead." I said the words aloud to my empty house. "She dead and ain't comin' back." No answer came. "Her baby is dead too." No tears came but I recalled each generous conversation I ever held with that fine woman.

I always knew she somehow knew more about my past than she let on; it was apparent in the ways she shared her own story. She never showed me cruelty, though and I expect, she treated most folks in that same carin' matter. She'd loved her baby thought it's time to enter the world hadn't yet come, she loved it with all her heart. Our town lost its saint.

I slept after my cleanin' and bathin' and grievin'. To my surprise, I slept the whole night through and woke to a bright sun glarin' through my open curtains. I slowly sat up; I think I was expectin' to feel ill or dizzy. I was just fine, though. I rubbed my eyes and looked over my little house. Then, I got up and went about my mornin' like usual.

My basket still held the salve. I tried ignorin' it though it sat in plain view no matter where I stood. Finally, I took it up and did what needed to be done. I made my way back to Joe's.

It was gettin' dusty with all the heat and no rain. I could see thunderheads gatherin' in the distance, settlin' right over the mountains but I doubted they'd make their way here. It just wasn't the time of year for no rain. I made my way slowly, deliberately contemplatin' what to say to Joe when I met up with him. I wasn't sure I needed to apologize. Then again, I wasn't sure I shouldn't apologize neither. I sighed. Comfortin' folks wasn't my strongest gift and the story of his Millie sent such a shock to my system, it lessened what I could offer even more. I told myself goin' back would be enough. I was nearin' the church yard. I forced myself to look.

New graves dotted the yard attestin' the losses suffered in the small community these last weeks. I didn't pray normally and certainly not every day, but I prayed for us all as I passed there that day. Like Joe, I didn't receive any response. I kept on my path, makin' my ways toward the store, forcin' myself to look away from the church yard. Just as I'd straightened my shoulders, I seen him, sittin' on his own, right at the edge like he'd said. I walked towards him.

He weren't cryin'. He weren't talkin' He just sittin' there near that overturned earth, not botherin' to look about him, though I figured he could me approach. I walked right up next to him and looked down where my friend lay then back at him. He had yet to acknowledge me or even look my direction. I wondered if he was mad with grief and gingerly lay a hand on his shoulder.

"Joe." My voice was soft. "Joe." He took my hand but took a moment to answer.

Finally, "Ruth, I apologize for telling you all about Millie and how she died. I realize you didn't even know we was sick. I hadn't talked to anyone since she passed, though and I needed to tell someone, anyone, the awful story. I can't tell if I done her right or not. There was so much going through my mind I just did what I could. I got them here." He indicated the earth before us. I sat down, keepin' hold of his hand.

"I know, Joe. I know. I can't say I wasn't surprised. I ain't never heard a story like what you told me yesterday. And you're right. I had no inclination you was sick or Millie was either. I guess I just expected you two were alright. I nearly went mad with loneliness durin' these past days so went to your place just seekin' out another human being. I didn't expect to find death."

I sighed. He sighed. And we sat, near our friend and his family for a long while like that. I didn't cry and he'd spent all his tears. There was nothin' more to be said, no more tears to fall so we sat together in our own grief. I couldn't tell how long we sat out like that, the sun beatin' hot and heavy on us when he spoke.

"I can't stay here, Ruth. I don't want to. The house, the store I don't want to keep it. I'm thinking of moving further west. I hear about the coal mining towns and figure I can bring goods out to one of them. They ain't so far but different from here." I nodded, unsurprised at such a revelation. Sometimes we outstay our welcome in the homes we build, its just a sad fact of life.

He went on, real soft. "I was so excited when she told me about the baby. I never thought we'd be blessed with a child. I can't say I didn't think of as anything but a bonefied miracle. For so long, I knew God was ignoring me, due to my own past. There was a time, I'd turned my back to him, just tryin' to survive out here. I killed a man, in cold blood. I won't tell you all the details but I'd done wrong. I paid dear for it and promised myself I'd never get too close to no one, I didn't want that to harm them, you see? Then I met Millie. No matter what I did, I couldn't stop myself of thinking of her pretty face or her cleverness. I never met a woman like her before, I doubt I will ever again." He went silent for a time.

"I told her I couldn't promise her much but she didn't seem to mind. We come here not long after we married and put in the store. We was real happy," he looked me right in the eye, assurin' me he was tellin' the truth. "We was so happy working together every day and then retiring each evening together. She was a good wife. She made sure I knew she loved me always baking my favorite food, setting up our home real nice. As you know, the only thing missing was a child of our own. I tried apologizing for it, but she wouldn't hear a thing of it. She was real generous like that." He stopped talking again and I waited patiently. Joe needed this and I was the only one around to hear it. A breeze picked up, gently stirring leaves around us.

He took a deep breath and continued, "Well, I know what a gift I got and I sure don't expect it twice. I thought we was doing all the things right and it showed when she got pregnant. You saw how pretty she looked these last weeks. I was given a good wife and child. The Lord, though, he gives and he takes. Well, he's taken so I am moving on. The reason I am telling you all this, Ruth. I need to move but I can't take it all with me. I figure I'll leave the house open; someone will move in who needs a place to live. The store, though, all the goods that remain, I can't take them. Now, there ain't as much as normal summers, not with this virus. I figure I'll take what I need but I was wondering if you might take it over." I looked at him.

To tell the truth, I was near as shocked as the day before hearin' about poor Millie and her stuck baby.

"Joe. I don't know about that. I just never planned…" my voice trailed away. I was thinking, though. So what if I never planned on ownin' my own store? I never planned most of what I already lived. I'd gone from place to place survin' and learnin' what I might improve. This might be the next opportunity I needed.

I would never again be lonely. Their shop always had a customer or two, each day. Folks needed their goods. I could keep a stock of my own salves on the shelf, that might keep me busy on Sundays. I could move into their buildin', leave mine as Joe planned doin' his. I wondered if I could live in the place that saw such sadness. It was bigger than my place and their vegetable garden was bigger too. I thought of my own little home. I couldn't see how livin' and keepin' stores in there would work. It may not matter what I wanted. Practicality demanded me move.

I was noddin' towards Joe. "That sounds real nice, Joe. I hope you know I never would have entertained such a thought before all this. I like this, though."

"It is the right thing, Ruth. I can't stay. You arc going to need an income sooner or later. Owning a shop won't make you rich, not like some of these miners or even some farmers. It is a real nice, steady life though. Even during lean winter months, folks still need their goods. I expect its always been that way and always will. I can teach what I know about it and when you're ready, we can move it on up to your place. After that, I think my Millie will rest real easy. She worried over you, you know that? Worried you might get lonely. Worried if you were going hungry." He smiled, a real genuine Joe smile. "She was hoping you and Jedidiah might fancy each other some day soon. Then, she said, she could stop worrying over the both of you." He shook his head a little at the memory unaware half of what she hoped for already was true.

I smiled back at him and silently thanked my friend layin' in the ground.

Joe and I set to work almost immediately though I didn't tell him my plans of movin' myself to their place just yet. There was enough to go over what with learnin' the books and orderin' of things. He gave me all the information he possibly could includin' popular needs and items during the different seasons. He even went over Christmas sales from the prior two years and what he and Millie did for the community to celebrate the birth of the Christ child. He showed me the garden, how it was all growin' and ready for harvest soon enough.

I soon understood how Millie had her hand in every corner of that place. She wasn't just a housewife or shop -keeper, she was everything to him and their home. It was her idea to sell my salve and her idea to give back to the community at Christmastime. She traded local as much as they could. Joe demanded nothin' in return for his generosity of loanin' me his time but I helped him clean the place and weed the garden after our lessons were finished. I also cooked him most evening meals and washed up afterwards. I felt I owed him something.

Chapter 23

Two weeks passed by in that manner and I found myself loving Joe. It was a love I hadn't experienced in a long time. It wasn't the same love I'd felt towards Jeremiah; I didn't seek Joe's company all hours of the day or even think about him too much when we parted ways for the night. No, it was a love much like the love I'd felt for my own sister. I wanted the best for Joe and to help him. I wanted luck to shine on him and life give him the blessings such a good man deserved. I felt as if I had a brother in Joe. I knew I would miss him when he moved on.

If I was real honest though, I was also excited to take over the store. I was excited to move into a proper place that would house me for as long as I needed. I was excited to be a bigger part of the community I now called home. The last weeks were so difficult and lonesome. I still didn't know about Jedidiah. I didn't know where he was or if he was safe from the small pox.

I wasn't too sure he would want much to do with me after all this. But I knew my own well being was at hand.

I had my own plans to expand the shop. The salve was real comfortin' for women on their sensitive areas when the need arose. Fact is, that was when I learned to make it, back when I was workin' for Evans. I knew it would be helpful on the freshly scarred skin of them that suffered the small pox.

After the small pox cleared, I expected it would sell real good to the ladies. No woman liked her agin' looks. I could sell somethin' that might ease the sagging skin. I expected it to be real popular. I experimented too, with different scents. My whole place smelled of the floral scents and I expected most would buy simply to smell that lovely.

As long as I was sellin' the salve, I figured I might make the same scents in soaps as well. I knew it would do real nice out here. It might be one of the finer things all the way out here. Plus, it would keep me busy during the dark, winter months. I think Millie would have liked the idea too. She liked the salve, said she even used it herself. I figured she'd like the soap and scents.

Of course, just like everythin' in life, when the time come for Joe to move on, no amount of excitement could stem the feelin's of loss that flooded me. I helped him saddle up, real early one mornin' and kissed his cheek farewell. I'd told him the night before I was plannin' on movin' in and he liked the idea. He even offered to help but I declined.

I could see he was needin' to go. He needed space from the sadness that would haunt his every wakin' second here. I'd waved him on, confidently tellin' him I didn't own much, that I'd manage. He was glad, I could tell, that I'd declined his offer. This way, the memories of his and Millie's home would always be theirs. Nothin' would interfere with 'em and each time he pictured what I imagined were his happiest days on earth, he'd only see them there.

He kept the good-bye real short. I knew he'd said goodbye to his wife and child the night before, I'd seen him down at their grave. I think he even spent most the night out there, talkin' to 'em. When the time came the next mornin', he'd gone west and didn't look back. I watched him ride on till he disappeared, then turned towards my new home and store.

The whole place was clean; he left the few goods still sellin' despite the epidemic. I walked through the shop first, takin' in all I'd so surprisingly inherited. I couldn't believe it. The shelves were most bare but I knew I'd fill them up soon enough. I walked behind the counter and touched each glass jar just waitin' on sweets. I touched the folds of the precious few yards of fabric left behind. Soon, the goods would all be goin' on to some other person but for now, all was mine. I'd never owned so much in my life. And the store was mostly empty.

After, I walked to the kitchen. The chairs Millie and I sat in for conversatin' were there, and her curtains still hung in the windows. I decided right then, I would keep the table and chairs. I'd sell mine in the shop, these were in better shape and there were more than I had anyway.

I went to their small sitting room. It was plain with two chairs and a small fireplace. All of it would stay the same, I just didn't have things for a sitting room. I headed upstairs.

I knew I would find one small room that would have held the baby Millie and Joe were expectin'. It was a bare room, nothin' at all inside it. I wasn't sure if Joe left it that way or they just hadn't gotten anything for it yet. I didn't ask and he didn't tell. Direct across from that space was the room in which Joe and Millie spent their most intimate moments. I expected this is where their baby was created in so much love.

They slept here. And of course, this was where Millie and the baby died. Joe never asked but this room was bare too. He must have moved the bed and linen and curtains out himself. I was glad he did. I wouldn't want to sleep in their bed or use her bedroom things. I sat in the middle of the floor and looked around.

I was a little afraid. I'd seen plenty of tragedy. I wasn't afraid of ghosts but I was wantin' a real peaceful home. I didn't like to infringe on Millie's spirit or memory. I didn't want her to think I somehow stole her happiness neither. I wasn't sure what to do and I couldn't quite explain it but I felt Millie there. I felt her quiet happiness with Joe and their thrill of their unexpected baby. I could just almost hear her tellin' me about their baby. She was so happy.

I heard a creak behind me but I stayed in my position trying to ignore it. "Houses make noises," I told myself and it stopped. I needed to make peace with my new room, my new house and all the ghosts of the past. I wasn't sure how but I had to try.

"Millie," my voice was hoarse from lack of use, I cleared it and tried again. "Millie." The creak sounded behind me again, closer. I stayed though my skin grew cold and goose pimples raised. "Millie." My voice was stronger though the room was cold as ice. I tried to keep from shiverin'. The creak sounded again. I took a deep, cold breath and tried again, "Millie. I want to thank you. I told Joe thank you before he left," the loudest creak yet sounded close enough to touch, "He couldn't stay. He missed ya too much. He would have spent his days over your graveside, missin' you and that baby. Now, no one wants that." I wasn't sure but I thought the room grew a little warmer. I went on.

"Now, I thanked him and he left. He left me the store to run and all of it. I told him I would. I want to keep the name, Millie's General Stores and Goods. But I want you to be alright with me here watchin' the place for ya. God knows I wish ya was here and I never wished ya gone." I paused to wipe a tear from my face. I did my friend.

"I wish I would have told ya that, how much I valued your friendship. I fear there ain't too many linin' up ready to befriend me. I miss your baby too," the room was growin' warmer all the same, there was another creak close by, "I do. Even though I never will have one of my own and I might have envied you growin' one in your belly. I miss it. I'd have loved it and I was lookin' forwards to holdin' the little thing." I breathed in deep and decided to finish up. I sat up straighter and dared look around more.

"Millie. I gotta ask you to go now. I know you and your little one are together again. I know you found your peace. It won't be long, Joe and you can reunite and be a family again. I truly believe that. I need peace here, though. Joe done taught me all he could about runnin' this place and how you worked in the community to offer up local goods and trade fair. I promise," I raised my hand to the square, "I promise to run it just how ya run things. I promise, I will take care of this home, just as you did. I promise not to forget ya, neither. Thank you, Millie. I love ya." I was too aware I'd sold my own soul to the Devil long ago to promise seein' her that last day when we all are called up. It sure wasn't fair but the Devil just didn't demand the same payment from us all. I just couldn't promise what I didn't have, so I didn't.

I stood, alone, and waited for some sign that might show me Millie listened. The room was warm, their was light filterin' through the windows and silence surrounded me. I stood til I felt silly, "waitin' on a sign," I chided myself silently and headed back downstairs. I let myself into the garden. It was warm and quiet out here too. I walked out and took stock of the plants already growin'.

I figured I'd keep both gardens this season and then switch all my interests to this one alone. I bent down to smell the ripenin' roses and stretched back up, hands on hips. A cardinal landed right near me and looked right at me. I smiled at him, wonderin' at how close he was. He bounced, on those tiny bird feet, nearer and nearer, till he was right up on me, nearly touchin' my own shoe. He looked up at me. And he stayed like that a good long moment.

He looked right into my eyes and I looked into his. I felt as if an old friend was visitin' me and I understood, "Millie?" I whispered. And at my words, the cardinal took flight.

I knew my house and my store was at peace and ready for me. It was time to move in.

Between introducin' myself to folks and tryin' to maintain both gardens, movin' took longer than I'd planned. I'd planned to re-open the store by the end of the week but moving in was more work than I'd thought it could be. I had figured it would take a day to get all my belongin's from my little place down to my new one but it took almost an entire week. I'd acquired more this last year than my entire life. Finally, finally, finally my little place was emptied. I swept it clean and took one last look around.

I was excited to move in and take over the store but this place had been heaven; I would miss it. It was small but safe and warm allowin' me to grow from all that I'd been forced into and believe about myself into what I wanted from life. I was lucky, I knew it and I was grateful for it. It was nearly one year since I arrived, more than one year since I'd left Evans. I wondered how the others were gettin' on and if poor Jo ever looked down on us. I was a different woman now a storekeeper. I straightened my shoulders and walked out the door, no longer a whore.

The next week was busy enough. I harvested what I could from my garden one afternoon and spread it out throughout my kitchen.

I figured I'd bundle it in the mornin', I was just too tired to do more work this evenin'.

As I boiled some water for washin' up, I thought I saw a shadow of someone standin' out in the garden. I tried focusin' my eyes to the dark world outside but I couldn't see anyone. I decided my eyes was playin' tricks. "It's time for bed," I said aloud, shakin' my head a little. It had been a long day and was time for me to retire for the night.

As I readied for bed, my thoughts turned towards Jedidiah, as they normally did this time of day. I wondered where he was and if he was alright. Memories of our four precious days crept into my mind, assurin' me there'd be no sleep for at least a little while. I thought of his arms around me and the ways we'd made each other feel so good. He was the one man I didn't find repulsive after all this time.

I laughed a little at the thought. He smelled like a man, said cruel jokes like a man but I missed everythin' about him. I finally started driftin' off, hopin' to meet him somewhere in my dreams when I began wonderin' if I'd ever even hear about him again. I had to face the truth; not only may I never see him again, I may never know his fate neither. I slept, hard, soon after.

But I didn't dream.

I woke up restless. I was sick to death of the epidemic and loss. I wanted to begin again. There was nothin' for it, so I went right to work.

The store front wasn't dirty but it was dusty. I swept and wiped down every bit of shelf and every inch of floor. Then, I worked on the window fronts and the counter top. It took me near til noon but the place absolutely gleamed when I finished. I had two customers too.

They was sorry to hear about the loss of Millie and Joe, one took it real hard. I found myself comfortin' a stranger when she was moved to tears. She bought three jars of my salve though, and showed keen interest in the small table from my old place. The next one also bought salve which reminded me of the harvest herbs and flowers waitin' on my in the kitchen.

I moved 'em to the store counter and left the door open welcomin' folks inside. I carefully tied each bundle off so the blooms and seeds were protected and hung 'em upside down behind the counter. I was surprised at how pretty it all looked. They lent their fresh scent to the store front too. It was nearin' evenin' time when I finally shut the door and locked the place up. I was hungry, I finally noticed. I hadn't eaten or drank much the entire day. I stood and surveyed the shop, proud of an honest day's work and the little pay I'd earned. I was tired, but not exhausted and I *was* hungry.

"Thank God its dinner time," I thought as I headed into the kitchen.

I pulled the small cooking pot down and set to makin' a simple but fillin' meal of biscuits and beans. I added some berries I found growin' in my newly acquired garden for dessert. I set down to the table makin' a nice meal of it when I saw a shadow against the back door. A chill went up my spine.

I didn't want no trouble, but if this was the same person as the day before, they was lookin' for a fight. I was tired, hungry and in no mood for much understandin' as to why someone might be lurkin' around my place in the evenin' time. I sighed and stood, lookin' longingly at the hot meal I was waitin' on. Takin' the few steps towards the door, I called out, "Now, look here, I don't want no trouble but I seen ya last night and I see ya tonight. Why don't you go on now, and not make any trouble!" I wasn't overly scared but I wasn't feelin' over easy about a stranger watchin' me neither. This epidemic changed folks, some were real needy but some folks was downright desperate. Desperate folks meant they was unpredictable.

They was tired of loss, tired of bein' sick, tired of bein' lonesome. If it was a desperate man on the other side of my door, I wasn' oversure I could hold him off, if he wanted in but I couldn't ignore the situation no more neither. Someone had been back there the night before and who knows if they been sneakin' around more than that. It was time to end the possible threat. I pressed my ear to the door, tryin' to hear if the person left.

A loud thumpin' nearly made me jump out of own skin! I wasn't expectin' a polite desperate person! I tried to catch my breath while I called out, "Who's there?" I could barely hear the low reply over my beatin' heart. I tried holdin' my breath to calm my breathin' and allow me to hear the person.

"Ruth."

I knew who that voice belonged to despite how quiet he sounded, despite how raspy his voice was and I threw open the door. Relief flooded my every being; physical and spiritual, Jedediah stood before me. My arms recoiled in horror, though.

CHAPTER 24

The man who stood before me was not the rugged, good looking man who I'd said goodbye to all them weeks back. Instead a pockmarked, aged man stood on my doorstep barely recognizable. I gasped, "Jedidiah! Oh my God, ya look as if ya lost half your mass!" As he stepped into the kitchen light, the full ravages of the disease were made visible. I couldn't help it, my hand went to my mouth as if I had no control over my own body.

We stood just like that for a few moments that seemed endless. I took in his appearance, sagging ill-fitting clothes, tired eyes and the scars that covered his entire face. I wondered if they reached over his entire body. His strong arms looked frail and his lips parched. I gathered my senses and stepped towards him and shut the door, finally wrappin' my arms around his thinned shoulders; I could feel his bones even beneath the shirt and coat he wore.

He leaned on me, real heavy and I realized the man was so fatigued he needed to sit or might collapse. I led him to the sittin' room and made him take the most comfortable of the chairs. Then, I stirred the fire some hopin' the room might warm quickly.

"Would you like some water, Jedediah? What about some dinner? I just made biscuits and beans but it looks like any food might do ya good." He was sittin' way back in the chair, leanin' his head back with his eyes shut. He straightened up to answer.

"I sure could use that, Ruth. Thank you."

I hurried to the kitchen to get both our dinners. I could hardly believe he was sittin' here in my home, never mind he looked like death warmed over, he was here. My legs trembled a little as I set a plate on his knee and handed him his water.

"What happened?" I was surprised to hear the emotion in my own voice, "Last time I saw ya, ya told me we might eat together that night. I can't even recall how many days ago you promised to see me at sundown. Tell me, Jedediah, what happened?" I found I wasn't over hungry, I was too nervous at the state of him, and how he'd spent these last weeks. I sat opposite him and looked deep in his eyes. He didn't answer straight away. He was eatin' as if it was his last meal.

"I wonder how long its been since he last ate?" I wondered to myself. I took a bite or two of my biscuit conscience he may request more; I'd gladly give him my share.

Finally, he looked up and smiled a little. "Ruth, them the best beans I think I ever ate." I smiled back at him. This was real, he was real, after them weeks of waitin' and wonderin', here he was, right with me, complimenin' this simple meal. He set his plate down beside him on the floor and leaned back again, sighin' real deep.

"I can't tell you how I missed you, Ruth. I left expecting I might not make it back that day but at least the next. It ain't much of a story neither. The town shut down, thanks to the small pox and I was out. When I left you that day, I rode out to see about some tales about cattle rustlin' out on the prairie. Well, it turned out to be horse theivin' and of course, that took me to the next town over." He closed his eyes, recallin' the weeks' events since he'd left.

"Well, we caught men responsible and I got 'em down to Laramie alright. They hang horse thieves, ya know." He shook his head a little, eyes still closed, "These guys, they was so young for their crimes. Well, I got them on their way down there and then got caught up in a long line of some of the natives movin' west. I wasn't over sure where they was goin', just a line of young, old, men and women all spread out tryin' to get somewhere's else. We rode up and down the line tryin' to find someone who might speak to us and by the time we figured out what was happenin' it was too late, we'd been exposed to the small pox. Well, by then, two guys ridin' with me already left back to their homes. I expect they took it with them and who knows who was infected after. It took me a few days, but I got sick. Real sick, I thought I might die." He stopped talkin' there. I waited, content to listen to the fire cracklin' and him breathin'. We was in the same room, it was hard to dare ask for more out of the world at that moment.

I reached over and took his hand. Even though his eyes was still closed, he smiled at the touch.

His voice was faint with fatigue when he finally spoke again, "Well, I took shelter at a home of another law man. It was terrible, Ruth. Every one of his family caught it, there was no one left to care for anyone. We took it in turns crawlin' to the well for water. Even the children took a turn. The thirst was terrible." He stopped and drew a deep breath, "All died, all of 'em, Ruth. One day, I don't know how many I was layin' there feverin' and thinkin' it was the end, the fever broke and I got up. Every last one of 'em was dead, just layin' all over. I was in no shape to do it, but I was the only one around, I got all the bodies outside eventually and set fire to them. I know it ain't Christian but they'd been gone awhile." He stopped, his eyes open finally, fixed on some point in the ceiling. He shuddered and stayed like that until I spoke up.

"The death hit here too, no one's told me exact numbers. I think it's a lot though. I never caught it myself but Millie did. I guess it ain't no secret, beings I'm here now and they's gone away." I hadn't talked to anyone about Millie or my good fortune at Joe's loss. I wasn't over ready but it was time to share it with someone. I was grateful it was Jedediah. He was watchin' me, waitin' for my next words.

"Well, Millie, she was expectin' a little one right around the start of this winter season. She weren't sick long, though. Joe, he caught it first and she cared for him all through his sufferin'. They helped close off the town too, hopin' to save folks. Well, he got better and she told him she was goin' to rest awhile one afternoon. When he got back, she was dead." I tried but failed to tell him about the baby. I just couldn't.

Instead, I said, "Well, he buried her, still expectin' near the churchyard. After that, he didn't want to stay. He offered me the store and house, sayin' its what she would have wanted. I made my peace with her, too. I've only been here a day or two." I took a deep breath, recallin' the lonely days of the summer. " I didn't catch any illness, and I feel real lucky for that but them were some lonely days, Jedediah. Real lonely," my voice caught in my throat. "Why, I didn't know where ya was or if I dare even hope ya might be alright. I didn't pray neither, I don't expect most my prayers are heard." I brushed hot tears off my cheeks. He grasped my hand a little tighter.

"I know Ruth, I was real lonely too. I was most afraid I might never see ya again." I was surprised to see a tear snake its way down his thinned face. "Life is short, we spend it chasin' dreams and work. If we ain't careful, we miss out." He looked exhausted after our talk, so I picked up the dinner dishes and washed up, quick-like for the night. When I returned, he was asleep.

I nudged him awake and helped him up the stairs. I washed him off, best I could before he laid down on the bed arms open waitin' on me. I didn't dream that night, same as before but there was no need, I was in heaven right there.

CHAPTER 25

I woke early, still excited for my own new ventures. Jedediah didn't notice me leavin' one little bit. I smiled at his sleeping form while I silently dressed. "He can rest all he needs, at least he's home," I thought as I walked downstairs. I ignored the small worries bloomin' in the back of my mind that he may need more than rest. "He's home. He can rest and that's all that matters," I said aloud.

It was early, too early to open the store doors. Instead, I busied myself with tidyin' the kitchen and preparin' breakfast. I walked to the garden breathin' in the high prairie fresh mornin' air. Nights were cool and most mornins brisk till near noon time. Mornin' was gettin' to be my favorite time of the day. Birds and other critters was out, welcomin' each day. The sunrise took my breath away streakin' the sky in blues and oranges. It was still quiet, nothin' too much expected of me and I found peace in the solitude. This mornin' was no different. I breathed deep and looked around the garden seein' this one was near ready for harvestin' too. I began pinching off blossoms and the vegetables that was ripe. From the corner of my eye, I saw the cardinal. I looked real close.

I was sure he was the same one as before, his tail feathers were a little bent on the one side, I recalled wonderin' at that the first time I seen him. Just as before, he stayed and stayed. I doubted he was afraid of me. "Even if ya are you can just fly away, can't ya?" I whispered to him. He blinked and bobbed his head at me as if he understood. He stayed put, watchin' me work much longer than any other birds I'd ever seen. As I picked the last rose blossom, he finally flew away. I raised my hand shadin' my eyes and watched as he disappeared into a thick tree.

I turned back 'round and picked up my basket. It was gettin' warm out, meanin' it was late enough I could open the store for business. I gave a little start, Jedediah was standin' right at the door waitin' on me. I grinned at him. "Why Jedediah, ya lookin' better already!"

He was leanin' on the door frame and didn't move as I approached him. His face was still lined and though his eyes were birght, I could tell he was still tired. He grinned back at me though, "Good mornin', Ruth. Thank you for the eggs and bread. It was mighty tasty." He took the basket from me and leaned in kissin' my cheek as I passed him by.

The entire mornin' he was right there, helpin' before I even asked. When I could see he was needin' a rest, I shooed him upstairs. By then it was near noon and no customers had visited yet.

I left the doors open but went to my kitchen to start some bread. It didn't take long and I had a nice dough risin' in a patch of sunshine landin' on the table. I laid out the mornin's small harvest, and made a big decision.

It was nice havin' Jedediah home. It was heaven on earth. I loved hearin' his deep breathin' night or now. I loved the fact I got him all to myself. I laughed a little, right out loud though, as I began heatin' water.

That man stunk to high heaven and needed a bath. I was gonna wash his clothes too. I got the water readied and decided to lock the store up while he bathed. When I re-entered the kitchen Jedediah was already there.

"You sleep alright?" I asked him.

"I did, thank you, Ruth. I am famished, we got anythin' to eat?" He looked around hopeful-like eyein' the risin' bread.

"That bread ain't done and won't be for awhile. Here have this instead," I gave him a plateful of beans and biscuits. "I know, it ain't as tasty as that warm bread is goin' to be but ya won't starve. After you're finished, you've got the bath waitin'. You stink." I winked at him and turned to clean up the dishes.

"I suppose I'll have to clean those clothes and the linens on my bed, now too." I laughed a little his way and gave him a little push towards the tub. "Now, I been warmin' water and it should be all ready for ya."

"Alright, Ruth, alright." He agreed and began peeling back the layers of clothin' he'd worn for only lord knows how long. I briefly considered burnin' 'em but took 'em and readied 'em for a good wash. Jedidiah leaned back in the water with a deep sigh. I lifted another jug of warmed water and gently poured it over his hair. I lathered up a good amount of soap and went to washin' him, tryin' to not gasp at the new scars erupted over most his body.

I hadn't yet gotten used to his scarred face and seein' the sufferin' he must have endured was just about more than I wanted to bear. His skin was no longer smooth beneath my fingers. Most of the scars were deep but his weight-loss was some sight, too. Before he left, his arms were full of hard muscle and the skin stretched across 'em nice and tight. His back was full and his chest and abdomen equally strong. Now, a shadow of his former self was all that remained. Skin hung off his arms and his stomach caved inwards. He looked like he needed a year's good feedin' and I told him so.

"Jedediah, ya know I missed ya and its real nice to have you home. I just need to get you fed up some." I scrubbed his back and under his arms more, "and get this smell off ya."

He laughed a little, his eyes closed and leaned back again, allowin' me to wash his chest and downwards. He seemed awful weak for havin' slept all night. I tried not to worry over-much as I scrubbed and rinsed and scrubbed and rinsed his skin till it was pink.

"That feels so good, Ruth. And you're right, when I look down at myself it seems I ain't half the man I was. How does the rest of me look for scars? I saw my face, in that little mirror you got in the store front there. I can't tell ya how worried I was ya might not recognize me. Or worse, ya might not want me around lookin' like this." His hand went to his face as if it were drawn to it, and he felt around like he was tryin' to feel the difference.

I just shook my head at his words and began washin' his filthy clothes. "Ya got somethin' else to put on besides these dirt-filled things?" He nodded.

"Yup, I brought the saddle pack in, I don't got much else. I guess I need to get the other few tings I from the jail- house." He opened his eyes finally, "That is, if I can stay."

I stood up, stretchin' my back and took my time answerin' him. "Let's see how ya smell first." He laughed and stood up, I was glad to see somethings hadn't waned on him. He caught me lookin' and smiled, "I saw you, probably seein' if I was changed all over." He wagged his cock at me a little, "Well? What do you think? Have I changed much?"

He stepped out of the water, drippin' a hefty amount on the floor and stepped close to me, not seemin' to care if he was wet, or if he got me wet and pulled me to him.

His arms was strong as ever and he seemed more than ready, more than needy as he kissed my mouth. He weren't as gentle as he'd been, this was different. His hands felt me all over and pulled one leg up around his hip, he was breathin' hard.

"Ruth," he murmured in my ear, his mouth open and breath hot on my neck, "I was scared. So scared I'd never see ya again." He pulled me towards the stairs, away from my chores.

We landed on the bed, him beneath me. He worked to undo the buttons on my dress and pulled off my pantaloons. He ran his hands up and down my bare leg and pulled my face towards his. I could feel him beneath me all hard, ready to penetrate.

I made him wait though. I pushed my pussy down on him, I liked it as much as he did. I could feel how wet I was, he seemed to get harder feelin' that. I still made him wait. I kissed his mouth, hard and gasped a little as his hips thrust upwards. I felt his chest with my hand and worked my way down towards his waitin' cock and grasped it a little.

"Ruth. I can't take it no more." His voice was raspy, his eyes closed. His entire being was tremblin' waitin' on me to let him come inside. I toyed with a little more until he opened his eyes and groaned, turnin' me right under him. He took what he wanted then, he was hard and he took his time. I gasped again and again, each orgasm thrilling my whole body.

Finally, he came warmin' my insides, leakin' down beneath me on the bed. I wriggled under him till I came no more, holdin' on till the end. He was spent, he rolled off me and very near fell right to sleep. But first, his hand found mine and pulled it gently to his mouth and he kissed it.

"I missed ya, Ruth. Those four days we spent weren't enough for me. I had to see ya again, no matter how bad the fever got, no matter how much I hurt. I had to see ya again." And with those words, his breathin' went deep and even. He was fast asleep.

I felt energized, rather than tired after our love- makin'. I wrapped my thin robe 'round me and softly stepped towards the bedroom door. I soundlessly found my way to the kitchen and then stole out to the store front. I wanted to check and ensure the place was all locked up for the night. After, I went back and finished his wash, hung it all up and finished bakin' that bread.

After, I fixed him some fresh fish caught by a visitor the day before and decided to serve him in bed. I laid the tray for two and headed back up the stairs.

"Why ain't you a sight," he said softly from the bed. I laughed as the robe fell from one of my shoulders, holdin' the tray high in front of me.

"I guess so," I smiled at him as he made room on the bed, "A near naked woman and food is probably every man's dream, ain't it?"

"It is when she is you," He whispered and took the tray from me.

I sat on the edge of the bed eatin' a little and telllin' him about my plans for the store. He listened without interuptin'. I told him all about makin' nothin' more than bagbomb and sellin' it.

"See, ya make the salve, it ain't hard. And even though its really for cow's udders, it helps on our skin too. Here, I can show ya." I just thought of how best to help his healin' skin. I grabbed some salve from the kitchen and ran back up the stairs. I began rubbing it into his back.

"I make the salve but when it's gettin' real hot, that's when I add the scent. I can add honey too, this one has honey. Honey has medicinal properties and it smells sweet. That's really the only difference between what we put on 'em cows and our skin, how it smells. I doubt any farmer is gonna waste time makin' his cows smell sweet." Jedidiah laughed at my little joke.

"That feels real nice, Ruth, the itchin' mostly stopped. And so has the burnin'." He lay back against the bed, lettin' me work ono his arms and legs and torso. As I reached his face I told him how I come to make it.

"Well, that line of work I was in, someone was always gettin' a slap or catchin' somethin' from some man. This helped heal all sorts of things. I began makin' it for us girls with Cook. She showed me how to make this and soap. She showed me how to scent it too and taught me about the honey. When I moved here, Millie took a real chance takin' it in; 'course I never told her it was nothin' more than bagbomb neither." We both laughed at my little secret.

I moved the tray off the bed and lay down beside Jedediah, restin' my head on his shoulder. We fell asleep soon after.

I woke earlier than him and started the breakfast and coffee. I wanted to open earlier today and work on gettin' more salve and maybe bar soaps on the shelves. I thought it might be real nice to have a rose scented soap and salve. I worked all mornin', a little surprised Jedediah slept so long. His body was healin' and it looked like it might just take time. "Rest was the best thing for him," I thought.

I worked on the soap, then worked on the salves and opened the door hopin' more folks would be needin' some goods. Not an hour has passed when my first one came in; I'd seen her a few times but never spoke to her.

"She was a lady, for sure," I thought as I greeted her a, "Good mornin'." She gave me a thin-lipped sort of smile.

Her hair was drawn up under a pretty little hat and her skirts full with petti skirts beneath. Her hands wasn't as worn as some women around here, and I figured she must have help with chores. She picked up the a jar of the salve and turned.

"What is this?" Her voice was neither kind nor unkind.

"Oh, it's a salve I make right here. That one is scented with rose. It's good for your skin or any malady on the skin." I held it close to her so she might catch a scent of the rose. I could see she liked that and wasn't surprised when she bought three jars.

"You know, I saw you and Mildred talking when I was in here one day. I can't say I was over impressed with you; after all what is a woman doing out here on her own? Why, I even went home and told my John." She looked down, and I saw her face flush. "I can't say I was over friendly to you then, nor did I encourage folks to be welcoming to you. Of course, Mildred, she didn't listen." She sniffed a little and looked me in the eyes. "There's a good number of women alone out here and I guess I know at least one reason. I'm lucky, my John is still here, he survived. He might not be as strong as he was but he's resting and he will be soon enough." She looked around the store and finished, "Thank you for the salve. I'll most likely be back soon for more and other goods. If I like it, I'll tell folks where its available. Good luck to you, running Mildred's place." And with that, she left.

I was amazed. I wasn't surprised folks hadn't been over-welcoming last year but that was almost an apology and a promise for more business. I felt good, like I was part of the community. I hummed a little as straightened up the store front and was surprised to see Jedediah standin' in the doorway, how long he'd been there, I couldn't guess.

"That was Mrs. Brown. Her folks helped establish this place, some might say they is pillars of the community. I guess they'd be right but for the most part she's not much more than a gossip. If she gives you praise that's good, she sure will talk to folks about it." He smiled at me. "You're doing well, Ruth. Real well."

I was elated. First, that Mrs. Brown gave, well if it wasn't praise it might be a compliment. Then Jedediah praised my work here. I asked what he was up to this fine day.

"I got to get my things from the jail house. I got to make room for the man takin' my place." He looked down at me. I was shocked. I had no idea he was makin' such a career move.

"Well, if ya ain't workin' the law no more, what are you doin'?" I asked.

He looked around the store and took both my hands in his, "I thought I might run this place with you. Do it in the same manner

Millie and Joe did things." My mouth opened but no words came out. He put a finger over my lips, real gentle. A few thoughts was goin' through my mind.

I liked runnin' this place. I hadn't even had it for a month and I wasn't ready to hand it over to someone. I had plans to grow it and really work in this community. Plus, Joe taught *me* to run this place. What could Jedediah know of my plans or runnin' a place? He just watched my eyes and kept his hand over my lips, as if to shush me for a few moments.

"Now, Ruth, I can see what you are thinkin'." He even laughed a little. "Its written all over your face. But there is no need to worry. Everyone knew it was really Millie runnin' things around here and I expect that's how it will be for you too. I don't want that. I want to help here. I want to spend our days and night together. I can't say I know too much about stores or orderin' or even sellin'. But I been to a few stores in my time, I see how they keep stuff real neat and displayed. I also see you, workin' so hard with the garden and your soaps and salves. I can take some of that from your shoulders. I can be a real help to you. What do you say to that?"

I was shocked and didn't know what to say.

How could someone this good and kind be here for me? It didn't seem real. Jedediah didn't seem real. His offer didn't seem real neither. I relaxed a little and took a deep breath. It was time I let love into my life, into my soul.

I didn't need Jedediah for survival out here and he didn't need me neither. I wanted him though. I wanted him by my side through the days and nights. Tragedies were all around us, the sickness killed off folks of all ages; kids with dreams, new mothers, expectant mothers, old and young. It taught me to hold on when I could because there might not be another chance. That's what the sickness taught me. It was a lesson I'd carry with me the rest of my life through; hold on to the good when I could because we don't always get another chance.

Jedediah stopped workin' law and made it official the next day. He moved his few belongin's to our place and began doin' the few repairs places always seem to need. Soon, autumn turned to winter one more time.

CHAPTER 26

We was sittin' up one night near the fire, he was readin' over an order and I was repairin' a hole in his trousers. It was warm and quiet, the wind howlin' with us outside its reaches.

"Would ya look at us," I smiled at his quiet words.

"Look at us?" I asked him, stoppin' my work for a few seconds.

"Well, yes, look at us. I can't tell if we got old these last few months or what!" He laughed his quiet laugh and went on, "Here we are, sittin' before a warm fire, everything neat and tidy. You sittin' over there pretty as a picture sewin'. I might need some readin' glasses before too long, goin' over these numbers." He winked at me and went back to his work. I laid his trousers in my lap and looked over at him.

Truth was, he *did* look older after his weeks of sufferin' the small pox. He gained most of his weight back but his hair had greyed and the scars on his face seemed to mark each hour he'd endured leavin' a permanent shadow in its traces. I picked up the trousers again.

"Well, that would make ya old, Jedediah," I told him softly.

The store was runnin' just great. Once folks started comin' out as the sickness lifted, our business increased ten-fold. The salves and soaps were found to sooth the pock marks left behind and I sold out each week. Every Saturday during the autumn season I made more and more.

I'd been right too in predictin' folks might like a bar soap with the same scent as their salve, I couldn't keep 'em on the shelf.

As the days grew colder and colder, we hurried to prepare for the cold winter that was promised. I was lookin' forward to those nights we would hide from it beneath layers of blankets together. Nothin' interfering with our lovemakin' or sleepin'. It was just us, just him and I warm against a cold world.

One mornin' I woke to him watchin' me. He smoothed the hair from my face, leavin' his hand restin' on my shoulder. He looked into my eyes.

"Ruth, I want to make an honest woman of ya."

"But Jedediah," I began. Then stopped. I thought back just one year. Then I thought back a little further.

Truth was there was years in there I wasn't an honest woman, the devil himself demanded that so I might live. Before that, though, I felt I'd been born an honest woman. I had parents who worked for us and loved me. I had a mama who made me clothes. I had a pa who kept the roof over our heads. I always thought I'd grow up, just like them, and be just like them. Life took them and sent me down another unchosen path though I'd born the blame and shame all on my own. I wasn't sure I was the marryin' type of woman, even if I'd been born to be. One thing was certain and I felt he better know before he talked anymore nonsense about makin' me honest.

I laid a hand on his face and began, my voice soft, "Jedediah, ya can't marry me and what's more ya don't want to neither. Ya might think otherwise but if ya just listen, I think ya might change your mind." I sat up and faced away from him. I could feel him pick himself up and lean over on the one arm, tryin' to get as close as he might to me. I kept my space though. "I can't have children." I waited a few seconds before I added, " I can't have your children."

He didn't say anythin' and I didn't add anythin'. My world was dashed in those few moments. I never heard of any man marryin' a woman he knew couldn't give him a child. All this time, I'd been pretendin' life was all roses and daisies but I'd only quashed the alarms some quiet little voice whispered once every while. I'd known the truth all along. Jedediah was stayin' hopin' for a future that I could never provide.

I didn't cry any more over it, I'd done all that grievin' long ago. It pained my heart that I would never look at a growin' girl that had my nose or a little boy with those dark eyes like his daddy's. I didn't grieve the loss, though. I'd moved on.

I was happy here. I was happy in the space I'd somehow inherited. I was happy with Jedediah by my side. Mostly, I was happy as I ever would be and I knew that. I'd known it all along.

I was as happy as I was ever gonna be and that was that. I doubted any man, even Jedediah would knowingly continue on this path being as happy as they ever gonna get.

I waited for him to tell me something, anything. I waited for anger or resentment at my dishonesty. It never came. He was quiet. Finally, he spoke. His voice was softer than I ever heard before.

"Ruth. I came back here for you. I came back from the brink of death for you. I wasn't thinkin' of anything or anyone more. I just wanted you." I finally turned to look at him and was honest surprised to see tears wettin' his face. I brushed them back. I could hardly understand nor barely accept what he was sayin'.

"I thought every many spread his seed hopin' for a family of his own," I told him.

"Ruth." He sat up too and we both faced front, our legs stretched in front of us. He turned his head towards mine, I could feel him lookin' at me without havin' to turn my own. "Ruth. Look at me, Ruth." I turned to him.

"I wanted children, of course. Like any human. I wanted you to have my children. I wanted to have girls that look like you and act like you. I'd be lyin' if I said otherwise. But Ruth. There's only one of you. I got to take you how I can get you. And if this is part of you, part of that awful past, I'm good. I want to share whole life with you. I can't live it any other way."

I just looked at him not knowin' how to answer or if I dared believe he was even tellin' me the truth.

"Look at my face, my arms, I ain't what you thought you was gettin' either. I come back half the man I was, all scarred up, barely recognizable. You never said a word about it, just went to fixin' me right up again. I think that's what love is, when we accept the surprises, good or bad, with what we know. I know I love ya. I can't change that. I can't change that ya can't have my babies but my love for you makes that alright. I like to think you like my face just as much as before because its me. I like to think you want me around awhile longer whether I work the law or not. I like to think you love me the same as I love you. You mean the world to me, Ruth." He swallowed a couple times. "You are the world to me, Ruth."

I ain't never had someone talk to me like that before, askin' what I thought love was or how I made their world.

"I like to think you're right, Jedediah." I touched his pock marked face. " I don't mind your scars because they are your scars. They're just a part of you and I wish they wasn't there, I wish you hadn't suffered so, but you're right. I'll take a scarred up you any day over the ones that don't have you at all." I leaned over and kissed and climbed right on top of him.

Our love makin' was more than ever before. I rode him, hard until I tired out and he finished on top of me. He fell asleep on me, nearly crushin' me but I left him there as long as my breath could take it. This was love. This was our love and I aimed to keep hold of it as long as each moment allowed.

We each woke up early and even headed downstairs together. He helped with breakfast and I made the coffee. We didn't talk, just enjoyed havin' the other there, occasionally touchin' a hand or shoulder. When we sat down to breakfast, he asked what was next.

"What comes next, then, when folks marry?" He inquired like I might know. I thought about it for a few moments, tryin' to recall the few memories I'd known when folks married.

"Well, I never sat in a weddin' ceremony, so I ain't sure about them. But I did see a few brides readyin' for theirs. I guess we got to get us a preacher or lawman to recite the vows for us. I don't want to go to a church to have ours, do you?" I asked him. He looked at me and laughed.

"I swear, Ruth, you didn't have to say those words out loud, your face said if for ya. If you don't want to go to church, I won't make ya." He shook his head and continued eatin' his eggs.

"I guess that means we go to the lawman, then," I answered. I thought a little while before addin', "I might like a new dress though. I seen a girl where a real pretty blue for her day. I can't see me wearin' white like some trussied up teenager waitin' to please her man with her virginity but I would like to be pretty for ya." I recalled the girl in that blue dress from a few years back.

I'd been standin' out on that rickety patio and watched her goin' right to the church. It was obvious even from my perch what she was doin' and who she was. She was frightened but excited, her eyes shone and her face flushed. That blue dress fit her just right, tight around her young waist with a full skirt. Her mama walked with her and a few other women and girls joined. The men-folk were already there waitin'. I remember envien' her a bit that day. I envied her future. I couldn't hate her though, as much as I envied her I couldn't hate her. I couldn't make myself even wish we might trade stations. She was too kind-lookin' to even wish such a life on her. She seen me watchin' and offered a quiet smile my way. Every time I seen her after, she did the same thing. I wondered what she might think of me now, runnin' my own store, marryin' a man. I kept those thoughts all to myself, though. I didn't feel like sharin' 'em with anyone, not even Jedediah.

"I want a dress and I want you to wear somethin' nice too. I think a new shirt would be alright. I want some sort of flowers too. What do you think about that? We might even have a little cake here for a few people to have to celebrate with us." I smiled as he nodded, excitement growin' in my heart.

"I can hardly believe it!" I threw my arms around him, "We gonna get married!" I kissed him, "When?" I asked.

He said that was up to me. I nodded and asked him to let me think on it.

It was a lot to think on, when I settled a little. I sure wanted that fancy dress and flowers and cake. I wanted to celebrate. I went into the shop and touched the soft blue fabric that would make a fine weddin' dress. There was plenty there for a dress with full skirts and sleeves.

I sighed and went to my garden. I was soon joined by my cardinal friend. He bounced around cocking his little head this way and that, bringin' a smile to my face. "How are you today, Millie?" I asked him. "I guess you know, Jedediah's asked me to wed him and I said yes. You know I can't give him children and now he knows that too. He said he don't mind, can ya believe that?" I thought for a second and added, "Well, I guess ya probably can, after all, Joe did the same with ya didn't he?"

I recalled that day Joe left, not so many weeks prior. He loved that woman so much; he just couldn't bear to be so near yet so far from her any longer. His head was bowed and though he seemed at peace, I think we both knew he would never find such a happiness again. The cardinal flew away, high up into a tree so covered in branches I couldn't see him any longer even though his bright red stood out so plainly from the dense green.

Then, all at once, two cardinals flew from his retreat. They flew together and round each other and up and down, til it was almost difficult to watch 'em too much longer. They were so happy with each other, just to have the other near. They cared little for how far or near the ground came, content to simply fly near the other's wing.

I stood and went back in my house.

"Jedediah!" I called out. He was standin' in the kitchen, I'd interrupted him helpin' himself to a cool drink of water. I walked over and wrapped my arms around his neck and looked into his eyes.

CHAPTER 27

"I don't want to wait. I don't want to wait even for a dress to be finished. I just feel lucky you're hear with me now and even luckier you want me to be your wife. Did I ever tell you about the Chinese woman who pointed out a crane one day? She told me it was bringin' me luck and I couldn't believe her. I just couldn't believe *I* might have luck on my side. 'Course then, they went on down there to China Town and that was just awful." I shook my head, tryin' to forget the poor folks stranded there that day. Images of Dan's face swarmed before my eyes too. I hadn't thought too much on him since I'd left. I shook my head again, I wasn't goin' to now neither. "Well, then I left though. I made it here and wondered if that was my luck. I wondered if it run its course. But good things kept happenin'. I found Millie and Joe. And you. I can't help but think it was luck that brought me here. And brought you back. I sure ain't deservin' of all this but I ain't goin' to waste it neither. So, let's do it, lets get married in clean, nice clothes but I don't want to wait. We can open the doors here and serve our customers cake the next day. What do you think?"

Jedediah brushed my hair to the side of my face and turned my face upwards, towards him. He leaned down and kissed me real gentle. "I want what you want but I think you are deservin' of a good life. And I aim to give that my best." And we stood like that awhile, arms 'round each other, contemplatin' a future I never thought I'd have.

We married in two days' time. Neither of us had survivin' parents or even siblings to attend. The sheriff performed the legal issues and signed our certificate. I hadn't wanted to marry in a church and Jedediah said he wasn't interested in that neither.

I wore my best dress, a real pretty calico print. I done my hair up and Jedediah put on his cleanest trousers and shirts. I thought we looked real nice and respectable. It only took a few moments for us to be pronounced husband and wife. We walked home, holdin' hands.

I was amazed what a few moments could do to a life. Here I was married after only a few moments. All those years ago that Indian attack lasted about the same time changin' my life. Even the massacre on China Town only lasted that day. A few moments could change everything; once again, I felt nothin' but luck was shinin' on me right then, these were good moments.

I opened up our store and laid out a cake. Folks was finally comin' out more and many stopped by lookin' for goods and wantin' somethin' different after the weeks spent apart. They all congratulated us; every single one congratulated us. They thanked us for the cake and the goods and by the end of the afternoon, I was tired.

Jedediah followed me up to our bed. He wrapped those arms around me and laid me down, "Now, wife are you ready to be married?" He whispered in my ear. He slid my legs apart and put his hand in between, searchin' for that little part that brought me so much joy.

Holdin' it between his thumb and fore finger, he kissed me, lettin' his tongue slide over my lips and on my teeth. It wasn't long before I was wet and panting, willin' to make him feel what I was. I pushed back and got him beneath me, lowerin' my mouth over him. Holdin' the back of my head right where he wanted he let me suck till he cried out. Then, he finished on top of me.

We fell asleep naked knowin' we would wake up to the other for the rest of our days. I couldn't help but cry, just a little as I was fallin' to sleep. I was so happy; my life was finally full of peace.

Winter moved in, swift and seemingly vengeful for spring and summer and all that comes with those months. A freeze finished off the last of my garden in one short night. Snow covered firewood another night and though we tried to keep the front of the store warm and cozy, winds blew in cold behind each customer. I wore a heavy shawl indoors as well as out most days just tryin' to keep from shiverin'. I kept my head covered and Jedidiah did much the same. 'Course, him bein' a man, he had the ease of wearing a heavy coat that never slipped from his shoulders while he worked. His heavy boots kept out the water and muck better than my shoes but he was still frail from the small pox. I noticed if he got a chill, he was cold to the bone till we went to bed. It didn't seem to bother me quite the same way, even without men's wear.

Our little store was doing wonderfully well. I had a larger harvest than I'd expected thanks to both gardens. Even though a small family moved into my place and I expected them to tend that garden, I was already plannin' on expandin' this garden. Jedediah was building some bee boxes so as to grow and harvest our own honey come spring.

Honey was the most popular salve yet. I knew honey could heal skin and it had a soft scent, so I wasn't too surprised but wanted to keep supply to the demand. Jedediah was right on par with the idea too. He took to runnin' the store front most days so I could make the soap and salves.

He was real good with the orderin' and keepin' shelves stocked. One day, I watched him from the doorway. I was curious how he interacted with the good folks sure, but my heart still took to flutterin' thinkin' he was my husband too.

He was real sweet to the older folks. He let them shop at their own pace, helpin' where he could but never over doin' it neither so they might take offence or think they was bein' coddled. One young mother came in with her baby girl who was new walkin'. He watched over her real careful, makin' sure nothin' was spilled or pulled down on her. No one stayed over long but all conversated real nice and said they'd see him soon enough. I recognized 'em from the weeks prior and figured they were all goin' to be regulars.

Life was peaceful but I also felt fulfilled. I'd first moved here searchin' for peace and found *that* easy enough. I kept to myself just as most did around these parts. I did find peace wasn't quite enough for a good life. Folks need something to keep them goin'. Its more than someone. I found that is an icing on cake but it ain't always what keeps us goin'. That drive comes from a place, deep within that drives us to rise each mornin' and dare to live. I think I'd found my drive in my soaps and salves.

There was just so much to do with that whole process, from harvestin' plants for their scent, to dryin' 'em to finally actually makin' the goods. Even then, the goods needed to harden or be jarred and most days I found plenty to do right in those steps.

Initially, I'd worried about Jedediah and his drive. I thought he might miss the law or excitement of the trail that so often called on his services. I was wrong, though. His drive was that little store. He liked greetin' his neighbors and was real friendly in ways I doubted he'd done before. He knew most folks by name and asked after their spouses, their kids and most times, even their kin. Each afternoon, he did the books and once again, I was surprised how neat his numbers and letterin' was.

It was just about heaven on earth even with the harshness of winter tryin' its best to freeze us out. We warmed each other each night and kept cozy dinners right there in our home. I was real surprised to learn that a man who lived on his own weren't too proud to mend things that needed mendin' or wash up. The winter grew deeper and darker, like all winters but we took little notice.

Our life was quiet and we'd settled into much sooner than most young folks. I accepted we might be beyond some of that immaturity havin' lived apart and then survivin' the small pox. February began with no promise or even hopes of an early spring. I doubted I'd ever lived through such a harsh winter my entire life. The winds continued to howl blowin' in a storm that lasted over a week only ended with over a foot of new snow. Jedediah had to dig us out of house and home and visitin' the outhouse was no small chore. Each time we wondered if might freeze to our deaths.

Hardly any visitors came in the shop that week. And, bein's was so late in the winter months, I had little to do for soaps or salves. I packaged the last ones and planned for an early beginnin' to them this next spring, just minus the scents if I needed. I worked on tidyin' the kitchen and was gatherin' things for the washin' next day when I heard the shop door open. Truth was, I was a little relieved to have a customer. I paid no attention to the small talk wafting through to the back, I was cleanin' and shinin' faithful in Jedediah's capabilities in runnin' the front. I was a little surprised, then, to see him standin' before me. I glanced up but paid him no mind in my zest to accomplish the chores of the afternoon. He cleared his throat and without lookin' up, I asked if he needed water.

"No. Ruth, I ain't need no water. I think we need to talk." He sounded serious enough, I finally gave him some time. I looked up only to see he was indeed very serious. There was no lingerin' smile playin' at his lips like I'd grown accustomed to, even the light in his eyes was gone.

"Look here, Ruth. I think we need to talk and its best if we sit down. I locked the front door. No one can hear what I am about to tell ya." I nodded, joinin' him at the table.

He sat silent for what seemed forever promptin' me to take his hand and ask what was so serious not once, not twice but three times over.

He looked at me, almost as if he was surprised I was there or talkin' to him.

"What is it, Jedediah? What could be this serious, durin' this storm to cause you this behavior? Who was in the store? What news did they bring?" I tried to keep my voice calm but I was irritated at the interruption and if he had somethin' to say, he may as well say it. Whatever it might be, we could figure it out together. He just needed to tell me what was goin' on.

"This ain't easy for me, Ruth." He began. He wasn't lookin' me in the eye, he was talkin' to the table. I took his hands in mine.

"Look at me Jedediah. Look at me. We can get through this. Whatever it might be. Why, look at what we been through! Together and apart. Just tell me what it is." Finally, finally he looked at me.

"You're right, Ruth. Right as rain. We been through an awful lot. Only a few things we done together. I can't change my past no more than you can yours. I like that about us. Fact is, its one of my favorite things about us. I don't like some of my past and I know how you feel about yours." He paused. Then he swallowed real hard. "This is so hard to tell ya. Mostly, I been truthful with ya. Some of it, I just forgot somehow. I never lied about how I love ya. I never lied when I told ya, you is all I need to be complete. Thing is though. Well." I was shocked to see a tear slide down his face. "I can't say I didn't know because I did. I just thought that part of my life was over and done." His shoulders shook with real sobs then. I had no idea what he was talkin' about.

"You ain't makin' much sense, Jedediah. Not much sense at all. Now, I can see how terrible you are feelin' and ya best tell me what is goin' on so I can help. Because as your wife, that's what I should do. Right?" I grasped both shoulders in my hands and got him to look me in the eye again. I was convinced whatever he was on about, we could figure out together. There was nothin' I could dream up otherwise. I just couldn't.

He rubbed his eyes and looked at me again. The man looked exhausted even in these early evenin' hours. Dark circles framed each eye and the hollows in cheeks were more pronounced than normal. "Alright, Ruth. But as I tell ya, try to remember what I just told ya first. I didn't aim to lie to ya or hurt ya. I was with a woman before you."

I almost laughed in his face. "With a girl before me," I thought, "Who wasn't with anyone before anyone?" He was awful serious though, so I tried not to grin at him beckonin' him on with his tale.

"I was with a girl that I loved. She loved me, I knew it and we lived for a little while, together. I had a little cabin outside of this town, that's where we first met." He paused again.

I still had no idea what was so upsettin' this man. I wasn't over-jealous of past lovers or love interests. I didn't care a fig if he lived with some woman before I was free and I told him so. He only nodded at the table again.

"Look me in the eye, Jedediah. Why are you so upset? Did she pass on? If she passed on and you're feelin' sad, I can't say that makes me over-happy because I want you to be happy enough here you never think of everything and everyone else. But that ain't how life works. I know that. You can be sad, I don't mind. If you loved her she must have been somethin' special to this world and I think its fine you mourn such a loss." I patted his hands.

"That ain't it, Ruth. She didn't die." He straightened his back and brought his folded hands towards his face and rested his head on them. "Like I said, I didn't meant to forget or mean to keep her from ya. I just.. I just moved on from her, from that time. Not too long in livin' there with her, I knew I would never stay with her, not like I wanted to stay with you. It was wrong. I should have left then. Hell, I should never lived there in the first place. I can see that now. I took advantage of someone needin' a safe place and all. I was kind to her but I let her pay me back with the only thing she had, herself." He sighed again. I didn't know what to say.

I didn't think the story was too terrible and certainly didn't think he was too terrible neither. But I sat up straight, emulatin' him and folded my arms in front of my chest. I waited for him to continue.

"It wasn't long before even I knew she was with child. I deluded myself, Ruth, into thinkin' it might not be mine. We weren't married. I didn't know her family. I told myself that baby could have been anyone's knowin' damn well it was mine. We couldn't talk over much, see and I finally grew tired enough of her, I just left one day. I left her out there on her own. I ain't even been back to that lean-to I fashioned for us. Not once." His thumbs were in front of his mouth now, hands still folded. He looked off in the distance, somewhere past my left shoulder.

"I left and I didn't go back. I figured her people would take care of her or she'd move on to someone else. Well, that was a lie I think I told myself so I might sleep at night. And it didn't matter then, and it don't matter now. No one went to look for her and she didn't move on. Her and the baby they been there ever since." I watched him, my arms still folded in my front.

Mostly, I was amazed at some girl darin' to live on her own in these mountains raisin' her baby. How she had the skills to survive was beyond me but I didn't say anything. I waited for him to tell me why this all mattered now.

Cruel as it might be, he might have been right. Her people might have finally come to her or she might have moved on, I wasn't too sure why he was talkin' to me about this at all. I tried not to dwell on the fact he had a child by someone else and that was all he would ever have;

I could never give him that. I forced myself to wait and see what more he had to tell me.

"The girl, she died. She must have gotten the small pox somehow. They found her, at the cabin where I'd left her. It was bad, she been dead awhile. No one ever went lookin' for her." Again, I wondered what he was tryin' to say and not say. I wondered why no one went lookin' for her. I felt my brow furrow and I leaned forward to hear his next quiet words, "You see, Ruth. She was Indian. She and I met one time in the forest. She offered herself to me and I didn't deny it even though we couldn't even speak much. We was caught, though. I think it was her brother that seen us. She refused to leave my side then. I took her to that little place and for awhile, it was nice. It was real nice to have someone all night and she never complained. She was young."

He stopped there and collected himself a little. I tried to understand just what he was sayin'.

"Alright, Jedediah. I think you are tellin' me you feel guilt over a girl you left. I understand, I really do. I think we can never predict how long she might have lived if you were with her or not. I might even be selfish sayin' I am glad you left her behind. I can't help that, though. I am glad. Your guild will fade." I reached out to pat his hand but he recoiled. I looked at him, wonderin' if this was the true Jedediah. A man who tired of his women after a few months. I tried to quiet my breath pushin' back the risin' panic in my gut.

I could make it out here on my own. I didn't need him, I'd proved that. I sure liked havin' him around though. I looked around thinkin' how just this mornin' I'd been so happy, so content and noticin' his happiness and contentment. What happened in a matter of hours that could change that? A dead girl? It didn't make sense. Once again, I waited for him to continue though I didn't reach for his hand again.

He breathed in and out. And in and out. It was all I could do, sittin' there waitin' wonderin'. Finally, he spoke again. "I can't feel too much guilt, even now. Hell, I feel more guilt not feelin' guilt, Ruth. She was just an Indian girl. She was probably cast out for somethin' that's why she was in the forest on her own that day she run into me. She took care of the home alright and like I done told ya, she took care of me too, every night if I wanted. Like I said, it was nice for awhile but soon I felt like I didn't want to be there anymore. I didn't want to be with her. I convinced myself she was evil somehow. I don't know how or why, I just felt it when I was with her. I felt like she might be waitin' to kill me. I'd wake up feelin' her stare on me. She wouldn't be in bed, she'd be standin' over me, just watchin'. I didn't like it. I convinced myself her baby wasn't mine. I think it was though. And now, it don't matter. She died and the child was left behind." As I listened to his story, relief flooded my being.

CHAPTER 28

Jedediah wasn't some hateful man who just left his women after tirin' of 'em. He left a girl for other reasons. I couldn't help but offer a small smile his direction.

"Well, no matter now. It sounds like she was right odd and you was fine to leave. I think it is a sad tale, for sure but sad for all of ya. What is makin' ya think of all this past? Is it the weather, the winter winds bringin' it all back?" I reached for his hand again. This time, he allowed me to take it.

"Ruth. It ain't the wind. I ain't thought much of her or the baby since I rode off three winters ago. Not till today. And a man just came in, ya know him. He wants to run for mayor next term. Well, someone has reported a child found, in the woods near a cabin. The child was the only livin' soul around, no one else was there to care for it or nothin'. I guess someone has takin' them in temporary-like but don't want to keep them." He stopped there and looked me deep in my eyes. I nodded.

It was clear now. A child, *his* child was found starvin' and alone in a winter fit for no man. I drew back my hand. I could see what he was askin' now, saw all too clear what the implications were and I couldn't answer. He would have to ask and I wasn't sure what answer I had.

He didn't though. He just sat there with his head in his hands leavin' me to wonder all sorts of things. I wondered if the child was a girl or boy. I wondered if they looked like him. I wondered if this was his debt for survivin'.

I wondered if this was a debt for my own survival.

I went to bed and didn't ask him to follow me. I needed some space and time to think.

I lay there, shiverin' in the dark. I'd grown accustomed to him bein' around at night sharin' the warmth of his body. I wasn't enjoyin' bein' apart, at least not with the cold. I lay on my back, eyes wide open to the dark wonderin' at this news.

It sounded like he was ready to take the child in and when he didn't ask, I figured he didn't want my opinion. That angered me right to my core. After all, I was the one who took him back in, nursed him back to health and shared my livin' space with him. He all but ran the store *I'd* inherited. All without a complaint from me. I wasn't too sure I was ready to give up more for him. I briefly wondered if he might do the same for me. I hardly slept at all and finally gave up sleepin' all together and went back down the stairs.

He was asleep in his chair before the fire. He looked rough, still completely clothed and his hair stood on end as if his hand raked through it a thousand and one times. I stood watchin' him until he woke a few seconds later. I took the chair opposite him. He struggled to sit up straight and rubbed the sleep from his eyes. It was still dark outside, the only light was from our dyin' fire. He stood and added another log. Then he looked at me and took his seat, he didn't sink in real comfortable. He mirrored me and sat on the edge. We watched the fire consume the new log awhile. He spoke first.

"I don't what is right here, Ruth. I can't say I ever did know. What does that make me? A man, capable of leavin' such a young thing on her own with a baby. What kind of man does that?" He watched me for my reaction. I just looked at him, my face drawn.

Nothin' I could ever say or do would change the past. I doubted it could take the pain away from him even. The thing was, I didn't think he was lyin'. That Indian girl might have been a real good time in the sheets but it was strange, the way she watched him while he slept, like that. I told him that.

"It is mighty strange the way she was watchin' you while ya was sleepin'. No one would like that, Jedediah. It made you uncomfortable, wonderin' what you might wake up to, maybe even wonderin' if you would wake." I nodded, at the fire, almost talkin' more to the fire than him. "Out here, well, its just like this fire. We all are drawn to it, it puts off all this heat, ya see. But if we don't feed it, it dies and can't give off more heat. Feedin' it takes more than we ever could have guessed. No man or woman out here can judge another's actions, we only see what we see and act accordin'. We all want to stay warm, no matter the cost. Life ain't easy out here, that we know. All we want is to survive, no matter the cost." I held out my hand without lookin' at him and he took it. We sat a long while, watchin' that fire until the log turned to ash finally and I stood to add another.

"What do we do now, Jedediah?" I stood before him, blockin' the fire, its light and warmth. "Do you feel like you need to care for a child you once abandoned? Could you abandon your child twice?"

He looked so sad then and I almost wished I hadn't asked but I wasn't tryin' to be hateful; it was an unspoken thought since he'd heard about the girl dyin' and that child bein' rescued. I think it hurt because it was my voice and I knew he didn't want to let me down. And this situation forever changed things for him and by default, it changed everything for myself too.

No matter what he chose, take the child or leave it, they would always be part of this world. And we would always know they were alive and livin' somewhere. I can't say this made me look at Jedediah much different, knowin' he was capable of cruelty. I already knew every person is capable of such cruelty, we just show it different ways and sometimes we are better at hidin' it. Jedediah was a good man. He just did a cruel thing.

I waited for him to answer my question. He sat a long while and finally spoke so soft I could barely hear him. I had to ask him to repeat what he said. He leaned closer, resting his head on his hands which rested on his knees.

"Ruth, I can't tell ya how this news felt. I feel like the most awful man leavin' them out there like that. Ya see, I always thought I was above such things somehow's. I tried to keep the peace. I kept mostly to myself. Even if that girl was strange, did she deserve abandonment? It ain't easy, life out here. The winters are tough and honest to God, the summers ain't much better. It's hot and dry and water is scarce. I left them that way, though. Left 'em to live or die, it didn't matter. I left 'em; to survive or die, it didn't matter. What does that make me, Ruth? A murderer? She died because of me, that child might have died because of me. I tried to forget 'em, ya know. I tried. I met you and I think I even did forget for a little while." He paused again. "Now, I have what I wanted, a good woman and all. Seems like no matter what I do, it might be wrong somehow. How can I ask you to fix my past?"

I nodded at his words, his questions. I took some time to think on what he was sayin'. He was askin' me to raise a child not my own. He was askin' if he was a good man or a man so terrible he did not deserve my love or any blessin's of this life. I looked at him and took my seat again. Keepin' my eyes on him, I told him what I thought.

"I don't think of myself as a whore no more, Jedediah." My voice was soft. I hadn't said those words out loud before. I said 'em again. Louder. Stronger. "I ain't a whore no more." He dropped his hands and made eye contact with me, his mouth open a little. He closed it and shook his head a little at me.

"Now, Ruth, I never thought of you like that."

"I know, Jedediah. And I don't think of you as a terrible man, neither. Life changes us, we grow and we learn. If we get real lucky some of us even get the chance to make peace with our pasts. Now, it don't matter what you choose, that child is free from her beginnin's. If you want to take 'em in, fine. I won't take issue with raisin' a child." I smiled a little and looked into the fire again. "I never thought I might be a mother. I gave up that hope a long while ago. I ain't just talkin', if ya decide its somethin' we need to do, I'll be alright becomin' a mother." I leaned back in my chair clasping my hands over my own empty womb. I knew what I hoped he would choose, but I wasn't goin' to choose for him.

We sat in the silence of the winter night a long while, just watchin' the fire, feedin' it and thinkin' to ourselves. When we finally rose to go to bed, we didn't talk neither. We kissed each other goodnight and held onto the other. Sometimes life just don't need words.

I was surprised that we both slept right through the night, neither of us woke, not even once. Jedediah smiled at me smoothin' my hair away from my face.

"I can't tell ya how lucky I am to have ya, Ruth. I sure don't deserve a woman like you."

"I feel just that way about you, Jedediah. That little Chinese woman told me that crane promised luck and I guess she was right because I never even dared wish for this life. Yet, here we are." I smiled at him recallin' that day by the river.

The woman was so sure of what the crane promised but I'd doubted her words. I shouldn't have, though. Before her, the woman with the cards promised a new life too. Lookin' back a little, I guess I was too afraid they might be wrong, that I might not deserve all this. One thing that devil demanded in whole, was hope. Once hope is gone it sure is difficult to see or even think good might come your way. I shook my head at all the changes in life in such a short time.

We rose and readied for the day. It was early and still dark outside. I could hear the wind promisin' more cold. I wondered what he'd decided but I didn't ask. I just set to makin' breakfast. He sat at the table, watchin'. I set two plates of steamin' biscuits and gravy down and took my own seat. The man hardly blinked though he was lookin' my way.

"I see you watchin' me, but I don't think you see me, Jedidiah." He didn't respond; I wondered if he even noticed breakfast was finished. "Jedidiah. Look, breakfast is all finished."

"What? Oh, yes. Thank you." And he began eatin'. I followed suit and we ate in silence.

While I ate, I began plannin' my day. I wanted to open the store and really clean some of the displays. We was set to get in a big order before too long and I figured space was goin' to have to come from somewhere. It was never too early to clean, neither. Spring would be here before too long and then I'd be busy again with the garden and the soaps and salves again. I looked out the window at the winter scene.

The garden was bare, nothin' at all showed the magic of the year. Rcallin' my thoughts from the night before, I hoped for an early spring and bountiful garden. I think I deserved it.

Jedediah was already cleanin' up the dishes so I stood and helped. Then I followed him into the store. He stood behind the counter, goin' over some numbers. I began workin' on the displays. It was still early but I unlocked the door anyway. "May as well," I thought.

We worked in silence awhile until Jedediah finally spoke.

"I decided, Ruth. I've thought about it and I think I know what I need to do." He just stood behind the counter, lookin' past me. I even glanced at the door, his stare was so intent, I thought I'd see someone walkin' through it. No one was there.

"What are ya lookin' at, Jedediah?" I asked him. He shook his head a little and finally looked my way. I walked to him. "What did you decide?"

"Well, I thought about what you said last night, how a person changes through life. I liked how you said we can sometimes make peace with our pasts too. I think we just gotta take the opportunities if and when they arise." He paused, watchin' me real close. "I want to give you the final say but I think we should get the child."

I grinned at him. "I was thinkin' you would conclude that, Jedediah but I ain't gonna lie, I wasn't too sure this mornin'. You didn't speak much and I ain't one to pry but I am real happy. I think we can be a real nice family. We have a safe, warm home. We have this business. I think we can provide real nice for the child. Speakin' of which, when will you tell me if it is a boy or a girl? Do they got a name?"

Jedediah strode over and picked me up, twirlin' me 'round once before settin' me back down. He kissed me and nestled his face into my shoulder, makin' me laugh. He didn't let go, so I gently pushed his arms until he stepped back a little and looked up at him.

"Well, what is the child?" I prompted him.

"It's a girl. They call her Ruth."

I felt my mouth open, I couldn't hide my surprise. I brought my hand to my heart, "A girl?" I whispered, "Who carries my name?"

I couldn't understand. First, I just expected a boy, no reason, I guess I just figured Jedediah would produce a boy.

When I was young I'd hoped for a girl. I wanted a little one to follow me around, copyin' my actions. I wanted to watch her care for a doll. After my own family was killed and I'd learned what girls were for, I'd stopped that dream. It was too much to bear. Now, that old dream was given breath and she even had my name. I felt a little light-headed.

"Well, I thought her mama was Indian, why she got my name?" I asked.

He was supportin' most of my weight now and he answered real gentle, "Well, the folks who took her in thought she deserved a name. She's so little and they don't think she speaks English or at least, she hasn't yet, they just called her Ruth. We may never know what her mother called her but I like the idea of keepin' her name as Ruth. I was a little worried what you might think. Did you have a different name you want to use?"

I looked at him. I didn't right know what to say at all. I didn't have names picked out. In my mind, when I thought the child was a boy, I'd figured on callin' him Jedediah. I needed to sit and I told him so, he helped me into the one chair behind the counter. Kneelin' in front of me he asked if I was alright.

"Well, I think so. I just wasn't figurin' on any of this. A girl called Ruth is goin' to be here and I will be her mother." I said the words out loud but more to myself than to Jedediah. He put a hand to my face.

"I am goin' to fetch you some water. You stay right here." I watched him hurry away.

I took a deep breath and closed my eyes waitin' on Jedediah's return. I smiled at him as he returned with the water. I accepted it gratefully and sipped.

"Thank you, Jedediah. I can't say what came over me just then. I knew it might be a girl but I think I was expectin' you to say boy. Then, to hear she carries my name…" my voice faded. "All I can promise is to do my best. I want her to have a life far different than mine even if she does carry my name." I looked at him. I was afraid of this next unplanned step in our life.

"I just can hardly believe this." I told him. "A few months ago, I didn't even know where you was. Then, here ya come, and we get this place. I can't say I ain't nervous. Little ones take a lot of care. It won't be just us." I watched his face, wonderin' what he was thinkin'.

Funny, not even twelve hours before I was so certain what we should do and what I'd hoped he would do. I wasn't disappointed it was a girl, I was just shocked. I was shocked that we would have a child and to hear she had my own name caused me to pause and really take in what her presence would change.

"I don't have to take her in, Ruth. I don't mind if ya don't want it. When I heard her name, I didn't know what to think." He looked down.

I put my hand beneath his chin, raisin' his face to mine. "I didn't say that, Jedediah. I said I was shocked. When do we get her?"

CHAPTER 29

That little girl changed our lives from that moment onwards. She came a few days after that conversation givin' me time to set up a proper bed and such for her. Jedediah left me runnin' the store on my own while he retrieved her. She was a day's ride away, he said and was gone most of the afternoon, through the night and well into the day.

I was real busy, we had more customers that day which I was real grateful for. I was so busy, in fact, I didn't really glance up when I heard the bell on the door indicatin' someone was enterin'. I was in the kitchen, and called out, "I'll be right there!" but took my time finishin' my water. I didn't hear Jedediah's steps enterin' the kitchen. When I finally looked over, there he stood with a tiny girl in his arms. He smiled at me and set her down.

She was so small and her mother's heritage was apparent. Her hair already was past her tiny waste, black as any night. Her skin was fair, more like Jedediah's though. Her features were dainty but I could see she shared his jaw line. Her eyes were dark but the shape was all his. She put her finger in her mouth and looked back at me.

"Well, my my." I kept my voice soft and gave her some time to see me. "She might be the most beautiful think I ever seen." I meant it too. She was absolutely beautiful. Jedediah crouched down to her height.

She was so little, he still towered above her but the gesture was one of the sweetest I ever saw.

"Little Ruth," I heard him say and he took one of her tiny hands in his own, "there's your mama." She looked at him, then looked at me.

I don't know if she understood him or was simply used to being with a woman more but she walked right to me, then. She looked up at me and I down at her. My heart was beatin' fast as it ever did as I looked over my daughter for the first time. Then, she raised her little arms.

I picked her up and said, "Hi there, Little Ruth. Ain't ya just a beauty." She put her one hand back in her mouth while she studied my face. I forgot all about runnin' the store and brought her right to our parlor. I sat with her on my chair. I faintly heard the door to the store again but I couldn't take my eyes off the little miracle sittin' there on my lap.

I touched her hair, it was still baby soft. I looked at each little hand and foot. Whomever found her must have been fond of her, she was clean and well fed. Her lips was bright red and moist too. She wasn't hungry or thirsty. I loved her more than I think I'd ever loved anyone before. Just like that.

I couldn't explain it but I felt a connection with her. She was my daughter, someone else had given her life but she was mine. I felt hot tears slide down each cheek as she leaned back into me. I rested my chin on her little head and silently thanked the girl who birthed her, the folks that found her and cared for her and I even thank Jedediah for fatherin' her. I wasn't too sure how to thank God but I did the best I could with that too.

As I prayed, that little girl fell right to sleep. I sat with her a long while, learnin' my new role. Her little body was warm and she warmed me as we sat. When the fire grew low, Jedediah miraculously appeared to check on us. I shushed him as he entered the room. He put another log on the fire and turned to watch us silently. Before he walked away, I saw him brush tears from his own face.

I don't know how long we sat there like that but when she finally woke, I was hungry. I expected she was too. I set her on the floor and held her hand as we walked to the kitchen. She pointed to the table. I figured that meant she was hungry. I sat her down while I hurried to get some dinner ready. I heard Jedediah close up the store for the night.

It was already darkenin' outside while I worked. Little Ruth made hardly a peep while I finished dinner up. She watched as Jedediah took his place at the table and I set her real careful on the other chair. I ladled a thick stew into three bowls and set each carefully down on the table. She grinned at the food. Jedediah caught my eye and we grinned too.

The next day or two passed in blurry stages of contentment and disbelief. Little Ruth was real smart, that was apparent from that first meal. She knew how to feed herself and even how to use the toilet. I bathed her each night and smoothed my salve into her skin. She allowed me to care for her and though I didn't think she understood what we was sayin' by the end of that first week, she was tryin' to copy our sounds.

I talked to her non-stop through each day. I pointed out items and told her what they was and how we used each one. I told her colors and counted things too. She followed me around more than she did Jedediah but she wasn't scared of him. One afternoon, I took a little break and went off on my own a little while leavin' just them in the store front.

I could here Jedediah talkin' to her, tellin' her how the store was and then I heard him talk to her about me.

"Well," he said, "You might hear us call you Little Ruth. We do that because you're so little," I heard a giggle and could see him tickle her tummy a little while he spoke, "And we call you that because your mama is also called Ruth." I heard him kiss the top of her head and I didn't think I might ever be any happier.

The days were nothin' less than magical spent with our Little Ruth. She brightened up our home and our shop and though she wasn't speakin' words just yet, her mere presence brightened up each person's day. Soon, all our customers met her and inquired after her each time they visited.

Nights were another matter.

Little Ruth would fall asleep on either mine or Jedediah's lap in front of the fire downstairs. We carried her upstairs to her own bed that first night. She didn't wake at all, not with the jarring steps or being laid down. I'd carefully covered her with the warmest blankets and carefully stepped away so's not to wake her. I figured she had to be exhausted from her journey and all the changes. She hadn't cried or nothin' all afternoon nor any time throughout the day time hours since that first day.

The first night, though not entire unexpected, she'd woke us both with her screams. It near broke my heart to rush in and see her clutchin' her blankets in sheer terror tryin' to find where she was in the dark. I took her to our bed that night and we slept that way since. I told Jedediah it was best for her and us. It was warmer and she didn't have to wait for someone to find if she was scared.

"And we will sleep better not listen' so hard for her, too," I'd whispered over her restin' head between us. He didn't answer, just laid a protective arm over us both and went back to sleep.

Each night, Little Ruth would waken two or three times, terrified and cryin'. I'd dry her eyes and Jedediah fetched her water. We spoke real gentle while she hiccupped through her tears and fall asleep again. Then, we repeated it each night.

Winter slowly edged towards spring time as we slowly edged towards Little Ruth wakin' less each night. After weeks and weeks, the sun finally warmed the earth enough to start the snow meltin', I could hear it as I opened the kitchen window for the first time that year.

It was glorious afternoon. Little Ruth had finally slept the night through. I wasn't too sure if sleepin' all night was what energized me or the fact spring was finally on the move.

"See!" came a little voice from behind me and I turned to see what she was piontin' at. "See?"

She was pointin' at the window to a real promise of spring, a bird appeared on the sill. He was somethin' all in red with bright eyes unafraid, it seemed of comin' right into the house.

"Hi, Millie," I whispered. Then, to Little Ruth, "That is a bird. A red bird." I told her. "Can you say 'bird?'" She looked at the bird, then to me.

"Burr," she said, pleased with herself.

I nodded to her, "Bird."

Years later, I was workin' in my garden one sunny afternoon durin' late summer. I was gettin' older but not real old. Little Ruth was grown and expectin' her first child. Jedediah was doin' alright, happily runnin' the store.

I was outside, weedin' and thinkin' as the wind ran over me. The garden had changed much as we had. The trees, once little more than tiny saplings, now shaded the house and garden from late afternoon sunshine. The white picket fence was still upright and gleamed white but only under continued care and effort. I laughed a little as the thought, "Just like me," danced through my mind.

The one tree, the oak that was already big when I'd moved in, and only thickened and strengthened throughout the years, reminded me of Jedediah, I thought that afternoon. It was strong and true, one branch twisted a little too much remindin' me nothin is perfect. It provided shade and shelter for our home.

The sun, though welcome each year, was hot and even deadly in this desert. The true ensured our home was almost always cool even in the early evenings. The winters had never eased and the tree sheltered us from brutal winds and high snows. Each year, folks in town had to dig their ways out of their own doors! Not us, though, thanks to the tree that took all the cold from us.

I stopped working and looked around the garden more. Through the years, the cardinal family still nested each spring. I still called 'em all Millie, likin' to think maybe they represented her Little Mildred sort of like my Little Ruth. Their happy chirpin' woke me each mornin' and none ever showed any sign of fear in my presence.

There were the roses, taller now and hugging the fence. Their scent drifted across to me enticin' me still. They reminded me of the girls I once worked and lived beside. They was better enjoyed from a distance, ya get too close, them thorns bite. Still, I couldn't help but look past the thorns, even forgettin' all about 'em most times. Their pretty blooms, all full and colorful, waved real pretty in any sort of breeze. No matter how harsh the winter, or hot the summer, they came back offerin' a gentleness uncommon to the land unafraid of what it might take to survive.

I was real proud of the lavender. If I had to compare it to someone, I think I'd probably compare it to my own mother. Most of the time, it grew all summer. Its scent was strong and fine. The tiny purple blooms weren't as bright as the roses but gentle and beautiful in their own right. It wasn't suited to this land though and each fall, it died away. I'd faithfully planted again each spring, though, simply because it was so enjoyable to have around. "This landscape needs somethin' out of the ordinary," I would think each year, "even if it needs more love and ain't gonna last."

Jedediah planted a few apple trees through the years. They was real nice producin' real pretty blooms each spring and of course, a nice harvest of apples all summer. I think they reminded me of Cook from so long ago. I didn't think they belonged here but they made it work anyway growin' even if it was difficult and bein' real useful later on. I wondered what happened to her, if she ever made a life as good as mine turned out. I sure hoped so.

Beyond the food bearin' plants like the beans and such, my garden wasn't all pretty and nice to see. Hemlock grew right outside the fence. I was careful to prune it and careful to leave it. Real nice to look at but poisonous to ingest, I was careful to keep a bit around just in case. It reminded me of Dan. Such folks and plants are necessary but they belong outside the fence.

I went back to my weedin' and only stopped when I heard a familiar happy voice.

"Mama!"

I smiled before I even looked up. There was my girl. She was most like the bees. Her love was pure as honey and just as healin' too. She was real busy, always had been, just like any bee bouncin' from flower to flower, leavin' love where ever she went.

"Why, Ruth," I tried real hard not to call her "Little" no more, she was too grown for such a nickname even if I did think of her that way. "How are ya feelin'?" I stood and embraced her.

My, how proud I was of the young woman standin' before me! "I think you grew since the last I seen ya!" I exclaimed. It was true, her pregnancy was nearin' its end and I had to bend over her growin' belly to hug her thin shoulders. She was grown but she was a tiny woman. I loved how she looked with that belly. Her little shoulders and hips seemed to small for such a burden.

CHAPTER 30

Ruth grew up, like all children do, too quick for my likin'. She'd been curious, still was and when it came time for marryin' I wasn't surprised she had several suitors. I was less surprised when she married the respectable young doctor who had only lived in town the one winter.

Since then, she practiced midwifery. That was more than three years ago and her and her husband had begun to fear they may never have children. She come cryin' to me one spring night just after the rain.

"Mama," she'd cried, "I can't help but wonder why? Why can't I have a child for John? Is there somethin' wrong with me?" I'd held her and kissed her head, just like I'd always done.

I listened to her fears and her sadness until she was all cried out. Then I quietly reminded her not all of life is so planned. "Somethings are surprises," I'd told her, "and sometimes, they are the best things you never dreamt on your own." She'd nodded then and even apologized for her selfishness; she'd always known she wasn't mine.

"I love ya, mama," she'd told me and never cried again to me over not havin' a baby.

'Course, none of that mattered no more, here she was nearly due all those fears left forever to rest.

"Come inside, lets get you sat down. Now, tell me. How are things today?" We went inside and she sat right at the table just like she'd done as a little girl.

She told me how the baby was movin' all the time, how terrible the heat was and how she just wanted to hold her baby. She told me all about helpin' her friend give birth just yesterday.

"She was in so much pain, I could see it, but she pushed through and delivered a healthy baby boy. I think both her and the baby are going to be just fine." She looked so happy thinking about her friend and new baby.

We talked awhile and decided she would stay for dinner; her husband was seein' to a sick neighbor and said he wouldn't be home till after dark. I loved these nights, when she was home with us. They reminded me of the years she was growin'. She'd sit and talk while I fixed dinner. Tonight, I gave her some beans to snap while she talked. I heard Jedediah lock up the store front and make his way into the kitchen.

He was still a good lookin-man after all these years. Time had softened him a little; his hair was a little thinner and his face wore the unmistakable lines of a happy life. Smile lines creased around his mouth and eyes showin' me and the world we'd had some good years. I hoped my face reflected the same.

Ruth stayed, long after dinner and Jedediah and I walked her home in the dark. A breeze cooled the day quickly. We stayed with her awhile, waitin' for the doc to get back home. I couldn't help but notice how tender Jedediah was with her, helpin' her to her seat and even takin' her shoes off for her. It was very sweet. I put a shawl around her shoulders and boiled water for tea. Soon, her husband arrived and shooed us on home.

"That was one of the most pleasant evenin's of my life," I told Jedediah as I undressed for bed, once we got home. "Ruth is such a lovely young woman and endin' the day with her tellin' me about the baby movin' and her day was real fine." I joined him in bed and he put his still-strong arms around me and kissed the top of my head.

"I can't say any different, Ruth. It was a perfect end to a day. Our daughter has grown up and it is wonderful we live so close. When do you think the baby will come?" As always, he voice was soft, gentle. It seemed even more so when he inquired anything at all to do with Ruth.

I smiled, even though I knew he couldn't see through the dark. "I don't know but I think soon. She told me she felt the baby drop today, that means its close. Real close. Or, least that's what she said. It means her body is preparin' to give birth. I could tell too, when she was standin' there. She's been carryin' the baby a little higher. She said its easier to breath now, though." I felt him nod into the darkness.

He kissed me again, and like so many times before our hands found the places to pleasure each other. I never tired of him and he never seemed to of me either. Our love-making was still freeing but gentler now. He finished on top of me and as I held on, I thanked the fates one more time I had such a man. We fell asleep, as we normally did; in each other's arms.

The next day or two went by fast as any. I tried but failed to hang on to each moment; they just came too fast. Later, I could never recall if it was the very next mornin' or the day after that when Ruth went into labor. All's I remember is it was mornin' and a young girl came by the store to tell me Ruth needed me. I'd asked why and it was her who told me Ruth's waters broke.

Jedediah nearly pushed the poor girl out of the shop and began collectin' the few things we'd set aside for this moment; he'd prepared clean linen strips and towels. I'd been sewing tiny clothes and blankets for months. We gathered it all up and nearly ran to Ruth's house. I was grateful to see her husband was with her.

Normally, a midwife would step in but Ruth was the only midwife around for miles. He would have to deliver her. Jedediah sat in the kitchen while I joined the doctor and Ruth in their simple bedroom.

I was so proud of her when I entered her room. Her hair was already damp with the sweat of her labor and her eyes shut tight in the pain demadin' for little ones enterin' our world. When she saw me she reached for hand and just said, "Mama," before another pain gripped her body and soul. I held on and smoothed her hair from her face. Hour after hour I wiped her forehead with cold clothes and even rubbed her back. She never once complained, though there were few tears when the pains grew real intense.

As the sky darkened for evenin', her grip tightened on my hand like no one ever held onto me before. She cried out. I can't lie, I was frightened but I held on. "Go on then, Ruth! Push! Your baby's almost here!" I told her.

I cannot describe the next moments. She pushed and he caught a moving mass covered in a little blood and water. Ruth and I watched together as he wiped off the tiny bundle. He turned it over and rubbed his back until we heard a small cry, then he laid it right on Ruth's chest. I covered it with a clean linen while the doctor worked on tyin' of the cord. I looked down at my daughter, holdin' my grandchild and was so overwhelmed to see such perfection, I was afraid I might lose my own conscience. I kissed her forehead again right at the moment she kissed her little one's forehead. A tiny hand wave from beneath linen. I turned and wetted a clean cloth to wipe off that little bundle and set to work. Ruth knew just what to do and started feedin' right away.

"Ruth," I whispered, "You done good, girl, so good. You got yourself a girl." I could hardly speak, I was overcome with emotion. I stepped back, so the doctor could hold his wife and new daughter but Ruth beckoned me over.

"Mama, can you get daddy in here? I want him to see." That was just like my girl, excited to share new joys with us. She was a generous spirit. I walked to the door and called Jedediah.

He must have been standin' right around the corner, I'd never seen a man enter a room so fast!

He came right in and went right beside her bed. His face already covered in tears and he kissed her cheek. "What you got there, Ruth?" His voice heavy, husky with emotion.

"It's a girl, daddy, we got us a girl," She smiled at her husband while Jedediah looked at the tiny face before him, now sleepin'.

"Just what I was hopin' for, Ruth." He squeezed her shoulders and my hand at the same time.

"Do you have a name for her yet?" I asked the new parents. I saw the doctor put a hand on his wife's shoulders and though he answered me, he never took his eyes off the baby; none of us could. She was simply the most beautiful thing we'd ever seen.

"We are going to call her Ruth."

I nodded, too overcome to answer but I felt it was perfect. Ruth, after her mama. Ruth spoke up.

"Mama, its after both us. I wanted her to carry your name, just like I was so fortunate to."

Jedediah hugged me. Life sure held its surprises but there were some perfect ones that changed life. Jedediah was one. Little Ruth was another and Tiny Ruth was one.

The biggest surprise though, was finding the ability to live outside a life I'd been forced into. I was no longer a whore and owed no debt to man, devil or God. I simply was and would be. After awhile Ruth tired of holding her daughter and I took her in my arms for the first time.

I couldn't recall the last time I'd held an infant and I'd never held one so new to this world. Ruth fell into a hard-earned sleep while Jedediah and the doctor stepped into the next room; I think they needed some fresh air. I stayed right there beside my daughter's bed and washed the baby clean and swaddled her. Then I lay her in the small basinet Jedediah built a few months back and set to work cleanin' up the room.

Gentle as I could, without wakin' Ruth, I removed the linens soaked in her waters and blood. I wiped her legs clean and covered her body in new linens. After I checked the baby one more precious time I brought the wash all into the kitchen.

"Jedediah, I need some water heated so I can get to these linens. I think its best I get this finished now. Lord knows between her healin' and a new baby we are goin' to need all the linens we can get our hands on." I kissed him on the cheek in thanks and walked to Ruth's door.

I didn't want to disturb mama and baby so I just stood, holdin' my breath, listenin' for any sound one of 'em might need me. Not a sound came from the room and I walked softly back to the kitchen. I was pleased when Jedediah helped with the wash then we brought in more firewood in case the night grew chilly.

By then, the doctor was in and out of Ruth's bedroom. I couldn't help but fear the next few days. More than a few new mothers spiked fevers after givin' birth. I wasn't too sure if it was the trauma of the body producing another living being or the labor that induced but I did fear it. I kept thinkin' the best thing for my girl to do was just rest and let us care for her. As I was readyin' dinner and Jedediah stoked the fire, I felt a small tap on my shoulder. It was the doctor.

I smiled at him. What with all going on, I realized I hadn't congratulated him. Or thanked him for keepin' my girl safe. I opened my mouth to speak but before I could utter one sound he put a hand up and softly started speaking.

"Ruth, I want to thank you and you too, Jedediah," he said turnin' towards him too, "Thank you for helping Ruth and I out. Each time I leave her on her own, I never worry. You are here. Now, I know you will be here for both my Ruths and I just wanted to thank you." I think it had been a long day; we three were all a little more emotional than normal. He went on, "I can see you both are worried about Ruth and you're right, these next few days she needs all the rest she can get. I wanted you to know the birth was perfect, though. I believe she's going to be just fine, there wasn't too much bleeding, she was over-exhausted and the baby," His voice caught, "well, you two have seen the baby, she couldn't be more perfect. I would surely appreciate one or both of you staying the night over or coming back in the morning but I don't want you to be over worried, mom and baby are both fine." I couldn't help but break down a little at his words and I saw Jedediah turn his back to us, wipin' his own face. He let us collect ourselves and went to check on his wife and baby. He wasn't gone long.

"Jedediah, I haven't seen you hold her yet. Would you like to?" He'd returned with that precious bundle in his arms. "I know Ruth wants you to hold her. She's asleep again and this little girl just ate so she's ready for a nice long sleep." Jedediah was already settlin' into a chair, arms outstretched ready to take the baby.

I never experienced my Jedediah holdin' an infant. Ruth was near three when she came to us bringin' every joy a child can but we'd missed out on this precious stage. Jedediah was a real natural and I told him so, though I wasn't too sure he even heard me. He was whisperin' to her, tellin' her she was as pretty as her mother. I walked near to them and sat beside him. Tiny Ruth was wide awake, just lookin' at him.

"Aren't you a beautiful baby?" He whispered, "and you got a real fine name. Your mother is the second finest woman I ever have known. And your grandmother," He looked at me, "well, just wait till you get to know her. She's made my life worth more than anythin'. After her I lived more than just survivin'." I looked at him, he'd never told me that before. I could hardly believe I was deservin' of such a compliment; it was how I thought of him. He went on, "You mean the world to me, Tiny Ruth and your mama means the world to me too." He lifted his head again, "And you too, Ruth. You mean the world to me."

We sat then, in silence, watchin' her fall asleep real peaceful.

Ms Ruth, you come through the coal fires of hell. Instead of burnin' ya they refined ya. I ain't over-worried about the past, and ya can't be neither.

The only thing tougher than whorin' was minin'. And the only thing tougher than minin' was whorin'. The town was existed only due the fact of the large,coal desposit uncovered a few years back. Men poured in from all over the world. All was lookin' for work that would make 'em rich.

It was real interestin' the way the town continued to grow. The coal just never ran out callin' to men to come get it. I'd never seen a thing like it before, least not that I could remember. Like most any society, there was a certain unspoken hierarchy that kept the order most of the time.

The mines ran the town. The owners ran the mines. Miners ran businesses. Women had charge of their families but submitted to their husbands. The families submitted to the church.

There was a good mix of people in that town. People from all over and like most towns around there, foreigners submitted to locals. It just was that way; locals didn't demand it but all followed it.